"I UNDERSTAND YOU SOMETIMES DO SPECIAL SORTS OF WORK."

"How special?" Darcy asked.

"Killing for hire."

"I'm not an assassin."

The Lemmant quickly corrected himself. "Not an assassin, no, but a soldier. Someone who wages fights with others in the same profession."

"The proper word is 'mercenary,' " Jade said. "I'm hired in situations where you need to gain an advantage over your opposition. I'm skilled in the use of weapons and unarmed fighting."

"I need someone's help desperately. It is a matter of honor. Three years ago, the Commancors invaded my planet. They wiped out my family. I am the sole survivor. Not in seventy-nine generations has such an assault been allowed to go unavenged. I shall strike back!"

"You and what army?"

"Myself alone, if I must, but I would like your assistance. . . ."

D0720022

THE REHUMANIZATION OF JADE DARCY

JADE DARCY
AND
THE AFFAIR OF
HONOR

by
STEPHEN GOLDIN
&
MARY MASON

A SIGNET BOOK

NEW AMERICAN LIBRARY

This book is dedicated to our son,
KENNETH SMITH
In the hope that he may live to travel between the stars . . .
with or without the Greest

NAL BOOKS ARE AVAILABLE AT QUANTITY DISCOUNTS WHEN USED TO
PROMOTE PRODUCTS OR SERVICES. FOR INFORMATION PLEASE WRITE TO
PREMIUM MARKETING DIVISION, NEW AMERICAN LIBRARY, 1633
BROADWAY, NEW YORK, NEW YORK 10019.

SIGNET TRADEMARK REG, U.S. PAT. OFF. AND FOREIGN
COUNTRIES REGISTERED TRADEMARK—MARCA REGISTRADA
HECHO EN CHICAGO, U.S.A.

SIGNET, SIGNET CLASSIC, MENTOR, ONYX, PLUME,
MERIDIAN and NAL BOOKS are published by NAL PENGUIN
INC., 1633 Broadway, New York, New York 10019

First Printing, October, 1988

1 2 3 4 5 6 7 8 9

PRINTED IN THE UNITED STATES OF AMERICA

CHAPTER 1

Nightmare

At first all was darkness around her, the silent darkness of the grave. He came at her, and she realized to her horror that she was naked. He seemed to be naked too, but a fine mist disguised specific details. His body was small but solidly built, and his face was strangely hidden in shadow. The smell of his sweat mingled unpleasantly with the tang of her own fear. He moved with the dazzling quickness only another carc could achieve, yet his approach was strangely slowed as though viewed from a projector run at half speed. Horrified though she was, she could not take her eyes from his body.

Her first impulse was to run, her second to fight, but she could do neither. She couldn't move. She knew intellectually she was just as fast and almost as strong as he was, but her body would not obey her. Her hands were held at her side by some invisible force, her feet were pinned in place. She stood helpless, struggling against her unseen bonds and gasping from the desperation of her efforts.

She screamed at him to stop, to leave her alone, but no sounds came from her throat—and despite the shadow that obscured his face she could tell he was beaming a salacious grin. His thumbs were rubbing the tips of his fingers as his large, calloused hands prepared to reach out for her helpless body.

Then the scene shifted and she was in the ingesterie, with its dim lighting and crowds of strange beings. The stillness was shattered by the deafening drone of alien speech, hundreds of simultaneous conversations, and still her screams could not be heard.

Most of the beings around her were strangers, but even so she saw many familiar faces. There was Rix in his accustomed box behind the glass wall, his multiple arms controlling the environment for his varied patrons. There was little Bab-ankh and slimy Lorpet, and so many others who were just a flicker of recognition in the back of her mind. Colonel Stavros, who'd never been within a hundred parsecs of this place, sat placidly at a nearby table, fingering his mustache and looking pointedly away.

She tried to call out, but her voice couldn't be heard above the din; she tried to reach out, but her arm would not move from its place. She could only stand there, naked and helpless, as the man with the shadowed face came toward her with lust in his eyes.

Then the man laughed, and all noise ceased. The ingesterie's patrons stopped what they were doing and riveted their attention on her. But not even the other arbiters made a move to fight off her attacker. Most of the patrons sat or stood where they were, and some even came around behind the man, ready to help him. She looked down at her own body and saw that strange arms and tentacles were now holding her in place. There was no safety, not even here. They had all betrayed her.

Her breathing was ragged and her heart was banging so heavily she thought it would surely burst through her chest. Her stomach was grinding at itself until she wanted to throw up, and yet she couldn't. Somehow that would be a victory for him, another bit of herself he controlled. She couldn't allow that.

The patrons were cheering silently as the man came menacingly toward her. Though she whimpered and twisted, she could not escape the inevitable moment.

Then the ingesterie vanished and she was in the woods again, naked on her back with her feet spread widely apart as he continued toward her. The ants bit at her, and she writhed on the damp ground but couldn't escape. The man's face was no longer in shadow and he knelt between her legs and reached up to grab her jaw with his strong right hand. It was a face she knew well, a face she'd cared for—once. Now it was twisted into a leering mask of sadistic lust, the lips swollen and red with passion, saliva drooling from the right corner.

Then his right hand pushed her head all the way back, so far she thought her neck might snap. She couldn't see what was happening now, but at least he'd stopped kissing her; of all perversions, that mockery of love seemed the most disgusting.

The man looked down and smiled in triumph, and kissed her and . . . and . . . and . . .

"Let me go, let me go!" Jade Darcy screamed as she opened her eyes and stared in horror at the gently lit ceiling panels overhead. Her screams reinforced her already heightened fear, producing an accelerating spiral that ended only when she ran out of breath. She struggled to sit up, but her arms and legs were restrained tightly at her sides and she couldn't break them free.

"Please read the numbers on the screen," said a gentle voice from the side of the room.

"Fuck you, Val! Let me go!" she shrieked.

"Swearing isn't good enough; you can do that in your sleep. Please read the numbers on the screen."

Jade turned her head desperately to the right and tried to make her eyes focus. The computer screen had a series of random numbers displayed on it. "Four, thirteen, twenty-eight, five," she said hoarsely, gasping like an asthmatic for air to fill her empty lungs.

"Good morning, Jade," the computer said as it released the restraints on her ankles and wrists.

"Motherfucking son-of-a-bitch computer," Jade muttered as she pulled her limbs in quickly, before the computer could bind them again. Her body was quaking from the aftermath of the experience, and her stomach was a pit of fire and nausea. As soon as she could control her arm movements well enough she reached for the plate beside her bed and grabbed some saltine crackers. She stuffed them into her mouth, nearly choking as she hurried to get them down to ease the burning in her gut.

Her body still felt slimy and dirty from the mauling by her phantom attacker. She remembered how bad the feeling was seven years ago when the nightmares first started, when she would stumble half blind from the bed, knocking over anything she hadn't already broken in her sleep, to reach the shower and stand under the running water for hours trying to rinse off the disgusting feel of his skin on hers. At least things had minimally improved since then.

"Shower, Val," she said when she finished her mouthful of crackers.

"Already running."

Her body was starting to feel more like her own again. As soon as she could trust her legs to support her she swung them over the side of the bed and stood up, then staggered into her tiny bathroom. She peed and stood under the shower for fifteen minutes, letting the hot water wash away her sweat and purify her skin. She didn't bother to lather just yet; she still had her morning exercises to do and some residual anger to relieve.

She walked naked into the second room of her two-room house, the special exercise room. For half an hour she performed the 108 movements of t'ai chi to center herself, to bring her back into herself, to reclaim her body from the possession of her dream attacker. She'd been taught to start from the center, the gut, then to place herself and her movement in harmony with this center. But it was this center that had been violated; it was the extremities that had been safely away, apart. These were all she owned after the nightmare. Starting from her fingertips, the exercises brought feeling in through her limbs and into her torso and feet, pushing out all unwanted intrusions and making her body and spirit whole again. Once she was back in control, she was ready for her real workout.

Walking to the set-in arsenal closet, she looked over her choices and finally selected a pair of long-bladed knives. She held one in each hand for a few moments, letting her fingers grow accustomed to their feel and weight. When she was ready she closed the closet and said, "Fifteen minutes, Val, mode A."

The lights dimmed to twilight level and the walls disappeared, replaced by an infinite plane of darkness. Jade Darcy forced herself to relax, running through the mild self-hypnotic tricks she'd learned years ago in Special Training. She put her conscious mind in the passenger seat, leaving the actual work to her subconscious, her training, and her computer-augmented reflexes. She'd watch and evaluate as a detached observer, not needing to participate unless an override was necessary.

From off to her left, barely visible in the corner of her eye, a faceless figure rushed toward her, and her body responded even before her mind registered the fact. Spinning on her left foot, she swung her left arm in a backhand slash that would have cut the attacker across his groin if he were a real person instead of a holographic image. The instant she delivered the disabling blow the image vanished, replaced by two more assailants coming from behind her.

Jade whirled and moved again, causing one of the attackers to charge past her. The second man came closer, only to receive her right-hand dagger up under where his ribs would have been. He promptly disappeared, leaving her to face the onslaught of his partner, coming around for a second pass. She didn't even need her knives for him; the back of her left hand hit him hard in the windpipe even as her right foot lashed out to kick him in the crotch. This attacker vanished and two more appeared, coming at her from opposite directions.

By ones and twos, holographic images of attackers charged at her, all faceless, all unarmed. All of them were dispatched with effortless blows her well-trained body delivered before her brain even had a chance, in most cases, to register the threat. Her body did not seem anchored to the floor. She moved in space from her center, not her feet. There were no separate motions, but fluid cascades along four, five, or even six axes. This was routine exercise for a carc, as mindless as sit-ups were for ordinary people; Jade's mind could revel in the sensation of her body behaving as it was supposed to, and the satisfaction of disemboweling and castrating the men who came charging toward her.

When she'd disabled the last adversary and no more came against her, the walls reappeared and the lighting came up gradually to normal level. "Fifteen minutes, as you requested," the computer told her.

Jade Darcy stood naked and sweating in the middle of the floor. She closed her eyes and took a deep breath before speaking. "Score, Val?"

"Ten dead, twenty-three incapacitated, three who might possibly have gotten up and caused further trouble."

"Replay those three."

Jade stepped off to one side as holographic images of her and her opponents materialized. She watched the movements carefully and saw she'd been a bit sloppy in a couple of her kicks. Viewed analytically, she realized she'd tried too hard to aim for the groin in cases where a lower kick to the kneecap would have been more effective. She knew it was still the aftermath of her nightmare—she *wanted* to kick men in the balls after that—but it disturbed her nonetheless. The spinal computer that augmented her reflexes was supposed to be dispassionate and separate from her mind and her emotions. If even *it* was affected by her nightmare, how deeply into her psyche had the rape been burned?

"Looks like I need some minor reprogramming," she muttered. "Too bad there's no one within five transfer stations who can do it."

She sighed as she put the knives back in their place in her arsenal closet. Almost anyone, even a carc, would be satisfied with that score, considering she'd remained uninjured, but Jade Darcy was a perfectionist. Fighting was her life's trade, the only thing that mattered to her anymore. "Pretty good" was not enough in the real world. There were only the perfect and the dead, and she was resolved to remain in the first category.

"Shower again, Val," she said as she padded to the bathroom. This time she lathered up and washed herself thoroughly, and douched as well to remove the last psychological traces of impurity left over from the nightmare. Finally feeling cleansed, she stood under the dryer and let the moisture be evaporated from the surface of her body.

"Let's have some breakfast, Val, while I'm deciding what to wear today. Just the usual."

The computer's programming could have synthesized eggs and toast, or cereal, or steak, or sashimi, or any of thousands of other combinations humans considered edible—but Jade Darcy's diet was rigid. She always had a breakfast of her own concoction, a milk-shakelike agglomeration of protein, vitamins, and all the nutritional necessities for human well-being. It was a meal devoid of taste or substance, but eating was a purely mechanical function, and Jade Darcy could see no reason to pamper herself by indulging in the decadence of pleasant sensation. A meal couldn't be good for her if it *tasted* good.

The bed reshaped itself into a table and bench in the center of her front room, and a slot opened in the wall to reveal a large tumbler filled with Jade's breakfast. Jade took the tumbler and sat down on the bench, staring at the computer screen in the wall. "I'm feeling purplish today, Val. Show me what you've got."

She sipped slowly at her breakfast as the screen flashed a number of designs and patterns, most of them totally inappropriate for her. She'd never told the computer to eliminate the frillier, more feminine designs from its catalog; she liked to look at them even though she knew she could never wear them. Finally the computer reached the more acceptable range and she saw a design she liked. "I'll have that one today, Val," she said.

Putting the tumbler with her half-finished breakfast down on the table, she crossed the room to the closet. The computer had used raw materials, both fresh and recycled from other clothes, to create the outfit Jade requested. The scents of fresh dye and the polymer catalysts were still dissipating as Jade reached for them.

She decided to give the smells a moment to fade while she did her toilet. She brushed her teeth and flossed thoroughly, then gargled her mouthwash as well. Her hair merely required two minutes' brushing with the special dryer attachment; the short cut Val gave her each month was designed for minimal care.

Her clothing was equally efficient. Breast bands built into the leotard were made of an elastic fabric designed to minimize both bruising in a fight and breakdown of tissues even during the most rigorous movement. The material of her tights allowed enough air circulation to prevent skin and other problems while still providing decent insulation from extreme temperatures. That these features also made the most of her sleek young figure was something Jade had told Val was an unimportant by-product. Over these basics she donned the clothes of a special breakaway design that couldn't be used to restrain her in a fight. After five minutes, Jade stepped out into the room once more. "Mirror, Val," she said.

The entire wall beside her became reflective, allowing her a full-length glimpse of herself. She looked her image over approvingly. Her hip-length long-sleeved silky shirt was lilac with subtle swirls of darker purples and had a deep-wine collar that circled her neck softly, leaving plenty of room to breathe and turn her head quickly. The slacks were a deep purple verging into black, tucked into thigh-high boots of lavender leather.

The ensemble fit closely to her short, slender body without ever restricting her total freedom of movement. In her job, movement was everything. She didn't bother with makeup. There weren't any other humans around here to impress, and aliens didn't care whether her features were artificially enhanced. She had her clothes impregnated with a neutral scent that soothed most pheromone-sensitive races, and that was sufficient as perfume.

Her jet-black hair was shoulder-length, curling inward just at her neck and framing the Oriental face she'd inherited from her Japanese mother. She had brown eyes, a straight, thin nose—the only feature she'd really gotten from her father—and a sensuous mouth. She'd once taken pride in her beauty, but she no longer thought in those terms. Hers was an efficient face, and that was good enough for her.

Deciding that she looked acceptable for the day, Jade sat back down at the table to finish her breakfast. "Any mail or messages, Val?" she asked as she took another sip from the tumbler.

There was one letter, all the way from Earth, and it bore the letterhead of Verdugo and Lance Detective Agency. Jade immediately sat up straight and read it carefully, but it was simply their monthly report on the activities of Mastersergeant Jeffrey B. Barker. The subject had spent his month entirely at the training base in Java with a corps of carc trainees. There had been no unusual activities. Along with the report was their monthly bill for 250 eus.

Jade snorted. "Motherfuckers are bleeding me dry, and all they send me is garbage. What's my credit balance, Val?"

"Fifteen thousand, three hundred seventeen energy units."

And rent was coming up next week, too, which meant another two hundred eus shot. This two-room detached house, with its gravity generator and distance from its neighbors, was the minimum she felt she could get away with—she needed the exercise room and the higher gravity to keep herself in shape—but she still felt guilty about the extravagance. She was tempted to write Verdugo and Lance and tell them to fuck off, but she knew she didn't dare. She had to keep tabs on Barker. She couldn't let him get away. In his position he could disappear at any moment, and she might never be able to find him again. She couldn't let that happen.

"Pay their fucking bill, Val," she sighed, knowing that and the rent would bring her well below fifteen thousand. She couldn't hire the kind of talent she'd need with that little money. No matter how hard she worked and how tightly she saved, the money mounted up so slowly. She'd never get what she needed working for Rix. What she needed was a few more jobs, a couple of big ones. But she couldn't go around creating them; they had to come to her, and she had to wait for them. It was very frustrating.

"There's also a message from the K'luune, Lorpet," Val said.

"Maybe the slimy bastard has a job for me. His last few tips paid off. Play it, Val, while I try to hold down my breakfast."

Lorpet's features appeared on the screen, looking like a mass of bubbling white jelly with a row of dark spots for eyes and sharp mandibles that clicked together to produce his speech. The computer translated his clicks for her.

"Greetings, worthy Jade Darcy. The humble Lorpet abases himself before your noble presence and begs your forgiveness for his intrusion into your privacy. Information has reached the attention of this unworthy one regarding the presence on Cablans of another member of your estimable race, just arrived today. Knowing this would be of interest to you, poor pitiful Lorpet hastens to contact you at your convenience to share his minuscule knowledge, and humbly awaits your decision to make an appointment. Once more, he entreats your forgiveness for presenting himself uninvited upon your notice." Lorpet's eyes blinked in a ritual of farewell and the message faded from her screen.

Jade Darcy sat frozen in place, staring at the blank screen. Another Terran on Cablans! An animal panic, kin to her nightmare fear, paralyzed her as no physical opponent could have. She'd come all this way, to the farthest transfer station she could find, specifically to avoid other humans. For five years she'd remained alone of her kind—and now suddenly another one had shown up. What could this mean?

Shards of her nightmare flashed through her mind, and her hand twitched so badly she put her tumbler down to avoid spilling her breakfast. Closing her eyes, she performed the t'ai chi breathing discipline to restore her body and spirit to calmness. *There's no evidence this person came for you,* she told herself sternly. *It could be a coincidence. You're not the center of everyone else's universe. Other people can come here for unrelated reasons.* This litany helped her stop the fight-or-flight reaction, but did little toward releasing the knot her stomach was tied in.

She looked at the small computer screen implanted in the back of her left hand and asked, "Time?" The screen showed she had little more than an hour before she was due to start her shift at the ingesterie—not enough time to meet and deal with Lorpet. She'd have to set something up for after work. This was top priority.

"Send a message to Lorpet, Val, as follows: The unworthy Jade Darcy gratefully acknowledges the enlightening message of the most honorable and exalted Lorpet, and while she is too lowly to aspire to his level of wisdom she begs his condescension to enlighten her further. She excuses the fact that her dreary . . . no, her dismal existence requires her presence at the ingesterie of Rix Kaf-Amur until seventeen hundred hours, but she would be most honored to grovel before him at a place of his convenience at any time thereafter. End of message." False humility was a power game to the K'luune. If she could outgrovel "poor, pitiful Lorpet"—one of the shrewdest data brokers on Cablans—perhaps she could knock his price down to something reasonable.

She went to her dresser and pulled out the accessories she'd need for the day. First was the u-trans, a small cylinder attached to a custom-molded earpiece. The curved cylinder fit around the back of her ear, making it nearly invisible. Without the u-trans she couldn't hope to make sense of the babel that surrounded her on Cablans. She rolled up her sleeves and strapped on her other accessories—two spring-loaded knife holders, one on the inside of each forearm. She tested them to make sure they were working, then rolled her sleeves down over them and tested them again. The proper muscle contractions in her arm would send the blade into her hand, ready for action; but in the meantime the knives were out of the way and unobtrusive.

That was all the weaponry she carried. If trouble arose that she couldn't handle with her training, her computer-augmented reflexes, and two knives, it would be such a big problem that she'd have to call for assistance anyway. There was no sense overarming herself.

She looked at herself in the mirror one more time, straightened her hair, and made sure the knives didn't show. Jade Darcy was ready for work.

"Maintenance configuration, Val," she said as she strode to the door, which opened obediently for her.

Standing in the doorway was a frizzlic, a small four-legged animal less than half a meter long and standing as tall as the middle of her calf. Its brown fur, streaked and spotted with patches of gray, was short and bristly. It had a small face with a long pointed snout, a white triangular marking on its forehead, and small black eyes that seemed to be all pupil. Jade had never seen a hedgehog face to face, but she could easily imagine that the frizzlic was an alien cousin to the hedgehog.

"You again," she chided the frizzlic. "How many times have I told you not to come around here?"

The frizzlic merely made chirping sounds and rubbed its long snout against the doorframe.

"You're supposed to be feral," Jade continued. "It says so right in my computer. I know some people make pets out of you, but you're supposed to take care of yourself in the wild. Why don't you do that instead of coming around here looking for handouts? It's not good to be domesticated. You get too dependent on other people, and then when they betray you, you die."

She looked at the screen on the back of her left hand and realized she had just enough time to get to work for the shift briefing. Her tumbler still had some of her breakfast left in the bottom—but her stomach was too queasy after Lorpet's message to digest anything more. It would be a shame to let the stuff go to waste.

"Get me a bowl, Val," she said. She placed the frizzlic on the ground away from the doorsill, then walked back inside and over to the wall slot, where Val had revealed a small bowl. The frizzlic followed her inside, adjusting to the higher gravity Jade kept inside her house, and trying to rub its eagerly wiggling snout against her boots. Pouring the remainder of her breakfast into the bowl, Jade strode back to the door and placed the bowl down outside, under the bushes that lined the walkway.

With a short, high-pitched squeal the frizzlic stuck its head into the bowl, getting some of the liquid up its snout. It snorted and shook its head, then began lapping at the liquid with its little green tongue.

Jade watched it with a scornful expression. ''Just don't expect to make a habit of this, frizzlic. This is not going to be a regular relationship. The last thing in the universe I need is a fucking pet.''

She walked back into the apartment and tossed the empty tumbler into the recycle slot. Shaking her head at the silly sounds the frizzlic was making, she strode off to work. Had she realized she was humming, and a lullaby at that, she would have been very annoyed with herself.

CHAPTER 2

Rix's Place

Jade made it to the ingesterie with a few minutes to spare. She slipped in through the back door and descended the broad stairs to the employees' area. Nodding hello to the kitchen help, she walked through the aisles between tables loaded with enormous cooking vats and the fresh fruits and vegetables that were one of the luxuries which brought customers to Rix's place.

On her left was a table full of those obscenely knobby, fluorescent chartreuse slime-eggs, oozing inside their gelatinous skins. Jade always felt slightly nauseated just looking at them. As she passed the next table, a Lemmant was unloading a shipment of pink dirda melons, and Jade frowned. Dirda melons meant two things. First, they were only transported by the Furgato sect of the Restaals, and the Furgatos always came to Rix's when they were on Cablans. Watching over them would be like dealing with a circusful of clowns.

Second, the only beings who really liked the dirda melons were the Palovoi, on whom they acted as both an intoxicant and an aphrodisiac. Since the melons had to be eaten quickly, Rix would be notifying his regular Palovoi customers of their availability right now, and they'd show up within a couple of hours—during Jade's shift.

She didn't relish the thought of facing drunken, lecherous Palovoi and thieving Furgatos when she was already on edge from Lorpet's call. Maybe she'd be lucky and the Furgatos and Palovoi would be in someone else's quadrant so she wouldn't have to worry about them. The way her luck was running this morning, though, she doubted it.

Passing through the kitchen, she came to the door of the security staff room, where the shift briefing would be held. She placed the back of her left hand against the security scanner so the door would recognize her computer's pattern, and waited for the familiar click as the door unlocked for her. When it came, the door slid open and she walked into the briefing room.

Even though she was on time, she was still the last to arrive. Her colleagues watched her as she strode across the room and settled on one of the soft, wide benches that were the universal seating arrangement on Cablans, built to accommodate most kinds of alien anatomy. Jade smiled, nodded, and looked right back at them.

As usual there would be four arbiters on this shift, including herself. On the bench beside Jade's chosen spot was Hiss!arr, the only arbiter on the entire staff who was smaller than she was. The Purrchrp was covered in short golden fur with black markings on his face, and his long prehensile tail was wrapped around his waist, as usual when it was not in use. He seemed rather heavyset for his height, but Jade had seen him move and knew he was scarcely slower than she was, with perhaps a bit more strength. He had a squashed-in face and wore only a wide belt for modesty.

The two coworkers on the bench behind Jade were considerably bigger than she and Hiss!arr. Kokoti looked like an enormous fat beetle sitting up, using two of his limbs for walking and the other four for manipulation. His shell was an iridescent blue-green, wrapped in a gauzy material that was spun around him fresh each day by a tiny symbiote. His head was in constant motion, sweeping back and forth; it was a trait that always disquieted Jade, even though she knew Kokoti needed it to see depth and achieve peripheral vision.

Beside Kokoti was Cyclad Arik, another insectoid. With long, oddly jointed limbs sporting razor-sharp serrations, she resembled a giant praying mantis except that she had a hawklike beak strong enough to rend meat from bone. Physically she was the most imposing of the four, yet Jade knew she was actually the calmest and most easygoing of the lot. Still, if Jade had to pick one other person to have at her back in a fight, she'd have chosen Cyclad Arik without hesitation.

Jade and her coworkers shared the job title of "arbiters," but Jade knew a more colloquial word for it: "bouncers." She and her colleagues were the security force for the ingesterie, one of the most wide-open public establishments on Cablans. Their task was to keep social frictions to a minimum and preserve the ingesterie's reputation as a gathering place among the many varied species that came to Cablans. The arbiters themselves referred to their clique, only half in jest, as the Ingesterie Diplomatic Corps.

Disson Peng-Amur, pod brother of the owner, Rix, noted Jade's arrival. He resembled nothing so much as a big blue tree with three main roots, and a ring of tentacles that always seemed to be busy on a dozen things at once. When Jade was seated he spoke in a loud, slow croaking voice that Jade's u-trans interpreted for her. "Since we're all here, even if it's a few minutes before the official shift start, I'll begin the briefing. Reservations for this shift are light so far. Hiss!arr, you'll of course have first quadrant." First quadrant contained most of the specialized environments, and Hiss!arr, with his short, lush fur, preferred that section because it was kept considerably cooler than the rest of the building. "Kokoti will have second quadrant today, Jade Darcy third, and Cyclad Arik fourth. So far, first and fourth look to be the busiest, but that's bound to change."

Disson next proceeded to discuss the reservations that had been made. Some of them were regular customers, about whom little needed to be said; the arbiters were already well familiar with their customs and practices. Others, either individuals they saw less frequently or members of races they were less familiar with, required more discussion.

A thorough briefing always started with physical details: what members of that race looked like, whether they required a special environment, what they ate and drank, and whether they'd requested any special items like privacy walls or screens. Then there'd be a discussion of how they could be expected to behave: what they considered a threat, insult, or a compliment, how large a zone of privacy the average member had, what other races they were antagonistic or subservient to, and how they were normally affected by the intoxicants and drugs they usually ingested in public. Finally the most practical aspects would be discussed, how to deal with them in a fight: whether they were normally armed and with what weapons, whether they had any natural defenses such as stings, venoms, or shells, what their fighting posture was, what their vulnerable points were, and—most important—what their surrender signals were. It was a huge amount of information delivered in a shorthand code peculiar to these highly skilled professionals.

Jade Darcy listened attentively to the briefings on the patrons who'd be seated in her colleagues' areas, since it was always possible she'd be called on to back them up in a tight spot. She noticed that an old troublemaker had been scheduled for seating in the second quadrant. Jade had discovered an effective way of dealing with her last time she was in, but had neglected to mention it in her report that day; she made a mental note to tell Kokoti about it before they went on shift.

When Disson came to describe the patrons who'd be placed in the third quadrant this shift, her worst fears proved justified: both the Furgatos *and* the Palovoi would be seated in her area. Jade braced herself. Neither group was especially dangerous under most circumstances, but they'd both be rambunctious in their own ways. She was good at handling both, but she'd have to be prepared for an active shift.

Then Disson added, "There will also be a triad of Commancors dining in Red 69 and 70, scheduled at fourteen hundred hours. Do you need a briefing on them?"

Jade frowned again and took a deep breath. "I'm quite familiar with Commancors, thank you."

None of the other arbiters needed a briefing, either. The Commancors were one of the most aggressive races in the known galaxy. They'd fought with almost everyone at one time or another, and as a result had made themselves and their culture well known, if not well loved. Commancors were always trouble; if they weren't causing it themselves, they were attracting it.

The rest of the briefing was routine, but Jade was still fuming inwardly at the notion of Commancors in her quadrant as well as Furgatos and Palovoi. She didn't need trouble today, not on top of the nightmare and the nervousness Lorpet's news was causing. She realized she'd have to keep a close watch on herself as well as on the patrons, because she'd like nothing better than an excuse to wade into the Commancor party with fists, feet, and knives. Still, the Commancors were patrons of the ingesterie, and as such deserved her respect and protection.

Disson closed the briefing with his usual admonition, ''Be careful up there,'' and the arbiters had a few minutes to relax before they were due to relieve their colleagues currently working the floor. Jade assumed a lotus position on the bench and performed some breathing exercises while the others talked among themselves.

Finally Cyclad Arik came over and knelt beside her. Although Jade knew intellectually that Cyclad Arik was a very mild and pleasant mantis, a slight trace of entomophobia combined with her enhanced reflexes to make her stiffen in expectation of a fight.

''My senses detected some agitation when you were apprised of the scheduled presence of the Commancors,'' Cyclad Arik said as the u-trans rendered her high squeals into English.

''I don't like Commancors,'' Jade said simply.

''Nobody likes Commancors,'' said Cyclad Arik. It was one of the bluntest and most unkind remarks Jade had ever heard this kind, polite creature make. The giant mantis continued, ''But that information by itself would not have created the intensity of your reaction. You don't like me either, but we function together without dissonance.''

Jade looked startled. "What makes you think I don't like you?"

"I've seen your body flinch and shudder when I approach. I try not to make such approaches frequently, but this afternoon I was concerned there might be trouble on the floor if this matter isn't discussed now."

"It's . . . it's just an instinctive reaction," Jade apologized. "There's a very predatory insect on my home world, and you look like a giant version of it. Even though I know you're a sensitive, intelligent creature, my instincts keep telling me to protect myself." The very reflexes that made her such a good fighter also exaggerated her instinctive reactions to Cyclad Arik, and Jade had to be constantly on override whenever her coworker came within range. "I . . . admire you and respect you greatly," she finished weakly.

Cyclad Arik tilted her head at a strange angle and clicked her beak a couple of times, a body expression Jade had never been fully able to interpret. "This still does not explain your reaction to the Commancors," Cyclad Arik continued.

"It's a personal matter," Jade said, and even she could tell her voice was a little too loud.

"It ceases to be personal when we're all upstairs working," the other said. "Our lives may rest in one another's hands. Surprises can be fatal. We must know as much as possible to prepare for all contingencies."

Jade sighed. Cyclad Arik was right, of course, but trusting still came hard, even after all this time.

"My planet was overrun by the Commancors," she said softly. "My father, brothers, and uncle all died fighting them. I swore then I'd get even—but right after I finished my army training, before I had the chance, the Greest ordered the Commancors to cede the planet to us and we weren't at war with them anymore. I still feel some anger and frustration, but I can handle those feelings once I know to expect them. I'll treat the Commancors like any other patrons."

"It's advantageous to know your sentiments on the matter," said Cyclad Arik, standing up again and turning to leave.

"Thank you for your concern," Jade said, so quietly it was barely more than a whisper. Cyclad Arik did not respond, and it was possible she didn't even hear Jade's comment.

Needing to shake off the emotional load that had just built up within her, Jade went over to where Kokoti was completing a discussion with Disson. As soon as was polite—etiquette being very important to the Kettcens—she said, "I heard you'll be having Marphle in your quadrant today. Would this be a convenient time to discuss something I found out about her?"

"Of course, my dear, any time for you," Kokoti replied. "I regret I have no refreshments to offer you right now. I do hope you'll forgive me."

Jade tried not to look directly into Kokoti's face as it moved from side to side; it tended to make her seasick. "Of course; I had no such expectations. At any rate, you were off duty the last time Marphle was here, and I had to handle a bit of unpleasantness involving her. During the scuffle"—and Jade felt that was a mild word for the brawl that erupted suddenly and caused three squares' worth of damage—"I noticed she always pulled her toes out of the way, even when it meant getting hit somewhere else. I ducked under all four arms and got close enough to stomp on her toes—and I told her I'd do it unless she behaved herself. She skittered away and cried, so I moved right after her and repeated the threat. She put down the tables she'd been about to throw and we settled the matter peacefully. I really don't think I could have done much damage through those heavy boots she wears, but she seems to have a deep-rooted instinct to protect her feet at all costs."

"Absolutely inspired, my dear," Kokoti said. Jade had always wondered whether the u-trans programmer had, on some strange whim, deliberately made Kettcens sound like stuffy British colonels, or whether that was really the way their grammar worked. "Phelphums are bottom feeders. They evolved in tidal areas and spend all their childhood there, living off what their toes can find and their hands can club. They're naturally very careful about them. The toes also play a major role in their reproduction. Why, to injure them would impair her in pairing.''

Kokoti began the high-pitched chirruping and head-bobbing that was laughter to his species. This attempt at an English pun, plus the up-and-down movement in addition to his normal side-to-side, was too much for Jade. She loudly pointed out she had to get ready for shift change, checked her gear, and walked away. Kokoti wouldn't be so bad, she thought, if only his species didn't think of multilingual puns as an art form—and if he weren't so wretched an artist.

A few minutes later it was time to begin work. Jade and the other arbiters left the quiet of the briefing room. They headed through the kitchen and up the wide stairs to the bedlam of the ingesterie itself.

Rix Kaf-Amur's ingesterie was the largest and best-known institution of its kind on Cablans. In a multi-racial society that conducted most of its business over computer linkups, the ingesterie was one place where social intercourse was possible on a personal, very public basis. Even those races whose customs forbade eating and drinking in public often came to meet business contacts from other races. It was considered the socially proper thing to be seen at the ingesterie occasionally, and members of all races and social levels mingled there on equal terms.

Physically the ingesterie was laid out like the floor plan of some enormous department store—a vast expanse of floor broken into discrete areas whose boundaries could be rearranged to suit the necessities of the moment. For administrative purposes the floor was divided into four quadrants, and in the center, where they joined, were the serving stations where food was brought up from the kitchen for the servers to distribute among the clients.

Within each quadrant the ground was marked off into basic square units roughly five meters on a side. If a patron required more room, one or more adjacent squares could be added to provide a dining area in the size and configuration desired. The first square was considered a basic part of the meal; each additional square cost the patron extra.

Within the squares, the furnishings were altered to fit the patron's anatomy and dining needs. That much was standard. Other services were available for a price. If the patron did not wish to be on display to the other diners, opaquing fields could be set up. If the patron wished, the closed-off section's environment could be almost totally controlled: atmospheric composition and pressure, temperature, sounds, smells, lights, colors, video illusions, and other requests could be specifically ordered, each for its own price.

Jade and her coworkers came out on the floor and relieved the previous shift of arbiters, who gave them a quick rundown on what had been happening. It had been a quiet shift, with no problems. Jade devoutly hoped her shift would be the same. Sometimes the ingesterie was the only neutral ground on which feuding races could meet in peace. It was the arbiters' job to keep it peaceful.

Jade Darcy stepped out onto the floor to begin her rounds. Looking up, she could see the glass wall of the control booth, where Rix Kaf-Amur spent virtually all his time. A tall blue tree like his pod brother, he kept the tentacles around his trunk in constant motion working the elaborate series of controls that made each dining area unique. A computer might have handled everything faster, but Rix contended his personal attention made everything the subtlest bit better.

The floor of the ingesterie was a cacophony of roars, bellows, clicks, whistles, squeaks, squeals, chirps, croaks, sighs, and miscellaneous other modes of communication, even though sound baffles had been used wherever possible. The smells of so many individuals from so many different races hung in the atmosphere and mixed with the savory and unsavory aromas of the foods they ate, despite the air purifiers' attempts to neutralize the odors. Since the ingesterie was open around the clock and was never empty of patrons, the constant clashing of noises and smells lowered a metaphorical haze over the whole establishment. Even after all the time Jade had worked here, it hit her fresh at the start of each shift.

She walked the paths between the occupied dining

areas with a casual gait, never hurried yet never daw-
dling. Her movements were graceful and precise. She
always knew where her next step would be and what
would be around her. As often as she could arrange it
her back was to a wall or an empty dining area. Her
eyes continually scanned the room, and she noticed
details without appearing to stare at anyone. Occasionally she would nod or exchange pleasantries with
a regular patron who greeted her, but most of the time
she was a shadow presence unnoticed by the ingesterie's patrons.

Her biggest hassle during the first half of her shift
was with the first wave of Furgatos, but they came and
went with only the usual minor incidents of casual
theft. They were friendly enough, but they didn't believe in honest trading—or in much of anything else,
for that matter. All was illusion, according to their
sect, particularly in matters of ownership. They stole
what they wanted and freely expected others to steal
from them in return. The results were seldom harmful
in these controlled surroundings and occasionally
amusing, since most people knew what to expect—but
it did mean extra work for Jade, who had to keep picking the Furgatos' pockets to retrieve items they'd stolen from other ingesterie patrons.

This much was routine. The pocketpicking required
a bit of dexterity, but Jade had enough practice that
she scarcely had to think about it. Her mind had altogether too much time to dwell on the unpleasant im-
plications of Lorpet's message. There was another
human on Cablans. There was *another* human on Cablans.

The Palovoi, enticed by the dirda melons the Furgatos had brought, would arrive at 1400 hours, about
the same time as the Commancors. While the Palovoi
wouldn't be staying more than two hours, they'd be
both intoxicated and insulting. They wouldn't hurt
anything except the feelings of some inexperienced
diner who took them seriously, but Jade would still
have to be prepared for trouble. It would be best to be
fed and refreshed before they arrived.

Through her hand computer she coordinated with

the other arbiters so they'd know she was on her lunch break and would cover her quadrant in case of trouble. Then she went downstairs and stepped into a small service cubicle that was there for the benefit of the staff. Pressing the computer in the back of her left hand against the scanning plate, she identified herself so the cubicle would know who she was. After a brief moment of reflection, Jade asked the cubicle for steak, rice, green beans, and coffee. While she was waiting for the meal to be synthesized, she used her hand computer to call home. "Any messages, Val?" she asked.

"Just one—Lorpet replying to your message. Do you want the entire statement?"

Jade didn't feel like wading through more of the K'luune's disclaimers and false humility, even though it would give her an idea of her bargaining position. "Just a summary, Val. I'll take the full text later."

"He asks you to meet him at Galentor's gambling palace anytime after eighteen hundred hours to discuss your business."

Jade nodded absently. Galentor's was a safe, neutral choice. "Call back and tell Lorpet that the unworthy Jade Darcy, who is so far beneath him that she dares not answer his invitation personally, acknowledges receipt of his far too generous request and humbly accedes to his wishes."

After lunch Jade went back upstairs to the main level. As she walked along the southern edge of the room from the eastern portion of fourth quadrant to her own quadrant three, she signaled her coworkers via her computer that she was back on the floor and working. There was no immediate sign of Hiss!arr, but Cyclad Arik and Kokoti both made the horizontal crisscross motion with their manipulators that meant everything was going well. As she passed Rix's glass booth high up in the south wall, he gave her a similar sign. This reassured her; nothing escaped Rix's notice.

As she got halfway around her own quadrant she saw Hiss!arr emerging from one of the environment tanks in first quadrant. When he stepped out and shut the locking door behind him, he saw Jade and also gave her the "all clear" signal.

A brief silence followed by exaggerated noise caused Jade to look over the meter-high central serving station and see that the second wave of Furgatos had entered the ingesterie. Bab-ankh, the ingesterie's greeter, was escorting them to their squares. Bab-ankh was a small ball of blue fluff with tiny hands and face on impossibly long stiltlike legs. He moved quickly, not letting the Furgatos dawdle near other squares, as he led them to a region near the back of third quadrant and under Rix's station, where they could be more closely watched. This also kept them away from the central serving stations and the servers' main paths; plates going past Furgatos didn't always arrive full at their destination.

Jade immediately changed her route to swing by the Furgatos' squares and was greeted by the top-ranking member of the group. Whoever had programmed the u-trans had decided that Furgato rankings were roughly equivalent to earth's naval ranks; the leader of this group bore a title akin to executive officer. He'd been to the ingesterie many times before and had become an admirer of Jade's. He exchanged a few pleasantries with her now as she went around the party, greeting former patrons and being introduced to a couple of first-timers.

The patting, hugging, and elaborate handshaking appeared affectionate to any but practiced "dips." Actually, pockets were being picked, counterpicked, and repicked as Jade went around the table, but this activity ended when a young Furgato touched Jade's implant wrong and the computer in the back of her hand sent up an alarm. The startled youngster dropped the bauble he'd been taking from Jade, who'd just taken it from another Furgato, who had, in turn, taken it from one of the patrons he'd passed on the way to this square. With a quick motion Jade caught the object before it hit the floor as the other Furgatos laughed at their comrade's mistake.

"Don't be ashamed, recruit," the Exec said through

his chuckles. "She's bested me more than once. Jade Darcy, you've earned a kung'an."

"I'm honored indeed," Jade answered. These riddles were a form of education to the Furgatos, and the more sophisticated ones were shared with an acquaintance as humans might share a snifter of fine cognac. Jade was, in fact, quite relieved; a night when a kung'an was put out led to deep discussion and little trouble.

"This is a kung'an that was actually presented by a member of your own race." Jade tensed at those words until the Exec continued, "I believe it's some three thousand of your years old. It was in a book of kung'an the Greest gave us; our replies to them were his fee to let us transfer through here with our shipment of melons."

Even through the carefully neutral tones of the u-trans the Exec's voice sounded exultant as he spoke the kung'an. "Listen: Two dragons fight over the lost pearl; which is victorious?"

"I'll give you my answer before you leave," Jade temporized. She noticed the Palovoi just being seated between the Furgatos and the serving station, and added, "But now I must see to those who'll be dining on your melons."

"Of course," the Exec said with excessive blinking. "Until then."

Jade bowed and started making her way to the Palovoi table, taking a small inventory along the way of the items she'd liberated from the Furgatos. Most of these she distributed back to their original owners with the apologies of the management, and the owners— knowing the Furgatos' reputation—accepted the situation. Jade ended up with one item left over—a small knife of the sort a Purrchrp usually carried behind his neck. She tapped a short message to Hiss!arr on her hand computer, but he replied quickly that his was still intact; this one must have come from some Purrchrp outside the ingesterie. Jade decided she'd better keep an extra-close eye on the Furgato Exec; it took both skill and nerve to steal a Purrchrp's stash knife.

The Palovoi's table and their saddle-shaped chairs

had been placed in squares close to the serving station, because delays in second and later servings of dirda melons had been known to cause problems. The Palovoi themselves looked like deformed, bowlegged centaurs suffering from rickets. Their quadrupedal bodies were about half the length of a gymnast's horse, with meter-long bowed legs whose feet pointed to the outside. From the rear came a two-meter long, bifurcated prehensile tail which, in such crowded places, was carried over a shoulder or wrapped around the "waist." The trunks rose from the front of their bodies perhaps half a meter before their two long arms branched out.

The Palovoi's two mouths and sensory organs seemed to be scattered at random on the smooth dome above the branching arms, but the creatures had full 360-degree vision and excellent directional hearing. They could see higher into the infrared than humans could but little past green in the other direction, which made their clothing color combinations seem strange to human eyes.

Their skin hung on them in deep folds, like that of a pampered bloodhound who'd recently lost weight. This disguised their sexual characteristics, except for the obvious beauty traits: Palovoi women were admired for the strength and size of their arms, men for their legs.

These Palovoi were old established customers of Rix's, a married party in the traditional grouping of two females and four males. Jade approached and politely inquired, "What ill wind blew you disgusting oafs in here? Is it just my bad luck, or do you want to ruin everyone's appetite?"

Migul, the dominant male, made an untranslatable sound with his left mouth, then said, "If we'd known you'd be here, tailless one, we'd have chosen another place to dine today. Anything's better than seeing you again." Migul's arms were on his back knees, a sign of battle-readiness—and respect.

Jade was about to reply when she noticed the Commancors enter the room. With that troublesome potential on hand she had little time to dally with boisterous but basically harmless Palovoi.

"I've got more important things to do than deal with scum like you," she told Migul. "I'll leave you in the hands of our inept server, who's still far better than you deserve."

"If you leave Rix's altogether we'll really have something to celebrate," Migul said in parting.

Bab-ankh escorted the Commancor triad to their dining area at his normal fluttery pace, which the Commancors, with their short, stubby legs, found hard to match. The Commancors were humanoid and, like most members of their race, were about Jade's height and built in stocky proportion. They had blue-green skin, bulbous heads, and bulging eyes set wide apart. Their tiny hands, with eight clawed fingers each, were very dextrous and deadly. They were among the most ruthless and aggressive fighters in the galaxy—but from the green cloaks they were wearing and the way they were looking at one another, this was a mating triad. They'd come here simply to eat.

As the group walked through the paths to Red 69 and 70, many heads and eyes turned to watch them. Commancors were not widely liked, and they drew attention wherever they went. Those who didn't stare or glare at them made a studious effort to look in other directions and ignore them completely. But Jade could feel the atmosphere in the room change abruptly, no matter what Rix's gauges said.

There was one patron who reacted more intently than the rest. He was a Lemmant, a tall, reedy biped whose body was clothed in swirls of crimson with a gaudy plumed hat. His smooth skin was pale blue, almost white, which Jade had been told was a sign of youth in his race. He'd come into the ingesterie alone some time before the Commancors, and had seemed content to eat his solitary meal in silence. Jade had dismissed him as not being any potential threat—but the arrival of the Commancors spurred her to a quick reevaluation.

When the Commancors entered and walked to their area a few squares away from his own, the Lemmant stopped eating to stare at them for several minutes before turning back to his food. Jade wasn't familiar with Lemmants and couldn't read his facial expressions, but the tensing of muscles throughout his body was unmistakable. He was preparing for some action.

"What are relations currently between Lemmant and Commancor?" Jade asked her hand computer.

The answer came back quickly. "The races are at peace with each other."

Then it must be a personal motivation, Jade reasoned, to provoke such a reaction. She asked for information about Lemmant social interactions and was told that the race, which so far inhabited only their native planet, was organized into strong family and clan units. Their behavior was highly formalized, and they had a strong sense of personal and group honor.

Jade worried as she continued to make her rounds between the Furgatos, the Palovoi, and the Commancors, paying special attention to the young Lemmant. Pride and honor, she knew from experience, caused more trouble and provoked more fights than greed and lust.

She asked for anatomical information, and learned that the Lemmants came from a low-gravity world and found even Cablans's point eight gees a little burdensome. That was comforting, since in a fight it would be harder for him to move than for her. The most vulnerable points seemed to be the leg joints, the soft midsection, and the neck. Jade filed the information in her mind as possibly useful.

Over the next half hour, nothing significant happened. The Furgatos stayed at their table quietly, discussing their kung'an. The Palovoi ate their dirda melons and became loud, but otherwise remained manageable. The Lemmant kept staring at the Commancors' area and ordering drinks, but made no overt moves to leave his own square. The Commancors, oblivious to his attention, casually pulled apart the raw carcasses of their food and ate it off the bones as was their custom.

Jade patched her hand computer into the ingesterie's files. "The young Lemmant at Red 23 has been ingesting many fluids in the last half hour. What is the nature of those fluids?''

"Blue Hazard is considered a moderate intoxicant for his species."

"What's the Lemmant intoxication level?"

"Unknown; such data have not been entered into my registers."

Jade brooded for a few moments as she made her circuitous route around the floor of third quadrant. "Isn't there a Lemmant working in the kitchen?" she finally asked the computer. "I thought I saw one as I came in."

"Yes. She is Cord du Dassenji."

"Put her on the line for me, please." Jade's concern increased as the patron finished his current tankard, slammed it down on the tabletop, and called his server to bring him another.

A polite voice came through the speaker. "You wanted me, Arbiter Darcy?"

"Yes. I need some information. A young male Lemmant is here, and so far he's consumed three and a half liters of something called Blue Hazard. I need to know the effect of that much consumption in about half an hour."

"He would be zhockened—that is, very intoxicated," Cord du Dassenji said with surprise. "That's an awful lot of drink that fast."

"What effects could it have on him?"

"It all depends on his mood and what happens around him. He could just fall asleep, or see things, or get into a fight."

"Thank you, Cord du Dassenji," Jade said, starting to sign off.

"Arbiter Darcy," her informant said timidly.

"Yes?"

"That intoxicated, he could even do something . . . dishonorable."

"Thank you for warning me. I'll try to prevent that."

She broke the connection with Cord du Dassenji and frowned. There'd be no way of knowing which way this particular patron would jump—though sleepiness did not appear likely. "Was the Lemmant armed when he came in?" she asked the ingesterie computer.

"Only a ceremonial dagger at his waist."

"What about the Commancors at Red 69 and 70? Are they armed?"

"They brought no weapons with them."

That, Jade knew, scarcely mattered. An unarmed Commancor was still likely to be more dangerous than a knife-wielding Lemmant. She took a brief moment to flash a message to her colleagues, describing the potential situation. They had to be ready to cover trouble in their own quadrants if anything erupted in Jade's—and to back her up in case the problem evolved beyond her capacity to handle it.

The noise level at the Palovoi table rose abruptly, and Jade started over there. The opening round of melons had been consumed and its effects were starting to show. The second round had been ordered, but, because the melons lost their effect very quickly after being exposed to air, they couldn't be prepared in advance. The time between consumption of the first round and delivery of the second was when trouble was most likely to occur. Despite their verbal aggressiveness—or perhaps because of it—the Palovoi seldom fought physically. When intoxicated, however, they were capable of major devastation—and the high price of the melons reflected this danger.

The Palovoi's tails were stroking their mates' bodies and braiding with one another in continually changing patterns. These melons must be from a potent harvest indeed; this behavior usually didn't start until the second round was half over.

The second round of melons arrived about the same time Jade did. Jade and the server were completely ignored as the sextet tore into the aphrodisiacs with their own knives. Jade started to breathe a little easier; the Palovoi would be pacified for a while now.

A gentle ciliated touch at the back of her neck caused Jade to whirl at full speed. Adrenaline pumped through her body and her right hand reached up in quick defense, even as her peripheral vision told her the touch was from the Furgato Exec. She caught his hand in a tight grip even as she controlled the rest of her reaction with an effort that taxed her to the limits.

"Arbiter Darcy," the Exec began, unaware how close he'd come to being killed. He gripped her hand as she let go of his. "My crew and I were wondering whether you'd care to discuss our kung'an at some length."

As Jade started to protest that she was too busy, the Exec continued smoothly, "Later, after shift, somewhere private?"

Jade then patiently explained that she didn't date customers. She had started to reclaim her hand from the complex caress of his two dozen cilia when a roar went up from the Palovoi table loud enough to cut through and silence the din in half the ingesterie. One of the melons had been very overripe. Jade pulled herself free with a hurried excuse and turned to the scene of the disturbance.

Migul was yelling at the server who'd brought the unsatisfactory melon. "You weak-armed excuse for a female! Get us some proper fruit now or the world will witness your fall from the trapeze!"

Much to Jade's relief, what passed for laughter was rippling through the group. They were noisier than usual, but just enjoying themselves. Talk at the other tables around them was just resuming normal levels when Migul spotted Jade.

"You're still here, I see, Arbiter Darcy," he said. "I'll bet you're as polite as that other human."

Jade's usual quick comeback was choked off as she realized what Migul had said. "What other human? Where . . . ?" she began.

Across the room the Lemmant jumped up from his seat, so abruptly his hat was knocked from his head, and uttered some unintelligible battle cry. He pulled his knife—a mean-looking curved-bladed dagger— from its scabbard and started charging across the empty squares between himself and the Commancor triad.

Questions about the new human on Cablans would have to wait. Jade instantly calculated the fastest possible route between the Palovoi table and the Commancors. She did not precisely run, but moved at a deceptively fast lope that covered the ground without the appearance of panic. If a square between herself and the Commancors was unoccupied, she cut through it; if there were patrons there, she took the path around. Even though she had a greater distance to travel, she arrived at the Commancors' area almost simultaneously with the Lemmant.

The Commancors had been involved with their own conversation and hadn't seen the Lemmant coming until he was almost upon them. They stood up quickly from their meal and spread themselves out within their area, presenting their foe with three separate targets. If he charged at any one of them, the other two would be quickly upon him.

Seeing this defense, the Lemmant hesitated. His drunken mind, while urging him to action, was inadequate to the task of planning tactical maneuvers. He stood unsteadily on his feet, anchored in place but waving his knife in a threatening manner.

Jade inserted herself into this formation, slipping directly between the Lemmant and the Commancors. This placed her back to the Commancors, which was not an enviable position—but all her attention had to be focused on the drunken Lemmant right now. She'd have to trust the Commancors were so startled that they wouldn't be as treacherous as their reputations warranted.

Although she had the spring-loaded blades up her sleeves, Jade stood openhanded facing her potential opponent. Her legs were slightly apart with just the barest bend to the knees; her arms were out at her sides in an almost universal nonthreatening posture. The Lemmant was already on a hair trigger; she didn't want to do anything to set him off.

Jade's voice was quiet and even as she spoke to the Lemmant. "Is there anything I can help you with?"

"They are murderers!" the Lemmant shrieked in a very high voice. "I am going to kill them!"

"No you're not," Jade said, just as quietly as before but with firm conviction. "This is an ingesterie, not a slaughterhouse or a battlefield. People come here to eat, drink, and talk, not to kill.''

"Let mudworm come," said one of the Commancors behind Jade. "We'll show him what is true fighting.''

Jade ignored the comment and concentrated exclusively on the Lemmant. "If you have a problem, if you have a grievance," she continued, "you can talk it over with me. I'll listen to you. Just put your blade away.''

"They are murderers, all of them," the Lemmant repeated, and slashed vigorously through the air with his knife to emphasize his point.

Jade put a firm override on her computer-augmented reflexes not to react to the gesture. Around her she could feel the ingesterie growing quiet as the other patrons turned to watch the drama. She hadn't asked for the other arbiters' help, yet; with luck, she wouldn't need it, but she knew they were there. She hoped they were keeping watch on the Commancors behind her.

The Commancors continued their jeering, as though trying to urge the Lemmant on. Jade tried to make the Lemmant focus entirely on her voice, ignoring the others.

"You obviously have a complaint," she said. "I'll be happy to listen to it. But you have to put the knife away first. We can't talk while you're holding that. Put the knife away and we'll talk.''

Jade was two steps away from him, out of arm's reach. With her speed and his drunkenness, she was confident she could close the gap and wrest the dagger from him if she needed to—but overt action was always the last recourse in her job. Decorum must be maintained.

The Lemmant's gaze wandered from Jade to the Commancors behind her, who were taunting him. With an incoherent scream he lurched a step to his left, toward the nearest Commancor. The other Commancors started to converge, and once again Jade physically interposed herself between the Lemmant and his enemies. She could feel the Commancors at her back, but she forced herself to stay calm.

She ended up a step closer to the Lemmant. His blade was within her reach—just as she was within range of its sharp edge. "You're a civilized being," she intoned. "You don't want to make a scene here."

"*They* are not civilized," the Lemmant said.

An idea occurred to Jade. "Does your family approve of brawling in public places?" she asked him. "Think of the dishonor it would bring to your name and your clan if you were killed as a common drunkard. You don't want that to happen, do you?"

A strange expression came over the Lemmant's face, and for the first time he lowered his arm slightly. His muscles were still tensed, but he was wavering. "But they . . ."

"The Commancors' behavior has no bearing on your personal honor," Jade said. "If you have a grievance, you must deal with it in an honorable manner. This doesn't become you. It's not honorable."

Jade watched with sharp eyes as his muscles began to loosen. Slowly and deliberately, making no sudden moves to alarm him, she reached up toward his knife hand. "You don't want to disgrace yourself in front of all these people. You can stop now. Nothing irreparable has happened. We'll talk, you'll tell me what your problem is, then we'll find an honorable way to deal with it. Trust me and no one will get hurt."

Her hand finally reached his and started to close about his fist. He trembled as her skin touched his, and then suddenly all the tension went out of him. The dagger dropped from his hand and Jade caught the hilt in midair before it could reach the ground. The Lemmant slowly pulled in upon himself and sank to the floor, making loud gasping sounds. He was oblivious to the world around him, lost in his personal grief. He was no longer a threat to anyone.

Jade tucked the dagger into her belt and finally turned to face the Commancors. "The management apologizes for this unfortunate incident," she said politely. "We're relieved to see that no physical harm has been done. You will, of course, not be charged for your meals."

"We knew he'd collapse," said one of the Commancors. "Lemmants always do."

The tallest and most authoritative of the Commancors, obviously the primal of this triad, asked, "What will become of cowardly Lemmant?"

Jade looked down at the Lemmant, still huddled dejectedly in a small pile. "He's obviously intoxicated," she said. "He'll be escorted from the premises back to his lodgings. When he sobers up and realizes his mistake, I'm sure he won't bother you again."

"Not sufficient," the primal harrumphed. "This creature has threatened us, and may again. Our future safety demands strong action. In Dominion, he would be killed—but on Cablans, I expect at least Greest's judgment."

The Commancors had every right to make that demand, Jade knew, but she really didn't want to go that far. Her rationale was that it would result in adverse publicity for the ingesterie—but deep down inside, her hatred for the Commancors made her unwilling to give them any satisfaction from this unfortunate encounter. Rix Kaf-Amur gave his arbiters broad discretionary powers to handle awkward situations—and what good were powers if they weren't exercised now and then?

"I really don't think such a drastic step is necessary," she told the Commancor.

"You're not person he threatened," the other responded. "My mates and I are now safe, but nothing stops him from ambushing us in dark spot outside ingesterie. Cowardly Lemmants act thus. I demand justice."

"Is safety your only concern," Jade asked, "or are you out to avenge your honor as well?"

Her question had the desired effect. "Let weakling Lemmants pule about honor," the primal said. "We wish only to travel through Cablans in safety.

"Not that solitary Lemmant is threat to Commancors in face-to-face combat," he added hastily. "But such cowardly creature might use impersonal weapon to kill us from safe distance."

"I understand," Jade said. "And if I can ensure

your safety on Cablans, will you then drop your demand for the Greest's justice?''

She and the primal stared at each other across the dining area for several interminable seconds. Finally the Commancor said, "How do you propose that?"

Jade turned back to the Lemmant and knelt beside him. Taking his chin in her hand, she forced him to look up into her face. "Listen to me well," she told him in stern tones. "You have violated both law and custom here, and the Commancors have a right to retribution. They've nobly agreed to drop charges against you if you guarantee their safety here on Cablans. You must give me your most solemn vow not to cause harm, either directly or indirectly, to any Commancors on Cablans.''

To a certain extent she'd been exaggerating when she claimed he'd broken the law—because there was no law on Cablans except the Greest's wishes. Since no one could know from day to day, or even moment to moment, what the Greest would think of something, most people tended to be conservative in their actions—but for all Jade knew, the Greest might decide to give this Lemmant a medal for his behavior here tonight.

Jade stared into the Lemmant's face, offering a silent prayer that he wasn't too drunk to realize she was trying to help him. At first the Lemmant looked back at her uncomprehendingly, but as she repeated her offer he began to nod. Pulling himself together, the Lemmant stood up slowly and turned to face the Commancors.

"I was wrong to attack you here," he said. "I will not cause harm, either directly or indirectly, to any Commancors on this world except in a matter of defending myself. This I do swear upon my honor, and upon the honor of my maternal uncle, and upon the honor of my clan.'' He looked unflinchingly into the eyes of the primal Commancor.

Jade rose to stand beside him. "If you know anything about Lemmants," she told the primal, "you'll know how serious his word is. Your safety is assured; he'd sooner die than hurt you or any of your race on

Cablans. Will you now agree to let him go without facing the Greest?''

The primal Commancor did not want to give in, but in the face of Jade's gentle insistence he could not find a reasonable alternative. ''Very well, cowardly creature may go,'' he said sneeringly. ''He's getting better than he deserves—but it's hard to sink low enough to give Lemmant what he truly deserves. Remove him from my sight before is ruined remainder of my appetite.''

After bowing to the Commancor, Jade hastened to comply. Taking the Lemmant by the arm, she led him gently but firmly past his table to retrieve his hat, then to the front entryway. The alien's steps were slow and wobbly, but he was in enough control that she didn't have to support him. Around her she could feel the tension in the air slowly ebbing as the other patrons realized the problem had been solved. Jade caught the attention of the other arbiters and nodded to let them know she had the situation well under control. It was then she noticed the too-casual return of the Furgatos to their table. They were stashing their weapons, not stolen baubles. Obviously they'd been prepared to come to her aid. This was atypical behavior, but Jade had no time to puzzle it out just now.

When she reached the entryway she discharged her prisoner into Bab-ankh's care. ''See that he reaches his lodgings safely,'' she said. ''Charge the Commancors' meal to his account and put his name on list four.''

''Not five?'' Bab-ankh asked, surprised. List four was for those people who could be readmitted to the ingesterie but kept under close scrutiny; list five was for those permanently barred until further notice.

''He's no fighter,'' Jade said, shaking her head. ''He's under some strain, but if we keep an eye on him we can probably control it. It'd be a shame to lose his business completely.''

She took the Lemmant's ceremonial dagger from the waistband of her slacks and handed it to the greeter, taking a close look at it for the first time. It was a beautiful blade, longer than her forearm, with a sharp edge and a hilt made of some material like gray ivory, engraved and set with jewels.

"Keep this here and let him know he can have it when he sobers up tomorrow. I'm sure he'll want it back; it's too good a blade to lose."

Her duty done here, she returned to her rounds in the ingesterie. Though her movements were as graceful as ever, she was emotionally a wreck. *I didn't need this,* she thought. *Not today. Let's just hope it's not an omen of bad news yet to come.*

Jade made the horizontal "all clear" sweep with her hands to signal her colleagues. Hiss!arr and Kokoti were already back at their rounds. Cyclad Arik, though, tilted her head back until her eyes weren't visible to Jade and spread her arms wide apart—the equivalent of a human's bow to a job well done. Jade was just as glad the mantisoid couldn't see her blush at the accolade.

Bringing herself back to reality, she started toward the Palovoi table to ask them about the "other human" Migul had mentioned—but it was too late. The Palovoi had risen from their rind-littered table and were staggering carefully toward the door. They were far too incoherent to make any sense out of—so intoxicated and aroused, in fact, that they were screaming about the utter lack of trapeze sets and trampolines a civilized establishment should have.

"Without privacy and proper equipment," one female yelled as she was helped out the door, "how could any civilized race enjoy the fruit properly?"

While this provided an interesting glimpse into the basically unknown sex life of the Palovoi, it frustrated Jade no end that she'd now have to wait for her meeting with Lorpet to get any real information about this development. She was also upset that the alien Palovoi should know about this other human before she did.

The Commancors seemed settled back to the rest of their meal, and Jade was just starting to relax when she saw the Exec headed her way, intent on an answer to his kung'an. Pretending not to see him, Jade walked briskly in another direction, meanwhile placing a discreet call home to Val.

As she'd hoped, her home computer's encyclopedic file had a number of replies to this classic riddle. Jade was too mentally exhausted to come up with an original one, so she memorized an old answer and hoped it would satisfy the Exec. Meanwhile she prayed that the last two hours of her shift—which had been average except for the Lemmant and the Commancors—would go smoothly. She had to be calm later when she met Lorpet and learned what he had to tell her about this other human who'd come to Cablans.

CHAPTER 3

Galentor's

Jade stopped just inside Galentor's airlock-style opening for a quick repair of the damage the wind and rain had done to her composure and outfit. A gentle fall night for Cablans: -4C, winds from the northeast at fifteen kilometers, and a centimeter of rain each hour. After work she'd changed from her adrenaline-sweat-soaked purple recyclables into what she thought of as her "merc suit"—one of the two she always kept in her locker at Rix's place. Tonight she was very glad for the water-repellent, insulated, comfortable jumpsuit with integral boots. A quick shake and brush got rid of the rain on the fabric, a rapid folding turned the hood into a thick cowl collar, and the gloves fit into one of the pouches on the heavy belt. The deep charcoal gray was hard to see at night. As she took a moment to survey the casino's interior from the half-lit vestibule through the etched-glass door, she was glad for the extra camouflage.

Galentor's gambling parlor was built on two levels. Most of the actual gaming was done on the vast lower level, with a surface area more than five times that of the ingesterie. It was broken up into distinct units, each with its own set of tables, benches, and paraphernalia for various popular games, though there were no walls between the units. Bright lights were always flashing here. There was a high central ceiling above this portion of the establishment, giving the noise and the odors of the gamblers on the floor a chance to dissipate.

Around the perimeter of this open floor was a series

of closed rooms that could be used for dining, rendez-vous, or private games. On the second level, above the closed rooms, was an open gallery where the less structured betting took place. This was where the high-stakes gamblers usually lounged, looking over the rail-ings at the frenetic activities of the people below them and making wagers on anything that struck their fancy.

Everything was wagered on at Galentor's. The hourly and daily attendance, hourly and daily take, or weekly, or monthly, or annually. You could bet on the next elections on various planets, the nature of the Greest, or the lifespan of a drowning kitten. Anything and ev-eryone was fair game. Fair, because Galentor stood for less than the average amount of rigging, and this reputation had made his fortune. As he often said, the house made so much on an honest game, rigging was a silly waste of time and bad customer relations.

Looking up at the gallery, Jade could see the usual long-term boards were up, though she couldn't make out much at this angle. The odds on the Greest's being male did seem to be dropping for some reason, though that was a sucker's game; Jade was firmly convinced no one would ever find out, so no one would ever win or lose any money on it. On the floor, the various games of chance weren't as busy as usual—the tables and domes were less than half full. That often meant a contest of some sort going on, though she couldn't see just what it was from here; she'd have to go in to find out.

She eased through the inner etched-glass door, hop-ing to slide in and out unobtrusively. She was well known here, and much of her extra work came from referrals at these tables. Tonight, though, she was in little mood for salesmanship—not with another human on Cablans, perhaps present here in the room. But since she didn't see very many creatures even vaguely humanoid from her vantage point at the top of the main room's entry ramp, she placed a bet with fate on her safety and started down the ramp.

Jade walked quickly across the elegant inner atrium that doubled as a security survey point. The manage-ment always knew who was coming and going, and a notice of her arrival was transmitted to the boards as Jade started down the last bit of gently sloping ramp *(the better to throw you out of,* Jade thought) when an overmodulated screech echoed from the back of the huge main hall.

"Jade Darcy! Jade Darcy, look over here! I have offers for you new! My employ you'll be soon in!" Galentor's screech cut across both the room and Jade's hope for a quiet night. She was in for a long session now.

"Galentor, my friend, I've often explained that I wouldn't risk our good association by such a mundane thing as employment. A contract I'll consider, but a job? I'm happy at Rix's." Jade tried vainly to slip through the hall before the galumphing quadruped could cut her off.

"Always this me you tell, my battling biped," roared Galentor as his four legs forced him through the crowd. Physically he somewhat resembled a griffin of Earth mythology, with head and wings like an eagle's but a body more like a horse's than a lion's. He had a disposition that, upon occasion, could make a harpy look civilized. "I have decided the job to expand. Not only would work you in the south annex, assistant head you would be of security—head when my Purrchrp retires."

That made Jade stop. "That's Miclavra's job. What happened to him?"

"The job would this way pay better, and even if you refused sex with some in the south annex, you—"

"What happened to him, dammit?" Jade's temper, drawn thin from the knowledge there was another human on Cablans, began to shred.

"—would still have work and so I would profit and bored would you not be. I have all thought given— *urch.*"

As the owner of the establishment had drawn close enough, Jade took hold of the capelet he used as both decoration and pocketbook and twisted it around his throat. She put her face close to his and shouted, "What happened to my . . . to Miclavra? Tell *now* me!"

She let go of him and stepped back, her posture loose and seemingly relaxed. She knew how dangerous he could be, but she was well past the point of curbing her temper. Galantor readjusted his cloak and his manner. The long-lost old friend gave way to the matter-of-fact businessman.

"Jeralvo a big purse offered for single combat to the death with a Commancor. Money needed Miclavra, and volunteered he for the fight. He lost. You the job is open to, with or without the south annex—the south annex more pays."

Assananziol Jeralvo varied between second and third on the list of people Jade would most like to see vanish painfully from the universe. The Reverdan was the center of unlimited corruption and grief on Cablans. He had no legitimate business dealings that Jade had ever heard of, and seemed to live for gambling—spreading dissension and death in the name of honest sportsmanship. Jeralvo was just the sort to sponsor a single-combat contest with a Commancor with a high purse, just to entice some sucker to enter. Jeralvo himself never killed anyone—but people died or were otherwise destroyed at his whims.

But Miclavra's too smart to kill himself in a lunatic fight like that, Jade thought. She had fought Miclavra many times. Those battles had earned her living the first weeks in Cablans, and the offer from Rix to join his staff. Return matches had become annual events and very profitable for all concerned. If Jade had had a comrade on Cablans those first hungry years, it would have been Miclavra.

"I need another job right now like another pair of legs." This sally brought expressions of humor from many of the quadrupeds in the room. "What happened to Miclavra's body?"

"It was recycled. No money for death rituals had he. It all he'd bet."

"And then he lost," said Jade very quietly.

"The bets he won, but money all went to his family as requested he."

Jade once again felt adrift in the multiple thought systems of Cablans. With the u-trans making the most alien speech seem like some type of English, she often started to feel she knew the other inhabitants—until something like this made her realize just how different their minds really were.

"You mean he bet against himself, and threw the fight?" Jade asked.

"No, knives with he fought."

"I meant he didn't fight to win—lost intentionally to win the bet."

"Never! Honor he had and won it till the thrust at the last. But against that one, won no one."

She set the incident aside as too alien to be dealt with now, and turned her mind back to the meeting she dreaded and hungered for. "I'm meeting the K'luune, Lorpet. What table is reserved for us?"

"The job offered is still pending, dear friend, sweet fighter. It is better than ever offered you I have."

"No, no, no! Not now, not tomorrow, not ever that foresee I can." Jade stopped short for a moment. "I'm even starting to talk like you. Just tell me where to meet—"

Her voice trailed off as a shout went up around the room. From this position she could see the gallery-level gameboard better, and on it was a symbol set she knew well—the Cablans pidgin for her name. Obviously even her taste in jobs was well known and the odds on her taking it weren't too high, but Galentor had still lost a bundle on her refusal. Angry at his arrogance—he thought he had an offer she couldn't refuse—but amused by what it cost him, she turned to face the owner of this madhouse only to find him beating a fast retreat.

"Room nineteen, north wing, biped who's costing me everything," he called over his shoulder, and slipped behind the tank of small sharks he kept for gaming.

Jade threw back her head and roared with laughter as the absurdity of it hit. The sound caused many players to interrupt their game and stare. Human laughter was very close in sound to a challenge of some other races. As the u-trans devices interpreted it as a pleasure signal, the other beings relaxed and returned to play. Jade, relieved her encounter with Galentor had been a quick one, proceeded to the expensive private room the K'luune had reserved. It was going to be a long and a costly night.

Galentor's flowed like a river; you never stepped in the same casino twice. Galantor had designed the gambling pit of his casino on rotatable sections of flooring. If a table wasn't doing well for him, it was moved to the back of the house. If a game became hot, it was often moved to the front in the midst of other play so that more players noticed and could bet along. The paths between sections changed frequently, the building arrangement was seldom left alone for more than a night, and the crowds were never predictable. Without the help of electronic guideposts every twenty-five meters or so, Jade could have wandered for an hour looking for a room that, despite its name, was now on the east side instead of the north.

Jade easily swung past the various games of chance, the randomizing computers, the neutrino detectors, and the roulette wheels. The sound of the immense hydraulic lifts that moved floor sections made her turn in time to catch an alien version of a bingo game being moved into her path. A quick check of the map told her this meant she'd have to detour through her least favorite part of the place, the zoo.

Jade understood speed races, and battles between sentients, and even using creatures carefully bred for such events. Yet many species preferred to bet on the outcome of violence between other creatures. Galentor didn't disappoint them. The zoo held the stock for such battles.

The zoo contained huge holding tanks for sharks and their analogs from many worlds. Pretty fighting fish, only ten centimeters long, in iridescent colors with tissue-weight fins, were housed next to screeching eels, next to multilimbed mammalian sea creatures, next to the nearby sentient plantlike creatures from some world Jade had never learned the name of. Jade found the actions of such violent eating machines too familiar and never bothered to watch their fights.

Weasels, insects, reptiles, and other land creatures

appeared and were used at a terrific rate. Jade thought it appropriate that one of the most enduring, and in its class the highest-rated creature, was the Terran brown rat. The rat colony here, despite frequent fights, numbered over fifty from the initial shipment of three. It had been a busy year. Sooner or later she knew one would get loose; she'd vowed to move off Cablans the next day.

Jade took the indicated turn past the aquarena and saw remains of the last battle. A large mammalian-appearing animal was being devoured by a thresher shark. The scoreboard showed it was the twenty-fifth battle for this veteran. As Jade hurried past, the shark shook loose a bite of its dinner, and the splash thus created landed in front of Jade. The portion of skull that was pushed out contained a large, now-clouding green eye. The green shade was just close enough to that of her vain cousin Loraine's eyes. With a curse Jade kicked the mess toward a cleaning robot and hurried through the last tanks to the hall of private rooms.

From the gallery above, Galentor noted her reaction, timed it from the video playback on the security monitors, and adjusted the odds on the board in front of him. On the main floor there was a flurry of new wagers.

Damm it! I know better than to be spooked by a fucking little thing like that. So it looked close to human, and Loraine had been so proud of her eyes and the way the boys flirted with her about them—when there were any. . . . Another goddamn human! What kind of military bastard would be assigned to a backwater like this one? Finally! The room! Fucking prissy son of a bitch and his remodeling!

Jade entered the room with too-casual slowness. "I trust this humble person will not intrude, oh, shit."

The room was empty.

Jade stepped around the two-meter spiral ramp that served as a chair for K'luunes and took the three stairs to the platform on the other side of the table at a single leap. The ramp, table, and chair on the raised back half of the floor were the main furnishings, all in a dull gold with edgings of deep coral. The walls were of a local wood the color of molten copper, with a fine grain of dark forest green. The sideboard with its holding oven, dumbwaiter, and ordering computer was of the same wood, with Galentor's logo inlaid on it in gold. Above it a screen was tuned to a picture of a mountain draped in autumnal foliage. With Jade's entry it began running instructions, in several languages, on how to order from it. These were made to appear as banners being pulled around the mountain. Jade ignored them for now.

The Nloian banquet captain had at least remembered her preference and put her back to the blank wall, but she'd arrived first and that would cost her money. Now she was in place, and Lorpet would beg forgiveness for his intrusion into *her* room. Well, at least she could place her order quickly.

"Kitchen, order to be billed to Greenstone account, number 30nn8. Coffee, usual Greenstone blend, small pot, with condiments—and K'luune rice." The last was an inspiration, if it could be delivered before Lorpet's arrival.

The door opened moments after the refreshments arrived via dumbwaiter. Lorpet slithered in and began his effusive apologies, only to be cut short by Jade's opening salvo in this strange battle.

"My most honored and revered host. Can you ever forgive the effrontery of this lowly creature? I arrived too early and invaded the room you reserved before you could take possession of it, thereby usurping your position. Surely such an insult cannot be forgiven even though it was unintentional, and so, most exalted K'luune, I am prepared to be banished forever from your august presence."

That ought to confuse him into at least one concession, Jade thought. *If he doesn't forgive me, I leave. If he forgives me, that means he has the power to do so, and therefore can't expect me to give him the excessive generosity a superior owes an inferior.* "I see this one who is less than dust beneath your . . . feet has distressed you. I shall regretfully leave your most estimable presence."

Lorpet squirmed on all twenty little feet and finally

conceded the point. "No, most illustrious warrior. You are not to blame. This pitiful data broker is late for our appointment, thus forcing you to be early."

"How can a lowly Terran like myself be so presumptuous as to expect punctuality when an important and prominent citizen like you certainly must tend to matters of far greater gravity than my meager concerns? The fact that you are here at all shows far more generosity than I have any right to expect. My hubris far exceeds my station, and I am forced to withdraw."

"Stay. This humble seeker of truth cannot withhold forgiveness when no insult was meant or given." Lorpet then began the slithering glide of his sluglike body up the ramp his race found comfortable for lounging and dining.

Jade walked around the end of the table and hit the lever that controlled the sideboard's recessed holding oven. The coffee service and a flan dish of the apparent mixture of rice gruel, stewed okra, and moldy breads that was called K'luune rice rose to the sideboard surface.

"This grateful and undeserving recipient of your generosity hopes her inadequate offering of refreshment in some infinitesimal way will compensate for her grievous wrong."

Lorpet began squirming again as Jade laid the dishes before him, serving him humbly as a subordinate would. This gave her hope that the night would cost her less than the week's pay she'd begun to fear it would.

This verbal sparring went on as they ate. Lorpet insisted that the information such a worthless person as himself could gather would probably be trivial and meaningless to someone as enlightened as Jade, and therefore he hesitated even to offer it to her. Jade assured him he was wiser and more insightful than she was, and that she would be honored if he shared it with her. Lorpet told her it would be his honor to give her the information for free if he thought it would be worthwhile to someone as illustrious as she was. Jade countered by asserting that the information gathered by so sagacious a being would be worth far more than she could possibly think of paying, and that she couldn't insult him by offering him a sum for such priceless data.

It took nearly two hours of haggling for Jade to "convince" Lorpet to tell her what he knew. He gave her the information for free, of course—but her convincing argument totaled 195 eus, including the rental of his room for the evening. Only then did she learn what she'd been after.

The newcomer was a woman named Megan Cafferty, in her late fifties with a hobby of appearing in amateur operas and operettas. Most important, she was a civilian, the major stockholder and chair of the board of directors of a multibillion-eu industrial conglomerate called Cafferty Technologies. She was known to be smart, politically well connected, and a recent widow with three grown children and four grandchildren. There was no reason that anyone could guess for her to be on Cablans—but she was at the Palazzo Hotel in the Regency Suite. In the forty-eight hours since she'd been on Cablans, she'd met with one clerk and a trade delegation of the Palovoi, though Lorpet didn't know what her business with them was. It hadn't gone well, he thought, because the session lasted nearly four hours. They both knew a long meeting was disaster with the Palovoi.

Lorpet gave Jade a picture taken by someone as Megan Cafferty had exited the transfer station on Cablans. It showed a woman in her fifties, with luminous white hair, green eyes with a laughing way about them, and a body softened by her years and good living, but obviously still athletic. She carried a large bag herself, and was wearing a designer suit and boots that, Jade knew from Val's recent fashion updates, had to be worth as much as Jade would make all year at Rix's. And Jade was well paid. She put the picture into a waterproof pocket and carefully fastened it. Further assessment and analysis could wait till she got home.

Jade arranged the credit transfer, begged the illustrious Lorpet to remember his benighted friend if more information came his way, and went through the parting ritual abasements with a great sense of relief and much suspicion. This wasn't the profile of anyone who might be after her—but what would a woman like this want on Cablans, so far from all other human contact?

Jade called Val after Lorpet left, giving her the data and instructing her to search whatever sources she could find for more information on this person. Then she left the private room, checked the guidepost at the end of the hall, and looked up to translate it into real-life terms. She made a mental note that one portion of the floor along her path would be moving, but it could easily be sidestepped. Then she set her mind to the question of Megan Cafferty. This puzzle engrossed her. She was so lost in speculation that she was a quarter of the way through the main hall before she noticed the riot.

Fights were always starting in Galentor's, which was why he needed good bouncers. People with large amounts of money at stake often took petty disagreements to great extremes. In the ingesterie, such unpleasantnesses were the exception, but here they seemed to be the rule.

Five large creatures were entangled in a melee over to her left, and like a wave the surge of violence was flowing in her direction. Jade looked up and saw that it was far enough away not to be a threat to her, so she relaxed slightly—but as she continued to scan the room she saw no signs whatsoever of Galentor's security force.

Where were they? There should have been at least six on duty right now, and they were usually more efficient than to let something this size develop. They couldn't all be on a break at once. Could there be some other emergency elsewhere in the building, something on so large a scale that this brawl could be ignored?

Her professional mind was analyzing the matter, checking to see where the dynamics of the situation were and how the fighting could be broken up most effectively with the least amount of damage. Then, as she realized what she was doing, she gave an angry hiss through clenched teeth.

Fuck it! I've already done that job today, and got

paid for it there. I ain't giving away no fucking free-bies.

She had started to walk on when she spotted the second brawl rolling toward her from the right, this one much closer. Again there were none of Galentor's bouncers to be seen.

Shit, if this is that bastard's way of suckering me into working for him, he's out of luck. It ain't going to happen. I'm having nothing to do with it.

A heavy metal chair came flying through the air at her head; without even slowing her pace she leaned the upper half of her body backward and the chair missed her by a good three centimeters, clattering noisily against a table. Some sort of mug—there was little time to appreciate finer details—also flew at her, but a graceful sidestep to the right caused it to shatter harmlessly against the plated hide of an elephantine Mororian.

In front of her, popping up like a jack-in-the-box, was a member of the race she called Jackals, since she could neither spell nor pronounce their real name. He had a long snout with pointed teeth, hairy ears, and shoulders that hunched over awkwardly. He snarled at her and charged with maniacal fury, death and de-struction gleaming in his red eyes.

Jade waited until he was almost upon her and then took one step more to the right, which put her on a section of the floor that was rotating counterclockwise just fast enough to carry her backward and out of the Jackal's path. The creature's momentum carried him past her into a quartet of beings who'd been quietly playing an electronic card game, and who were not at all pleased with the unexpected intrusion. Jade took two steps forward, then a step back to the left onto her original path and kept walking.

She sensed, more than saw, someone rushing up at her from behind, while her way ahead was blocked by two beings grappling at one another's throats. There was no open ground to step on either side, so she made a quick leap to her left, onto a table where a group of people, ignoring the brawl around them, were tossing multisided, irregularly shaped objects that made dice seem trivial. The creature coming from behind her ran through the spot where she'd been, running into the brawling pair ahead of her and instantly transforming it into a threesome.

Jade muttered a quick apology to the gamblers she'd interrupted, then started hopping from tabletop to tabletop on an irregular zigzag course toward the exit. She passed over or dodged the rapidly expanding melee until she reached the table nearest the door and dropped lightly back to the ground. The only obstacle remaining in front of her was a pair of combatants rolling on the floor, intent on killing each other.

Jade was prepared to step calmly over them when they suddenly rolled toward her, arms outstretched and grabbing for her legs. Making a quick off-balance leap, she vaulted past them and tucked herself into a ball, landing on the other side and rolling forward in a somersault. She rose gracefully beside the door, then turned to survey the chaos behind her.

Galentor's was a mess. Nearly half the patrons on the ground level were now involved in the brawl to some extent, while the rest tried gamely to ignore the disturbance and carry on with their betting. Bodies were lying sprawled on the floor or on tabletops, either dead, unconscious, or just too tired to go on with their fighting. Furniture was smashed, though the gambling machines themselves were unharmed; Galentor had had them made virtually indestructible.

Glancing at the upper gallery level, she saw that the pidgin symbol for her name was still on the betting board, and her anger flared again. She didn't know whether Galentor had deliberately started the fracas or whether he had merely taken advantage of one that started conveniently, but he'd obviously been willing to allow some damage to his establishment to entice her into a fight.

Galentor was standing next to the board, glaring at her. He must have lost even more money on her tonight, a thought that comforted Jade a little. With satiric exaggeration she made a deep formal bow to him—and as she did so, the drink from someone's glass flew in her direction, dousing her face and hair. The stuff smelled terrible and stung her eyes, making her give a little yelp, cough, and snort.

Gathering what dignity she could while still coughing and wiping her eyes, Jade straightened up, turned her back on the riot, and walked out the door.

CHAPTER 4

Fastal ip Fornen

There was an irregular lump lying on the walkway in front of her door as a drenched Jade arrived home, her feet slurping where she had dug in some of the paving stones to trip a stranger on the path. The gloomy downpour and the night darkness obscured the shape, making it impossible to recognize. Jade slowed her pace and quickly checked that her knives were loose in their forearm sheaths. When her nerves were this shot, any tiny deviation from the ordinary was a cause for alarm. She stepped up to the curb, glad for the textured boot soles that gripped even the slick granite blocks. Silent as any drop of the falling mist, she advanced, watching for the possible baiters of this attention trap.

The shape didn't move as she approached. She recognized the shape just before the sickly scent brought recognition of its condition. A frizzlic. A very dead frizzlic.

Daski, Cablans's ecological equivalent of coyotes, commonly preyed on frizzlics, and a frizzlic caught in open ground was easy prey to those vicious, snapping jaws. Jade's arrival must have scared the dasko off before it finished devouring its catch.

"No. Not you too." The moan escaped Jade but didn't register on her ears. Jade's heart seem to swell and her mouth went dry. "Every damn thing in this fucking shit-ass world has to die. In front of me. I told you to go away."

Jade knelt beside the body, still moaning as she looked for any markings in the dim light of the security system Val monitored. The frizzlic's hindquarters had been chewed, and bare bones protruded from its rear legs. She took a pocket flash out of one pouch and shone it on the corpse. Though the fur was streaked with blood, it was obviously mottled gray and brown in an irregular pattern, with no marking on the forehead. She sucked in a deep moist breath and was silent. This was not *her* frizzlic.

The wave of relief was followed quickly by a burst of anger. "Goddamn motherfucking little son-of-a-bitch parasite deserves what it got. I don't have time to waste on a fucking fur ball. No reason to care which one of them gets caught by their betters. Damn fool thing to waste time on."

She straightened up, wiped her nose on a handkerchief from her pocket, and kicked the dead body into the bushes. "Let the dasko have the rest. To the hunter go the spoils." The last steps to the door were taken in a firm parade-march step.

She palmed the door, and Val admitted her. Once safely locked inside she stripped off the wet jumpsuit and flung it with the ease of practice into the hole in the wall that Val provided, where it was promptly cleaned, folded, and stored away until its next use. Jade stepped under the dryer in the bathroom until even the psychological moisture from the rain had evaporated from her skin and hair. Finally feeling at home again, she returned to the main room.

"What've you found on Megan Cafferty?" she asked her computer.

"Just the *Who's Who* listing, about two years old. There's a printout on the table. Other references are available from the central library and will be forwarded within the next week."

Jade picked the sheet up and looked it over. Megan Cafferty, age fifty-six, chair of the board of directors of Cafferty Technologies, on the boards of several universities and charitable organizations; husband Liam Cafferty, also involved in numerous businesses and organizations—he had his own separate reference that Val had also printed; three children, four grandchildren; hobby, opera singing . . .

Jade wadded the paper into a ball and threw it disgustedly against the screen. She began striding about the apartment, slamming her fist into the walls hard enough to bounce the cupboard doors open; she flung them closed again with such violence they ricocheted back to hit her fist. "Lorpet! The fucking, slime-snorting bastard sold me an old reference book. All he had was a name and an entry photo. I could have gone to the fucking Greest for that. He played me for a moron, but he'll pay for it. I'll take those mandibles of his and stick them so far up his asshole he'll rip his own throat out from the inside. If it hadn't been so important . . . if I hadn't fucking freaked and just checked it out as usual, like I should have. Three days' pay for a goddamn name and entry photo?"

Jade's voice had climbed to a barely audible screech. She froze with her fist an inch from her practice mirror. Her voice had been one of rage; the face she couldn't see through her suddenly full eyes was one of terror and despair. She melted to the floor, knees akimbo, her legs forming a perimeter for her safety. "I can't take it, Val, not today." The whisper was too soft for even the computer's mikes to pick up clearly, so as programmed, it didn't respond. "This is just one thing too many, one fucking thing too many." Her body trembled with barely restrained emotions, and she wrapped her arms around herself to stop the worst of the shaking.

Head bent down, body quivering, Jade Darcy sat silently in the middle of her fighting floor rocking gently back and forth, while the computer that was the nearest thing she had to a friend waited patiently for the next order or question. And waited. And waited. . . .

There were nightmares again tonight, but not *the* nightmare. These were fantasies of flight and pursuit, of shadows lurking behind corners, of an unknown specter looming over her with white hair and piercing green eyes, and no matter where Jade ran she could not escape that confident gaze. Lorpet was laughing at her, Galentor was placing bets on whether she could outrun the shadows . . . and somewhere unseen was *his* presence, lurking, waiting, always waiting. . . .

"Jade," came Val's patient voice from Rix's mouth. "Jade," came the voice from behind her, intruding gently into the corners, dispelling the clouds of uncertainty and fear. "Jade, wake up."

The universes of dreams and reality intermingled momentarily as the one dissolved and the other took its place. Jade liked to pride herself on her soldier's ability to come instantly awake and alert, but too much had happened yesterday and she was too dragged out to respond properly.

"Huh?" she mumbled. "Is it morning already?"

The bonds on her hands and feet unstrapped themselves; there was no threat of violence to require them. "Not yet your standard wakeup time," Val said, "but you have a visitor waiting outside."

That brought Jade fully awake. She sat up instantly, heart pounding, feeling suddenly naked rather than just nude. "Is it the human, Cafferty?" She was already calculating whether she'd have better odds fighting unarmed or with the five-shot tucked beside the bed, or whether she should hit the arsenal first.

"The creature is not a Terran human," Val said, "but I do not recognize it."

Jade closed her eyes to steady herself, letting the worst of the fighting rush work its way out of her system. She could relax a little, but not much. Visitors did not generally just drop in on her. "Who is it, then?"

"It hasn't announced itself. It hasn't even approached the door. It stands outside in the rain, moving back and forth, as though uncertain what to do."

"Put it on the screen."

The screen lit up, showing the dark, rainy scene outside the door and the indistinct, but definitely humanoid, figure lurking in the shadows. "Put a little more light on the subject, Val," Jade said quietly, her hand reaching for the comforting feel of her gun.

Val increased the circle of light outside the door, and Jade's eyes widened. It was a Lemmant—the same one, she was sure, who'd caused the commotion at

Rix's. What was he doing here? Looking for revenge because she'd stopped him from attacking the Commancors?

"Is he armed?" she asked.

"I detect no energy-based weapons. He could be concealing chemical-based or mechanical."

"I'm not worried about them. Get me my gray kaftan."

Val produced the loose, flowing garment, and Jade felt immensely better with the clothing over her body. Soft though the fabric was, it was armor between herself and the world.

She put the u-trans in her ear and briefly considered picking up a knife, then discarded that notion quickly. The Lemmant had no energy weapons, which was her biggest concern. She'd seen his fighting skills—or lack thereof—at the ingesterie. In these close quarters and in the higher gravity of her home, she could counter anything he tried hand-to-hand. Her trained body should be weapon enough, though she pocketed her five-shot pistol just in case as she stepped into her firm-soled slippers.

Taking up a position behind the heavy console, out of line of sight of the door, she said, "Open the door, Val. Slowly."

As the door slid quietly into the wall and light streamed out from her apartment into the rainy night beyond, she watched the figure of the Lemmant on the screen. The increased light a moment ago had already startled him; now he looked as though he wanted to run, yet he remained rooted in place.

"Either come in or go away," Jade said. "Your standing there makes me nervous—and you don't want to make me nervous."

Her words broke the spell of paralysis. The Lemmant took a hesitant step forward, stopped again, and said, "Pardon, please. You are the being called Jade Darcy?"

Jade quickly discarded a dozen witty comebacks. She was too tired for repartee, and the draft from the open door was too cold. "Yes. What do you want?"

"You are the one who . . . who disarmed me at Rix Kaf-Amur's ingesterie yesterday?"

"Yes."

The Lemmant took another step forward, stopping just short of the doorsill. "I . . . I must thank you."

Jade frowned. "What for?"

"I behaved in a most dishonorable fashion in public. You stopped me from irredeemably disgracing myself."

Jade shrugged, even though the Lemmant couldn't see her and might not correctly interpret the gesture even if he could. "I did my job, that's all."

"Still, I had to come see you and express my gratitude."

"In the middle of the night, in the rain? There's more on your mind than just gratitude. You could have phoned that in. Either come in here where I can talk to you face to face, or go away and let me sleep."

The Lemmant took the big step over the threshold into Jade's apartment—nearly stumbling, as everyone did who wasn't expecting the higher gravity inside. Once he was fully in Val slid the door shut again, trapping him in Jade's home territory.

The fellow was taller than she remembered him—but this time he wasn't drunk, which meant he might be standing straighter. He was more than a full head taller than she was, with long, lanky bones and a deceptively soft, flabby appearance that the dense subcutaneous fat gave all his race. His movements were slow and labored, particularly in her apartment with its heavier-than-normal gravity. He wore a three-piece outfit of a long-sleeved bronze vest that came to midtorso, a midriff wrap that was like a triple wide gold cummerbund, and tight red trousers with a strange black embroidered design woven into them. In a scabbard attached to the cummerbund was the beautiful ceremonial dagger she'd taken from him before. He must have retrieved it from the ingesterie before coming here.

The Lemmant looked around, a little mystified. Jade, feeling more secure with the situation, stepped forward, allowing him to see her for the first time.

"You have the advantage on me," she said. "You know who I am, but I know nothing about you."

The Lemmant spread his arms widely, head thrown back—perhaps his race's equivalent of a bow. "I am Fastal, with the honor of being ip Fornen. I am of a line of seventh-rank nobility, though of a side branch without title or fief. My parents united the lines of Fornen and Distalba, and my grandparents on my father's side—"

"I'm sure this genealogy is important to you," Jade interrupted, "but it ain't worth shit to me. I've had a rough day and you cut short my sleep, so you'd better open up soon or I'll throw you back out in the bushes just like that damn dead frizzlic. What do you want from me? Kitchen conformation, Val."

The bed folded into her table, and two benches rose out of the floor. She perched lightly on the end of one bench, but left Fastal ip Fornen standing. She deliberately did not invite him to sit.

The Lemmant opened and closed the fingers on both hands; there was no mistaking it for anything but a nervous gesture. "I understand that you sometimes do special sorts of work."

"How special?"

"Killing for hire."

"I'm not an assassin, no."

Fastal ip Fornen waved his right hand vigorously in front of his mouth, as though cutting off his previous words. "I must have expressed myself badly. Not an assassin, no, but a soldier. Someone who wages fights with others in the same profession."

"Who told you all this?"

"A K'luune named Lorpet."

That slimy grubworm's had a busy night, Jade thought. "I hope you didn't pay him too much to learn that."

"A hundred eus."

"You were robbed. Anyone who knows me could have told you that for free. I don't hide my services; that would defeat the purpose of being in business."

The Lemmant looked abashed and started to say something, but Jade cut him off. "The proper word is 'mercenary,' " she said. "I'm hired in situations where you need to gain the advantage over your opposition. I'm skilled in the use of weapons and unarmed fighting."

"Lorpet said you were very good."

Jade gave a slight nod. "I'm alive."

"How much do you charge?"

"They say if you have to ask, you probably can't afford it."

Fastal seemed to fall apart all at once. "I need someone's help desperately. It is a matter of honor. You were so skilled in the ingesterie, so sensitive, I thought I could . . . that is, I thought you would—"

"Sit down over there," Jade said, indicating the opposite end of the other bench. "I can see I'm not going to get any sleep tonight anyway. You may as well tell me your story. Just keep it entertaining so this isn't a complete waste of time."

The Lemmant sat obediently, still floundering. "Where should I begin?"

"If you start more than one generation back, you go out the door real fast."

Fastal took in a breath to steady himself. "You should be aware that it is not easy for my people to expand to other worlds. Our home planet has a lower gravity than those of most other intelligent races, and we need a particular atmospheric chemistry and low level of solar radiation. Finding the right combination has been impossible until just recently.

"Several decades ago, the Greest opened up a new world called Haldek, attainable only through the Cablans transfer station. This world was ideally suited to us. There were not even any other intelligent races living there. Other peoples could settle there, but it was most perfect for Lemmants. We applied to the Greest and, at great expanse to us, he agreed to let us colonize Haldek.

"I cannot explain to you how much this meant to my people. We had been within the Greest's network of civilizations for over two centuries, watching other races expand onto new planets, and our peculiar circumstances forced us to limit ourselves to our original world. Our social scientists blamed the rise in crime, despair, rioting, and general malaise on our world to a feeling of hopelessness and overcrowding. We desperately needed this new world of Haldek so our race would grow and flourish.

"My family emigrated to Haldek when my father was a young man, and I was born there. Since we were seventh-rank nobility, we had a sufficiently large homestead out in the country, though not too far from Detalla, the capital city and transfer station. We had many servants to work the land, and everyone was prospering. I won't say it was paradise; there were problems with weather and some strange diseases, and one year when the crops did not grow at all. But for the most part it was a change from our native world, and the settlers were proud of their role in Lemmantine evolution."

Jade didn't bother to stifle a yawn. She'd had little sleep after a very trying day, and the Lemmant's pedantic style only made the matter worse. Only the knowledge that he had a dangerous blade in his sash kept her remotely awake. The odds were the alien wouldn't interpret her yawn as a sign of boredom—and if he did, perhaps it would spur him to liven up his story.

"About three years ago," Fastal continued, "I was sent back to Lemmanta to obtain a more formal education, as befitted a young man of my rank and station. When that was completed, I would return to Haldek and take up my rightful place within the family structure. Only before I could return, the Commancors struck."

Jade sat up instantly. Suddenly this dull story had taken on a very familiar, very personal, note.

"Yesterday was the second anniversary of the Dominion's invasion," the Lemmant went on, "which is why I was in so . . . susceptible a mood. I do not know why the Commancors decided to attack us. They have plenty of worlds of their own; they did not need ours as well—"

"That's never stopped them before," Jade said quietly.

"—and we had paid the Greest extravagantly for the right to settle there, so we do not know why he agreed to let the Commancor Dominion make war on us. But one moment everything was peaceful, the next moment Haldek was invaded.

"I was not there, or I would not be here talking to you now. I cannot describe what happened. . . ."

Jade needed no descriptions. The images came unbidden to her mind. Images of Toranawa. Houses erupting in towers of flame. People lying facedown in the mud, their backs burned by the Commancors' energy beams. Children screaming with terror as they ran helpless into the unfriendly night. Her brother dying in her arms, blood dripping like tears down his face from his sightless eyes. The sounds of sirens, the smell of decay, the taste of ozone. The images came unbidden to her mind. Jade needed no descriptions.

". . . and so my family's honor demanded they stand and fight," Fastal was saying. "The Commancors wiped them out down to the last child. I am the sole survivor of my family."

"You're very lucky," Jade said quietly, her face turned toward the door.

"I am humiliated and embarrassed," Fastal said, and Jade assumed his trembling was a sign of agitation. "The Council of the Families and the Delineator all made great noises about what a tragedy it was, and how we were humiliated by the Commancors and betrayed by the Greest, but in the end they took no action. 'The Commancor Dominion owns many worlds and has many resources,' they said. 'We could not fight them and win. Perhaps they would even set their sights on Lemmanta itself. Let us not provoke them into even worse action.' So spoke our wise council, and in the end our people did nothing against those murderers.

"After a year of talk, when it became obvious that our government would do nothing, I came here to Cablans. I took a regular job to earn my keep, and in my extra time I have made detailed inquiries about the Dominion's occupation of Haldek. I have studied and I have planned at great length."

Jade felt a chill of premonition. "And you want to strike back at the Commancors." It was not a question.

"I must avenge my family's honor. They were attacked in a brutal and cowardly manner, and their bodies sing out for justice."

"Dead bodies don't sing," said Jade Darcy. "They rot. I've seen enough of them to know."

"You mock me, yet I must tell you that not in seventy-nine generations, along any line of my family, has such an assault been allowed to go unavenged. I shall strike back!"

"You and what army?"

Fastal's body slumped a bit. "Myself alone, if I must, though I would like your assistance."

Jade let out a great sigh. "I've done some studying, too, you know. I've studied specifically to fight Commancors. I know something about them. The smallest attack force they've ever sent against the tiniest, undefended planet was thirty battalions. The smallest occupation force they've ever used is ten battalions. Their battalions are at least sixteen hundred strong, which means you're looking at sixteen thousand, minimum, against one or two of us. Those are not my idea of favorable odds."

"I know something about the occupation forces," Fastal said. "There are three battalions stationed in Detalla, the capital; the rest are scattered in various settlements many kilometers away. But I do not intend to retake the planet. I know you must think me foolish, but I am not as foolish as that."

"You have a more practical goal in mind?"

"Yes, I do. Most of the Dominion's troops are mercenaries from among their subject races, engaged in honorable battle solely because their masters ordered them into it. I have no grievance against them. But from what I have learned in my studies, Commander Horsson—the Commancor officer in charge of attacking my family's estate—is noted even among his own race for his brutality and sadism. Some of my family's servants who survived and escaped from Haldek say that he took cruel delight in destroying our estate and torturing my family. He is the one I want to kill. His death will symbolize a strike back against our ravishers, a blow to restore my family's honor.''

''Well, at least you understand the concept of a limited, obtainable objective,'' Jade said. ''That's something.''

''I will kill Commander Horsson myself,'' Fastal said, ''but I would like some help in staying alive while I do it. You have been, as you said, specially trained to fight Commancors. I would pay you to accompany me and protect me while I achieve my goal.''

''How much?''

''Most of my family's wealth was tied up in the estate on Haldek. Of that I can reclaim only household furnishings, clothes, and such. I have little personal fortune, but I will give all of it—''

''How much, not counting the chairs?''

''One thousand eus.''

Jade stared at him with unabashed wonderment. ''Is that all? You expect me to nursemaid you through this vendetta for one thousand fucking eus? We'd have to slip onto this planet past sixteen thousand Commancor troops, find this one officer—assuming he's still on Haldek, of course—kill him, and then slip away safely back home, without anyone hunting us down for being murderers in our own right. One thousand eus doesn't go that far these days.''

''It is all I own. Even much of that has been borrowed. I could—''

''You're missing my point. I'm a mercenary. People pay me to take risks. That I understand and accept. But there are limits. I have to believe there's a reasonable chance I'll come back to spend the money. This is a suicide mission. I don't approve of the odds, and they wouldn't get significantly better even if you offered me more money.''

''But—''

Jade stood up. Small as she was, she seemed to tower over the seated Lemmant. ''Let me tell you something else. You don't have any corner on the revenge market. I hate Commancors just as much as you do, maybe more. I can't forget or forgive some of the things they've done, either. If someone gave me a good, clean shot at a Commancor's back, with the chance to get away and no reprisals, I'd do it in a second. I wouldn't even charge him for it.

"But I don't propose to die for a cause. This 'honor' of yours is nothing more than disguised pride. Your family ego was hurt. Big fucking deal. You'll do your family more honor by going away and living a productive life and leaving the Commancors alone. Your scheme is certain death, and I want no part of it."

"I will go on my own, if I must," Fastal insisted dramatically, standing up and making some sort of formal gesture.

"Then go die gloriously," Jade told him. "But remember, there's nothing as silly-looking as a dead hero."

Jade stared at the door long after it had slid shut behind her visitor. Fastal's story had brought back too many unhappy memories, too many vows left unharvested and rotting in the vineyards of her mind. Her fists clenched and unclenched as though with a will of their own.

"How much time before I go to work, Val?" she asked.

"Two hours."

"Shit." Not enough time to go back to sleep, too much to stall. That Lemmant had really ruined her night. And there still was the matter of this Megan Cafferty person to deal with.

"More t'ai chi. A workout and some meditation, I guess," she muttered. "Maybe if I can compose myself a little better I can help the day go more smoothly."

But some part of her mind, way at the back, refused to let her believe that.

CHAPTER 5

Cyclad Arik

Lunch break had seldom been so welcome. Every move Jade made seemed to hurt. Her truncated morning workout had only accented her fatigue, rather than relieving it as it usually did. She often had days more physically exhausting than yesterday, but few with as much emotional baggage thrown in.

It could be four or five days before she learned more about this Megan Cafferty, and until then life was as interesting as the old curse would have it. The tension had drawn her nerves as tight as an old E string on a hard-played guitar. On this edge, once again, she lived and functioned.

During her otherwise routine briefing at the beginning of shift, Disson surprised her by mentioning that the Furgato Exec had arrived just before shift change and asked to see her, and then had sat to wait for her without the usual pilfering except for a few passing fruit garnishes. Jade couldn't think of any reason for it, unless he wanted to reclaim the Purrchrp knife she'd taken from his crewmember the night before. Just in case, Jade slipped it into her pouch before heading up to the floor.

As usual, the noise and smells of a busy night at work started her adrenaline pumping, and Jade felt almost normal as long as she didn't move too fast. She deliberately set up the initial cruise of her quadrant to cover all but the section the Furgato was in. Some of the regulars asked specifically about the oddly restrained zen pirate, and, propelled by their curiosity as well as her own, she slighted the last five tables and went to his.

The Exec's greeting was as ebullient as always, but there was none of the dipping she'd normally expect. He grasped her arms and placed them at his side as if assuming a formal position, then spoke in measured, even gracious tones.

"Jade, my imperial stone, the food at your establishment is as edible as you are lovely. It is always the aphelion of my travels to see you again, and to be challenged by your skill and wit."

"Thank you, officer. You always make my evenings interesting." Jade wondered at the quiet voice, for a Furgato, and the elegance of his language. The rough-and-tumble manner that had served them for years hadn't prepared her for this. Cyclad had begun to drift closer to the boundary of Jade's quadrant, obviously troubled by this behavior as well. Many races were quiet only before a killing. With that thought chilling her, Jade unobtrusively flexed her spring-loaded wrist knives to make sure they were ready, and rolled her head to signal Cyclad to remain wary.

"I had only a short time before travelling to our next station," said the Exec, "so I wanted to give you another challenge."

Jade reached for her pouch, and hoped he'd take only what she could retrieve, or ask a kung'an that Val knew how to answer.

"My glorious gemstone," he continued, "would you come to our retreat and celebrate with us?"

Jade froze for an instant, awaiting the threat she'd primed herself for, then realized she hadn't truly heard what was said. "I'm sorry, I'm not sure what you mean."

"Jade," he said, touching her arms gently, "our annual festivals of First Snow are coming soon, and I would have you travel to them as our guest."

Jade had heard of the festival, and knew that politicians and scholars throughout the civilized universe would sacrifice their firstborn to attend. Only a very few outsiders ever had. It was an intriguing possibility.

"I might like that. When are they?"

"In only two more of this planet's years. You are welcome to come anytime before that. You are a worthy student."

Two Cablans years would be more like three and a half Terran years; the Furgatos' home world, with its highly elliptical orbit, had a long revolutionary period. Jade tried and failed to figure out exactly what kind of invitation was being issued—but at least it wasn't for the immediate future, or for a battle. She waved Cyclad back to her own quadrant, surprised at the feeling of warmth her offered help had created.

"I'll consider and give you an answer soon," said Jade as she tried to pull her arms from his. Since all was illusion with the Furgatos anyway, "soon" was a safe and meaningless concept. "I must get back to my duties now, if I may?"

His parting embrace was so enthusiastic and sudden that Jade barely restrained her reflexes from starting a counterattack. His ciliated touch ran over her breasts and down her belly, and she tensed involuntarily; then he turned and, without another word, left the ingesterie. After he was gone she found the Purrchrp knife was missing . . . and a small figurine had taken its place in her pouch. Without looking at it closely, she tucked the statuette back in the pouch for later inspection.

At lunch break Jade examined the carved piece again and then called Val at home, using the security camera linkup to show it to her.

"It appears to be a carp," the computer said, "an ornamental fish from Earth, carved in the manner of the late Sung dynasty. If it is not a replica in other materials, is it of stone?"

"Yes—heavy, dry, and somehow cool, and," said Jade as she tried and failed to scratch the bottom with her pocketknife, "very hard."

"Then it is certainly imperial golden jade."

As she turned it over in her hand, Jade realized this was only the second piece of her namesake she'd ever held. The small pendant her mother had given her had been left . . . back there. Jade closed off that memory firmly.

The fish was swirling around some sort of plant. The piece, smaller than her palm, was graceful and marvelously detailed. There was something very restful about gazing at the dainty antique. Jade would enjoy the gift. With reluctance, she put it in her locker and returned to the floor.

With the exception of this incident, the first half of her shift had been busy but routine, a capacity crowd. Jade moved smoothly among her tables as the second half began, and even the regulars saw no break in her professionally calm facade. All was quiet for the next hour.

The problem began silently. Jade had been patrolling the sector farthest from the special-environment section, where Hiss!arr was working. He had entered the tube suit of the largest methane tank, where, according to the briefing, some important negotiations were going on, and had been in there awhile. This wasn't too unusual, but Cyclad Arik had moved closer to cover the rest of his section better—SOP. The first indication of trouble was a clear bell-like sound as something very hard hit the inner surface of the tank.

Conversation stopped in most of the hall, and the arbiters began edging toward the first quadrant. The red light flashed on top of the tube-suit entrance, and a wounded Hiss!arr came running backward out of it, followed by a methane cloud.

Jade was in motion immediately. A blur to most witnesses, she wove through her sector so quickly the environmental alarm bell came on only after she'd cleared her last occupied tables in midsector and was aimed across the bare floor to the injured Purrchrp's side. Before anyone could pinpoint the source of the problem, Jade was on the edge of her colleague's section.

Up in his glass-walled booth overseeing the ingesterie, Rix had hit the alarms and activated the bulkhead system. Instantly strong exhaust fans began pulling the methane vapor up toward the ceiling of quadrant one as wall panels rose from the edges of that section's floor and descended from the ceiling to cut the quadrant off and protect the other patrons.

Cyclad Arik plunged over the rising barrier and ran to Hiss!arr's side. Jade took a deep breath and held it, then leaped and spun between the walls as she heard them close with a sharp clang, rolling to her feet on the other side. The condition had worsened.

The sharp clang she'd assumed was the closing of the security walls had actually been the outer wall of the methane chamber cracking; some sort of weapon had been fired inside and had struck the wall. A suicidal alien was trying to murder the lot of them.

Jade ran behind the chamber to the right, looking for other oxygen breathers needing rescue, as Cyclad moved to the left toward Hiss!arr.

Hiss!arr shrugged off Cyclad's help, grabbed the oxygen masks from the rack on the side of the chamber and fitted himself with one, then used the others to help evacuate the oxygen-breathing patrons through the small airlock doors which could open only to an arbiter's code in this kind of emergency. These doors led back into the rest of the ingesterie, and safety. The other non-oxygen-breathers were secure for the moment in their own tanks, and other walls were rising around them to protect them from further danger.

The methane stank and obscured Jade's vision as she came around the chamber—but worse than this was the supercold gas that sucked the heat from the room. Rix was shutting down as much as possible in this quadrant to minimize the resources at the suicider/terrorist's disposal. Jade saw that all the patrons at risk from methane poisoning seemed to be leaving with Hiss!arr, and she had started for the exit herself when she heard a scream so high-pitched it seemed to drill right through her skull.

Cyclad Arik had slipped in a puddle of water that formed as the escaping cold gases turned the water vapor from the air into slush. The mantis was struggling to rise when another blow from inside the methane tank cracked open a wall panel and a tentacle snaked around her, pinning her to the frozen surface deep within the billowing poisonous cloud.

The insectoids of Cyclad Arik's race had lungs, but retained some of the skin respiratory system found in their smaller Terran look-alikes. Cyclad was incapable of holding her breath in this noxious cloud and was being poisoned; otherwise, she could easily have cut through the tentacle instead of sawing at it feebly with one edge of a serrated forelimb.

Jade forgot escape and ran toward Cyclad. The stink and cold ate at her lungs and nasal passages even through the cowl she unrolled from her collar up over her mouth and nose. Her eyes burned like ignored toast, and the floor was becoming even more slippery. It took a nightmarishly long time to reach the side of the tank even at full-out carc speed—and as Jade got close, Cyclad stopped her struggles altogether.

The tank lines kept pouring fresh methane into the system to sustain any beings who might still be alive inside—but the enormous crack merely meant that methane came out under pressure into the rest of the quadrant. The general ventilation system, trying to pump it out, was overwhelmed by the task. Jade faced a critical decision—whether to save anyone left alive inside the tank, or to save Cyclad.

She barely gave it an instant's hesitation; the only creature she knew was alive in the tank was an enemy. Jade hit the emergency gas feed cutoff switch on the side of the tank and reset the chamber's fans to reclamation. As both the internal and external ventilation systems began to pull in the methane, the tentacled creature dropped Cyclad and tried to flee from the oxygen/nitrogen mixture that now rushed in at him.

Jade grabbed the falling arbiter and tried to pull her away—and promptly fell into the puddle on the floor. The insectoid was deceptively light, and the overcorrection and slick floor had betrayed even Jade's reflexes. Using the floor for leverage, she came up with Cyclad's huge forelimb around her neck. She then moved quickly toward the door, only to realize she couldn't drag Cyclad through the hatch.

Rix was using the short-range channel to broadcast over the speaker in her hand computer, ordering her to leave before she died, too. Jade ignored the increasingly obscene orders to give some of her own.

"Listen, you vegetable, raise tank number whatever

I'm on, now! As soon as the walls are up, pump in O_2 at double pressure and percent. Move, you fucking poor excuse for manzanita!''

Later Jade wondered how the u-trans dealt with the insults, or whether Rix even thought them insults—but at that moment she was just glad to see her instructions followed. The chamber walls rose around her and Cyclad, followed by a sudden gale blast of fresh air. Jade lay Cyclad under the strongest part of the blast and was trying to figure out how to give CPR to a praying mantis when her hand computer chimed twice for an urgent message and proceeded to give the instructions. The pressure points were easy to find, and in less than a minute a sort of cough resulted as Jade pushed and Cyclad started to breathe on her own.

The insectoid then turned her head and vomited up one whole and one barely halved frog-type creature. She then tried to stand, but failed.

"Easy there," Jade said as she slid her comrade away from the disgusting mess. "Hold still, I'll help you. You'll be okay. . . . What the fuck!"

Jade turned toward the startling noise and then began to laugh, which set off a fit of violent coughing as her injured mucous membranes rebelled at this new demand. The ubiquitous robotic cleaning arm had been automatically activated and was busily vacuuming up the mess. Cyclad began the leg rubbing that produced the rasping pleasure noise for her race.

"It's sure as hell back to normal now," Jade exclaimed between coughs and giggles.

Cyclad nodded, and tried to speak, but could only wheeze. As Jade queried Rix on the need for a medic, the gale of incoming air subsided and the temperature within their isolated cubicle became more bearable.

Jade asked Cyclad Arik if she had any idea what had happened to cause the disturbance, then Rix, but both proclaimed their ignorance. Jade had just finished her request when the ingesterie's staff medic came into the chamber.

"What . . . how did you get here so fast?" Jade asked. Dr. Olokak lived clear across the city and worked at a hospital a good fifteen kilometers away.

Even in the direst emergencies he usually couldn't make it to the ingesterie in less than twenty minutes unless it happened to be those hours when he was on duty here. "Fix her, then explain."

The four-armed physician was usually prone to long-drawn-out speeches. This time he opened his mouth twice, saw the angry look on Jade's face, then said, "The Greest summoned me here half an hour ago."

Jade went colder than the remaining chill in the air could account for. If the Greest was involved in this, whatever it was that had happened, then anything was possible, and not even the Old Loquacious Quack himself had the nerve to speculate on what it might be.

As the adrenaline washed out of Jade's system, she noticed the cough that she'd acquired from the gas, and the exhaustion. "I'm getting too old for this shit. Is she going to be all right, or do I have to take you apart too?"

The doctor kept his eyes firmly on his patient and spared not a glance for Jade. "Her voice will return, and all else will be fine by morning. In cases like this the hyperbaric oxygen is of course an aid, and the—"

"Enough! That's all I needed to know, dammit." In softer tones, Jade asked Cyclad if she needed help standing. Together they stood up and opened the large chamber door, leaving the lecturing medic in midsentence.

They were greeted by applause. Noisy hoots, clacks, hisses, poundings, whistles, and other noises of approbation flooded them and almost sent them back to the doctor. The quadrant walls had been withdrawn, and except for the damaged tank and the applauding customers, it looked like a normal night at Rix's once again.

Jade, following Rix's signal, helped Cyclad into the lift to the briefing room, where a transport team was waiting. Cyclad was to be held overnight in the local hospital, mostly to treat her damaged respiratory system. Jade refused treatment herself. She'd had colds that made her feel worse, and hospitals were too damn expensive and confining. She lingered in the quiet of the briefing room after Cyclad was rushed out, wishing she didn't have to head back upstairs. Too many surprises and too much reassessment made for a bad ambience, as Rix would put it. She was on her way to the lift when a group of five Purrchrps walked in, one of whom she recognized: Mwrrhungh, Hiss!arr's brother and occasional relief arbiter.

Disson Peng-Amur spoke up for the first time since Jade had come down. He seldom spoke unless business required, so Jade was startled by his sudden pronouncement.

"My pod brother and I wish you, Jade, to go home. You need rest. You will be paid for the shift. Hiss!arr's family will take over."

"I'm fully capable of finishing my own shift." Personal pride and a sudden fear of losing her position drove adrenaline into her system and became expressed, as always with Jade, as anger. "Damn it all, I handled that as best as can be expected out there, and with no oxy casualties in the biggest special-gas leak this dump's ever fucking seen. I'm worth two of any raw recruits, and to replace me you'll have to do better than these . . . newcomers." Even in extremis, Jade remembered the danger of damaging Purrchrp pride, and that these kids weren't to blame. She was starting to gather strength for her next blast when she realized Disson had continued right along, taking little notice of her outburst.

"Jade, it is the right of Hiss!arr's family, under their customs, to decide how to compensate for the assistance you gave their brother. Also Rix and I agree you have earned a day off early. Enjoy the rest and we'll see you in two days. Because of the prompt actions taken by you, Hiss!arr, and Cyclad Arik, the only being killed was the terrorist who started the trouble, and we don't count him, so there will be the usual bonus for hazard-with-no-casualty posted to your account within the hour."

Jade began to tremble as the last burst of adrenaline fled her system and the accumulated stress made itself felt. Wordlessly she turned, gathered the figurine from her locker, and started out. As the door was closing she turned, braced it open with the leg she'd bruised when she fell, winced at the pain, and asked, "Cyclad . . . you'll call if . . . ?" Jade wasn't sure how to finish the question.

"If your friend is anything but healthy before morning, I will call you."

"She's not my friend, she's just . . . well, you know." Jade fled the definition as Disson answered a call from the floor above. Troubled by her own lack of precision, she concentrated on another subject entirely, trying once again to make sense out of Megan Cafferty's presence on Cablans as she treated herself to the luxury of a solo cab ride directly home instead of a shared hub-route conveyance. Using the cab phone, she ordered Val to prepare for her early arrival, and to have the tub ready.

The Greest knew it was going to happen, she thought as she rode, too tired even to be angry. *He knew enough to summon a doctor half an hour before he was needed. He knew there was going to be a blowup, and he did nothing to stop it. Nearly killed Cyclad, and me too. Someday that bastard'll go too far, and someone'll take payment out of his four-dimensional hide.*

Jade walked the block from the cab stop, dragged herself through her front door, and headed straight to the bathroom, shedding her clothes as she went. The pull of the heavier gravity added to her exhaustion, and only her intense discipline kept her from ordering it turned off—that, and the effort it would take to form the words. At this moment it was beyond her.

"Jade, there's a message—"

"Stuff it." Jade pulled off her boots and added them to the rest of the items she was putting into the burn chute. She didn't want to recycle anything that smelled of this night. At the last moment she remembered the figurine, the Sung imperial-jade carp, and gently pulled it from her breast pocket. She stood for a moment looking at the way the light melted through the edges, as though the light were inside the carving and illuminating the room rather than the reverse. Again the strange timeless peace began to creep into her flensed spirit. She took a small flat-bottomed bowl out of the cupboard and carried it into the bathroom.

Turning it upside down on the side of the tub, she placed the carving on this improvised pedestal. It seemed to shimmer and almost come alive in the fog as the steam condensed on the carved scales. She then climbed the couple of steps up to the lip of the steaming tank.

"Jade, the message is from—"

"I said, 'Stuff it,' and I meant to put it in the most uncomfortable bit of RAM or ROM you've got until morning." Jade's voice was nearly a whisper, the vehemence of the words only another habit. Jade sank into the water, just this side of painfully hot, turned on the air jets, and gave a deep shuddering sigh of release as the near-scalded skin gave up its tension to the delicate powerful pounding of the air blasts. She arranged herself on the bench so that her back and legs were braced without effort against the force of the seemingly fragile bubbles, and laid her head against the integral neck rest, warmed by a tube of heated water that ran just underneath it.

By turning her head slightly she could see the carving as the pearls of dew flowed over it. The tail fins seemed to float over the plant in tissue-weight curves of light. A smile played about the koi's mouth, as though it were still amused after centuries of observing humans. Its age seemed to put the last days into perspective as tiny bubbles in the immense ocean of time this fish swam in. Almost, Jade could forget the tensions of the night. Almost she could welcome sleep.

"The Greest," Val said.

Jade jerked upright, splashing water all over the floor. "What?"

"The message is from the Greest. He wants you to come to the Pale House for a meeting, tonight. He didn't specify a time exactly, but I think he meant soon . . . I think."

Only the Greest could cause a computer to stammer. Jade slid back into the tank, thought a moment, and slipped under the water.

I shouldn't come up. First the Cafferty woman, then Galantor's bet, then that damn fool Lemmant, the Furgato, Cyclad, and now the Greest. Jade exhaled, held for ten seconds from habit no longer thought about, then rose up when her bubbles hadn't brought bullets. The carp was once again just stone.

"Val, call and tell him I'll be there in two hours. At least try to get some idea why he wants me, and good luck trying." Jade sank under again before Val could deliver any more news, and wondered what load of recyclable organics she was about to wade through in that perceptual horror called the Pale House, the home of the Greest.

CHAPTER 6

The Greest

The Greest lived in a crooked house, a white building constructed especially for his use that followed no pattern discernible to the architects of any race. The building, as far as anyone knew, contained no right angles or circular arcs. The bright white walls were of irregular sizes, some as high as seven stories, joining at odd intersections, seldom even standing upright, but leaning inward or outward and defying gravity through the sheer will of their occupant. There were no windows, because the Greest never looked outside; there were some who theorized that the Greest had no eyes and therefore couldn't look at all.

Perhaps the building made sense when viewed through the fourth dimension. And then again, perhaps it was as crazy there, too. No one ever accused the Greest of either consistency or common sense. The Greest, for his part, apparently neither knew nor cared what these strange flat creatures thought of his home—or if he did, he took a strange perverse joy in befuddling them.

The Greest's domicile did have a door, however—a very wide, tall one. Many were the beings who visited the Greest on a variety of errands, and all could be accommodated within those strangely jutting walls. But none of them were comfortable; no one could be comfortable in the presence of the Greest.

Jade Darcy approached the Greest's home with more annoyance than trepidation. This was not unknown territory, as it was for some. The Greest had summoned her to his presence five times before—a fact that astounded her acquaintances, for personal audiences with the Greest were not easy to come by. He conducted most of his business over the telecom. There were potentates of planets and rulers of vast financial empires who had never been permitted in the Greest's presence. Six invitations was virtually unheard of. Jade wondered what she'd ever done to become so blessed—if that was, indeed, the proper word.

The weather was overcast but dry as she walked up the path to the lunatic-designed asylum. The gloom hid most of the building's crazier features from her sight, and the tinted glasses she always wore to the Pale House dimmed it even more. The noise and confusion of the adjacent docks and transfer station were muted from this side of the Pale House. She could almost believe it wasn't real. She sure wished it weren't.

"Please enter, Jade Darcy," came the Greest's low voice from the speaker beside the door. "We have been expecting you."

Of course you have, Jade thought. *No one ever turns down one of your summonses. The only question is how often they trip over their own feet getting here.* Nevertheless, she obediently entered the building when the door slid open to admit her.

The Greest's home was no saner inside than out. The walls were pure white, almost blinding in their intensity. After her first visit Jade had bought the deep-gray glasses—actually, snow goggles—she wore gratefully now. Her eyes felt poached with sand after the near-sleepless nights she'd had lately.

There was no furniture in here, nor upper-level floors, nor interior walls—nothing that made any concession to a visitor's comfort or welfare. The place was barer than a barn and, except for its singular occupant, far less interesting.

Jade look around her, wondering how the Greest would appear today. He had never looked the same twice on any of their previous meetings, and he did not disappoint her this time. He was now in yet another of his seemingly endless cross sections.

The Greest was floating about five meters above the floor, his body looking like a flexible tube of jelly, about a meter in diameter, that had been bent into a Y-shape. He appeared to be floating there without support, but Jade knew better. The Greest was standing, or sitting, or lying, on something; it was simply not something that anyone from our dimension could see.

She'd once had it explained to her by a teacher in military training. "Suppose that you, a three-dimensional creature, paid a visit to the two-dimensional beings of Flatland," Captain Chiu had said. "All they know is life on their plane; they can't see you in your entirety. What they see is the two-dimensional cross section of whatever part of you is intersecting their plane. For instance, if you stick a finger through their plane, they'll see a roughly oval shape. If you stick two fingers through held together, they'll see two ovals side by side. If you hold your first two fingers apart in a vee, the Flatlanders will see two separate and apparently independent ovals a few centimeters apart. Holding all five fingers apart will yield five different ovals, and any Flatlander would call you crazy if you suggested that these independent shapes were really all part of one and the same creature; there is no apparent connection, and indeed each can move independently of all the others."

All anyone could ever see of the Greest, the captain went on to explain, was whatever three-dimensional cross section of his four-dimensional body happened to be intersecting our space at any given time. Despite numerous attempts to plot the shape of the Greest based on known cross sections—attempts made by leading topologists of many different races—no clear image of the creature had ever emerged. All anyone could ever tell was that the Greest must be huge to have so many different cross sections—or else "he" was in reality several creatures acting in unison. The Greest was unknowable in his/their totality, but the mathematicians and physicists kept trying.

"Welcome, Jade Darcy," said the Greest, his voice rumbling out of speakers, for his mouth probably did not exist within this three-dimensional representation. "We greet you with the kindest felicitations."

"Cut the crap," Jade Darcy said to the most powerful being in the known universe. "What do you want from me now?"

"Ah, ever in a hurry, ever willing to violate even the social customs of your own race. Is it little wonder we treasure you so highly?"

Jade had learned quickly that she could neither shock nor offend the Greest. The more blunt she was, the more he seemed to enjoy it. Naturally, she kept that bit of information to herself. Everyone else was afraid of the Greest; this gave her a leg up on all of them. "Look, I've had a shitty couple of days. I just want to go home and sleep. What's so fucking important that you had to call me all the way down here?"

"We presume you refer to the incident with the Lemmant in the ingesterie, and the riot at Galantor's, and the Lemmant's visit to your home, and the fight this afternoon at Rix's."

Jade didn't bother to ask how the Greest knew of those things as she paced about the room. The Greest knew everything of importance that occurred on Cablans, and perhaps a lot of the unimportant stuff as well. Maybe an army of data brokers like Lorpet kept him constantly informed and updated, trying to curry favor—or maybe he simply monitored sophisticated eavesdropping equipment in every room on the planet. If anyone had ever successfully hidden information from the Greest, it was a well-kept secret indeed.

"Among other things, yes," Jade replied. "You knew about that assassination attempt at Rix's, and you made no move to stop it. That's fucking criminal."

"We have heard that you humans thrive on a certain chemical in your circulatory systems—ah, adrenaline, we believe it is called. We would not wish you deprived of so vital a nutrient."

Jade planted her feet and faced the turning sausage from the fourth dimension. "I don't believe the whole performance was for my benefit. Cyclad Arik nearly died."

"The purpose of the universe depends entirely on perspective. You flatlings, of necessity, have such a limited scope. See here how Bab-ankh makes that satellite sing? In four dimensions the lines of causality are far more apparent.''

''Not more of your fucking philosophy. I want answers, dammit.'' Her voice ragged, Jade vibrated with frustration.

''The patterns are beautiful in four-space—and is that not what life is about? Patterns? Even you hopelessly handicapped flatlings impose patterns on your interpretations of the universe. Your patterns are so stunted and limited, yet the pattern known as Mozart, when viewed alongside that of fractals and de Chirico, reveals such promise. This is why we have chosen the task—or perhaps avocation would be the proper word—of shaping and molding the patterns into the most aesthetic designs. As one of your patternists said, 'We would die for our blue china.' You, of course, can see only the grossest details of our plan when they intersect your reality, but we assure you—''

''I've had enough of this bullshit. Talk about something *real* or I'm leaving.''

''Where the pond and night sky meet, two moons kiss. Go bring me the one that is real. That one I'll shape—''

''That's it. Open the fucking door. I'm leaving.''

''The door will not open for you until you're finished.''

''I'm finished now.''

''See how little of reality you do see? You cannot see the truth of your own pattern, nor how beautifully it glows. You see not the golden arches sweeping the vistas, but only the dim shadows where the crux points intersect and loop over one another—''

''Who is Megan Cafferty?'' Jade asked suddenly, taking a step closer to the Greest.

The Greest actually paused, as though taken by surprise. ''You have been given many facts—''

''And they're facts only,'' Jade said, pressing her advantage. ''To use your own analogy, I've been give a two-dimensional picture. As a flatling I might not be able to understand a four-dimensional image, but I'd fucking well like at least three.''

''What dimension are you lacking?''

"Why is she here?"

"An interesting philosophical point. As many of your race's wisest philosophers have asked, why is any of us here?—although had they been capable of seeing the problem fully they would know it is the lily which compels them to create the nebulae."

It was just as well the Greest had no furniture in his house, or Jade would have broken something. Instead, she resumed her nervous pacing. "What's her relationship with me?"

"Revealing all yet hiding much in her mists, Time retreats."

"That sounds like Furgato drivel."

"Far beneath the frozen earth lies the seed that with the—"

"You're not going to tell me anything, are you?"

"Nothing you could understand."

"Because of my limited perceptions?" Jade asked sarcastically.

"Because the pattern as we perceive it requires gradual enlightenment, unlike the Mandala," said the Greest. "But mostly because we choose not to."

"At last, the first honest thing you've said. But if you don't want to talk about Cafferty, what *are* we talking about? The Lemmant?"

"Different patterns, different intersections," said the Greest.

"But are they important ones?"

"All intersections are important to different people on different travails."

"But are they important for me now?" Jade persisted.

"Did you eat your breakfast? Go wash your bowl."

I think you mean yes, you sneaky bastard, Jade thought. *How can I word things to get answers out of you?* She swallowed, trying to convince her dry mouth there had been moisture there. "Fastal ip Fornen told me you charged his people a great deal of money for the right to colonize Haldek. Is that correct?"

"All such things are purely relative to arbitrary standards."

Another yes. "And then you turned right around and

sold them out to the Commancors. Is that part of your grand pattern?''

''For a flatling, you sometimes make leaps of fourth-dimensional intuition. Of course, they cover only the grossest of details, and are probably based on incorrect assumptions, which in the end will invalidate even the most accurate suppositions.''

Jade stopped and stared at the door, her back to the Greest. Impersonal chance was one thing, but having the fate of millions decided by this sausage was too blackly humorous to deal with easily. ''You allowed thousands, maybe millions of people to die because it fit some fucking pattern?'' *And my family?* she only dared think.

''Some branches pruned are lost. Yet how bright now is the poppy it reveals?''

''Who gave you the right to make those decisions?''

''The privilege of the artists is to shape that which exists into patterns only they perceive, and in the aesthetic perception is all the permission.''

Yeah, and there's any number of dictators who'd go along with that, Jade thought, but didn't even bother saying it out loud. She wasn't afraid to tell the Greest to his face that he was a tyrant, but nothing would be accomplished by it. The Greest would simply agree. The Greest was totally honest about the power he wielded over interstellar commerce and politics, even if he was devious about how he used it.

She was getting nowhere with generalities, so she decided to narrow her questioning to specifics. ''You said you knew about Fastal ip Fornen's visit to me. Do you know what he intends to do?''

''He had to explain it to us at some length before we would consider giving him permission to transfer to Haldek.''

''And you gave him permission?''

''We sold him two round-trip passes.''

''How much?''

''Ten eus.''

''Ten eus!'' Jade exclaimed. ''That's pocket change to you. That won't even pay for the energy to turn on your machine.'' She paused. ''You say you sold him *two* passes?''

''He asked for two. It was a reasonable number.''

''He asked me to go with him. Did you think I would?''

''The patterns around this particular interstice are turbulent, though yours surely intersects it.''

''Does my pattern show me to be a blithering idiot? Do you want me to go on this suicidal quest?''

''The forceful cutting of sentient life is always a sorry business—''

''Spare me the piety. You just admitted starting a war to fill out your precious pattern. Now you want to send this Lemmant to his death, and you want me to go with him.''

''If it eases your feelings, your imminent death, though but a trivial flourish on the overall design, is not the optimum shape we envision for your universe.''

''I love you, too. Let's go dancing sometime. Assuming I survive this whole fucking mess.''

Behind her, the door slid open. ''Your sarcasm,'' said the Greest, ''is wasted on us who can see the four-dimensionality of the total universe, because we—''

Jade gestured at the open door. ''I presume that means we're finished.''

''Nothing can ever be truly finished, for the great pattern is a process of life, of change, of evolution. It isn't. Is is.''

''Wonderful. Keep that in mind. Because I intend to shape patterns for a good while to come, and my pattern's going to be a beauty.'' Without waiting for the Greest to spout any more jabberwocky, Jade stomped out of the twisted house and returned home wondering what the purpose of the whole visit had been.

''You have a message,'' Val said as soon as she walked through the door.

''Fuck it, of course I do,'' Jade said wearily. ''Not an hour can go by without some new catastrophe. Play it, Val. I might as well get it all over with at once.''

Obediently the screen lit up to display a face. A human face, a woman's face. An attractive face of mature years, with dazzling green eyes, pointed chin, and round red cheeks, all surrounded by a mane of white hair. The face Jade had seen only in a photograph so far: the face of Megan Cafferty.

"Hello, Ms. Darcy. I finally managed to track you down. My name is Megan Cafferty. I'd like very much to talk to you. Please get in touch at your earliest opportunity."

Jade stared at the screen long after it went blank, and finally had to remind herself to breathe. Now, after so long, had the moment she'd dreaded finally come? And in so unexpected a package as a middle-aged woman with white hair and rosy cheeks?

"I could run again," she muttered. "I did it before."

"Would you like me to prepare a list of the pseudonyms and planets where your accounts are?" Val asked.

"Huh? Oh no, not yet. I was just thinking out loud."

She sat down at the table and took some deep breaths. *Where else can I go?* she thought. *Cablans is the end of the line. Anywhere else just takes me nearer, not farther away. I can't run* toward *them!*

She looked around her. The house was small and spartan, but it was the only *home* she'd known in seven years—and if one discounted army barracks, the only home she'd had since she was thirteen. She could still fit all her most valuable possessions in a single duffel bag. She could leave Cablans this minute with barely a ripple to mark her passage.

"What more have you learned about Cafferty?" she asked.

"The inquiries are still out," Val replied. "Nothing's come back."

Jade stared out blankly for a long time, until finally she realized she was staring at her arsenal. She could not remember standing and walking here, nor asking Val to open it for her.

Of all her possessions, these were the ones she most

treasured. She'd spent years acquiring such a complete collection, weapons for almost all occasions a single warrior could handle. And these were precisely the things she'd have to leave behind if she ran. She couldn't carry more than a few of them with her and still travel as fast as she'd have to.

A couple of small blades, she thought, reaching out into the cabinet. *The soldiers at Customs won't let the big stuff through, but Commancors understand the need for personal armament. Some basic innocuous tools and a few loops of nylon wire inside my belt. Anything else I can forage when we get there.*

"Call the Lemmant Fastal ip Fornen, Val," Jade said. "If he's prepared to leave right away, tell him I'll come with him for the price he names." *And God have mercy on our souls.*

Chapter 7

Fornen-Dakk

"I know you must think I am a total fool," Fastal ip Fornen said as he and Jade rode in the back of the speeding cab. "But I have given much thought to this matter. I have made some plans."

Jade leaned back in her seat and folded her arms across her chest. She thought about the Lemmant's one thousand eus, already securely transferred into her account, and how obliging the other arbiters were to cover her shifts for the several days she'd be gone. She turned and watched the shadows of the passing buildings play alternating light and dark across her companion's features. "How much formal military training have you had?"

"All Lemmantine males of decent birth receive strict instructions in discipline and military honor—"

"Yeah? What about guerrilla tactics, hand-to-hand combat, the care, handling, and use of weapons?"

Fastal fidgeted. "I can use a knife. All Lemmants can, even our women." He patted the beautiful dagger at his waist. "This is not just ornamental. We start practice when we are very young."

"Good for you. Now we just have to hope the troops let us get close enough to use a knife. Tell me, with all this practice, have you ever killed another intelligent being?"

"I will kill when the time comes," Fastal said resolutely.

A virgin. God help us, thought Jade. She grew very quiet as she said, "Look, Fastal, enthusiasm and discipline are all very nice, but experience counts for a lot, too. Why don't you stay back here on Cablans, nice and safe, and let me do the whole job for you? I'd feel much more secure if I didn't have to nursemaid you at the same time.''

Fastal waved his left hand vigorously side to side, equivalent of a firm headshake. "No. I am avenging my family. It is my honor at stake. I must perform the deed myself. It would be cowardly to stay behind and just send you. That is not honorable.''

"No, just smart,'' Jade muttered.

"Besides, you do not know the territory. I grew up there, I know the land well. I have done research, and I know where we can find Commander Horsson. I must go with you, if only to save us weeks of fruitless effort.''

Jade considered. "That's the first thing you've said that makes tactical sense. A native guide is handy. I just hope I don't keep tripping over you.''

The cab stopped as they reached the transfer dock, and the two passengers got out. The dock area was crowded all the time with cabs waiting to pick up new arrivals at any hour, would-be guides and data brokers, shippers with automated carts and trucks, and street hustlers who scavenged on the bits that fell through the cracks in the system, performing odd jobs for the diverse beings scurrying about. The sights, sounds, and smells always reminded Jade of a bazaar in ancient Baghdad.

Fastal had said the inhabited parts of Haldek were hot and muggy all year round, so Jade wore a lighter-weight version of her merc suit, gray mottled with black for good night camouflage when needed. She strapped it in at the waist with a narrow belt that was more than just decorative. In her backpack were two identical versions of the same outfit, as well as a lantern, small portable range, and other camping necessities. Her knives were at her ankles, one inside each boot. The Customs officials would probably spot them, but even if the blades were confiscated, Jade was not worried. There were plenty of weapons to be found on Haldek; all she had to do was liberate them from their owners.

Fastal ip Fornen was wearing a loose-fitting navy-blue blouse of some silklike material and a blue-black wraparound kilt that looked terribly impractical, but that he insisted was quite comfortable and good for fighting. His beautiful jeweled dagger with the inlaid design was tucked inside his inevitable cummerbund, and his feet were shod in sturdy slippers.

Together, Jade fervently hoped, they did not look like a pair of people posing a serious threat to the security of the Dominion's regime on Haldek.

"We should not have any trouble in Customs," Fastal said. "I have all the documents proving I am not one of the 'subjugated peoples,' as they call the Lemmantine survivors on Haldek—and as a former inhabitant, I can legitimately go back to claim incidental personal property. We don't have to worry—"

"Don't tell me the obvious," Jade snapped. She was mad at herself for agreeing to go on this crazy venture, and she didn't need lectures from a young whelp determined to get himself killed. "I've visited Dominion worlds before. And you're dead wrong, We *do* have to worry—about everything."

The transfer docks dominated this area of Cablans, a vast, blocky complex of buildings squatting solidly beside the Greest's Pale House. Jade gave a quick glance at the cockeyed structure next door, wondering precisely what game the Greest was playing with all of this. But worrying about the Greest only gave her headaches, and she had enough worries of her own just to keep herself and her client alive. *Leave the big "pattern" to him,* she thought. *You concentrate on survival.*

Fastal stepped up to the gate of the transfer-dock complex and announced himself. Jade didn't even bother; the Greest's scanning machinery knew every inhabitant of Cablans, and identification was automatic. There were some races in which Jade had trouble distinguishing between individuals, but the Greest somehow knew everyone.

"Passage for two to Haldek," the computer said as the gate slid open. "Round trips prepaid. Enter through building number seventeen."

A moving walkway took Jade and Fastal down a long portico to the right. The transfer dock was enormous, as by nature it had to be, for this was the sole method of interstellar commerce, the lifeblood of galactic civilization. These buildings had to accommodate everything from private travelers such as Jade and Fastal to tons of merchandise destined for new worlds—or whole armies set to invade a planet. The Commancors could not have sent their battalions to Haldek without going through these same transfer docks—and thus they had the explicit consent of the Greest. No matter how whimsical or vague he pretended to be, Jade could never forget his coldly vicious nature.

The docks were crowded around the clock, for they were the source of all commerce in the interstellar community. Shipments of merchandise and groups of people were constantly coming through these buildings and usually going out again through a different building, for Cablans was seldom anyone's final destination. The walkway had carried Jade and Fastal past large crates of machine parts, boxcars of stock animals being transported to some new world, and a dozen other items that neither of them could identify, as well as bins of food arriving on this world, for Cablans had little agriculture of its own. Jade took this all in stride; Cablans was a distant and comparatively new transfer station, and the traffic here was less than in most of the others she'd visited. Fastal had been here before, too, though he had little else to compare it with. Both passengers rode the walkway through the turmoil around them with little comment.

Building seventeen was one of the smaller ones, and still it towered over them, an enormous hulking mass. This building was primarily for passengers, handling everything from a lone traveler to large parties of colonists settling a new world. Jade and Fastal stepped off the walkway to stand in front of the large steel door, which slid slowly open to admit them. Still feeling a sense of doom about this mission, Jade stepped cautiously inside and looked around.

There was a small vestibule, as barren of decor and

furnishings as the Pale House. Ahead of her was another door, slightly smaller. No one else was in the room; Jade and Fastal were the only passengers right now traveling to Haldek. *And the Greest charged only ten eus,* she thought. *He must really want this mission to happen. But does he want it to succeed or fail? Which is best for his "pattern"?*

As Fastal entered the vestibule behind her, the outer door closed and the inner one opened. The two travelers walked across the entry room and stepped into the actual chamber that would transport them to Haldek.

Again an empty room, but this one was huge, a vast warehouse of nothingness. The Greest made no concessions to the comfort of his passengers. Everyone had to stand or else sit or lie on the floor. "Nothing is more versatile than a bare room," the Greest had once told Jade.

As the door clanged shut behind them, Jade walked purposefully across the vast room to the door on the opposite side. Her footsteps, even as quiet as she made them, echoed loudly in the huge chamber. When nothing had happened by the time she reached the door at the far end, she sat down cross-legged on the ground, closed her eyes, and tried to meditate, soothing her nerves for the ordeal that was to come.

Fastal came up noisily and sat down beside her. "I wonder how long it will take," he jabbered. "I am told it is never the same twice. Sometimes the trip will be over by the time you can cross the room, and other times you have to wait an hour or more before it even starts. And once it starts it can still take different amounts of time, even between the same two places. Very odd, don't you think?"

"Perhaps." Fastal was very hard to ignore, but she tried valiantly.

"If only the Greest would let people make scientific observations during transfers. But we cannot. There is a legend of someone who tried to see what was beyond the room while it was in transfer and has been stuck out there permanently. We call him the Lost Uncle. Have you heard of that legend?"

"The Flying Dutchman," Jade said distantly.

"I have heard the theory that perhaps all of our space is in motion through the fourth dimension, and that the 'distance' between one spot and another can change, leading to different transfer times. What do you think?"

"The Greest like to keep us guessing."

"That much is certain. Even his very nature is a mystery—if indeed he is a 'he.' No one even knows whether the word 'Greest' is singular or plural. There is always exactly one Greest at any transfer station, and he seems to know everything all the others do. I know some people have speculated that there is only one Greest, with different three-dimensional cross sections intersecting at the different transfer stations. I personally prefer the theory that there are a number of them, but they have a hive mind or telepathic mentality. Their constant use of the first person plural when speaking suggests—"

"Fastal, I will say this once and once only." Jade's voice was low and measured, each word carrying complete authority. "You're talking to hide your fear. This is understandable, but not excusable. Nervousness is contagious, and I don't need it. Save your energy for the enemy, as my serg—as a teacher once told me."

Fastal shut up, and instead began checking through his pack for the fifth time. Even with her eyes closed, Jade could feel the nervous vibrations radiating outward from his body. He couldn't completely control his fear, despite his boasts about the discipline he'd trained under. In this mode, though, he was at least moderately ignorable.

She had almost reached the trance state when the floor lurched, as though the entire room were a roller coaster that had just dropped down the first hill. The feeling steadied almost immediately, and after a few seconds there was no sign of motion except for the slightest of vibrations she felt only because she was otherwise so totally still. Jade gave up trying to sink any deeper into her trance and just maintained her current level. They would reach their destination soon, and she had to be ready for trouble.

Within minutes there was a slight jolt and the vibrations stopped. Jade opened her eyes and rose to her feet in one fluid motion. Beside her, the lanky Lemmant scrambled upright as the exit door opened, welcoming them implicitly to Haldek.

The Customs office was expecting them. There were neither Lemmants nor Commancors here, but three lower officers within the Dominion's mercenary forces. Two were humanoids from a race Jade was not familiar with; the third was a Rozhin, a squat, scaly biped with glowing eyes and a short snout with sharp teeth. They had been told the passengers were coming—the Greest normally charged quite a bit extra for surprise transfers like invasions—and they were not expecting any trouble; they stood casually facing the door, their 481-Zendaris—standard Dominion issue—snapped firmly into their holsters.

Jade glanced around her. It was a simple setup, a large room with three desks and a couple of flat inspection tables, plus various detectors. To the left were large swinging doors, probably leading to a bay where any cargo could have been unloaded. Straight ahead were the doors that probably led out of the building. And over to the right was a small enclosed office where the Commancor who ran this operation must work.

Despite having a large—and ever-growing—empire, the Commancors themselves were fairly few in numbers. They managed their conquests with large armies of mercenary troops culled from the races under their dominion. Service to the Commancor Dominion was one of the few ways a member of the "subjugated races" could ever achieve position or wealth. The mercenaries were never put in positions of ultimate authority; there was always a Commancor around somewhere to supervise them.

The Rozhin was obviously the leader of this trio, though, for he stepped forward and hissed something that the u-trans interpreted as "What have we here? A runaway Lemmant come to give himself up? And what are you? A little small and oddly colored for a Lemmant, aren't you?"

"I am Fastal ip Fornen, a citizen of Lemmanta,"

Fastal said with dignity. "As a former resident of *free* Haldek, I have returned to claim miscellaneous personal property. This is my servant, Jade Darcy."

The Rozhin looked at Jade, his golden eyes trying to see right through her skin. "What is your race?"

"Terran. We are not at war with the Commancor Dominion. Currently."

The Rozhin was mildly amused by Jade's addendum, since almost everyone was at war with the Commancors eventually. "You have the documentation to prove these statements?" he asked.

Jade and Fastal held out their arms to present their computer implants, and the Rozhin gave each a quick check with a miniature reader. When he had verified the information he gestured them over to the table in front of them. "Empty your packs and prepare for inspection."

The visitors did as they were told. The belongings in their packs were innocuous, but the detectors quickly found the blades they had on their persons. "Three knives," the Rozhin said. "You must surrender them now before being admitted to Haldek-fief."

"This is the dagger of my family, my lineage," Fastal said. "I carry it with me at all times."

As the Rozhin snorted with contempt, Jade spoke up. "Commancor law allows anyone to carry defensive weapons. Do you expect us to overthrow the Dominion with three knives?"

"You must surrender them," the Rozhin insisted.

Jade had seen this sort before—a member of a subjugated race given some measure of control and trying to compensate for his social inferiority by lording it over anyone in his jurisdiction. She had no great concern about the knives, but she refused to yield to this petty tyranny. "Please let us speak to someone in authority," she said quietly.

"I am in charge, and I say—"

"Is that your office there?" Jade asked, pointing.

The Rozhin faltered slightly. "No, but that's irrelevant. I am in complete charge—"

"You assert, then, in front of your two aides, that

you are the ultimate authority within this office, capable of establishing policy?"

The Rozhin clapped his jaw shut with a loud click and turned to look at the two humanoids standing obediently behind him. From what Jade knew of hierarchical structure, either subordinate would happily report to the Commancor in charge that their immediate superior was assuming unwarranted airs. Nothing would earn demotion faster than for a subjugate to pretend to powers reserved for his rightful master. Much as he would hate giving in to this upstart visitor, the Rozhin knew where his long-term career lay.

He hissed a command at one of his subordinates, who walked briskly to the office on the right-hand side of the room. After a moment he reemerged, followed by a Commancor in military uniform. His insignia gave him a rank equivalent to lieutenant—low-level, but adequate for this post. "What is problem?" he asked the Rozhin.

The Rozhin quickly explained the situation, and the lieutenant looked from him to the two visitors and back again. "Whole big fuss over three knives?" he asked. "Nines take it, you are most incompetent fool I ever deal with. They could get three more in any kitchen on Haldek-fief. Let them keep knives for all it matters."

Then, for the first time, he turned to look directly at Jade and Fastal. "I worry, though, about 'property' you wish to recover. Dominion does not give up what it has rightfully conquered."

"These are mere personal effects, of no intrinsic value," Fastal said. "I am told the Dominion's officers have already combed the estate and removed everything they considered important."

"Still, it is irregular," the lieutenant said.

"We've submitted the matter to the Greest's justice," Jade spoke up, "and we're acting with his approval." It was a flagrant lie, but not one that would be lightly challenged by a mere lieutenant. Besides, the Greest had charged only ten eus for a transfer fee; if that wasn't approval, what was?

The lieutenant bared his teeth at the mention of the

Greest, but otherwise gave no immediate reaction. After a moment he said, "What is name of estate you'll visit?"

"Fornen-Dakk," said Fastal.

"Let me check." He returned to his office and closed the door. After several minutes he came back out.

"Estate's buildings have been declared abandoned and worthless. Its lands are being worked for good of Dominion by Lughflin family, neighbors who aided our occupation. Take what you want from house, but leave lands intact."

"I understand," Fastal said with a stiff bow. "I seek only personal items. My visit should be no more than five or six days."

"Then welcome to Haldek-fief," said the lieutenant.

Jade and Fastal repacked their gear on the inspection table and left the Customs office. As soon as he was sure they were out of earshot, Fastal turned to Jade. "Thank you for standing up to them. I did not want to give up my family blade."

"If you want to thank me," Jade said testily, "don't ever call me a servant again. Commancors don't respect that. I'm your assistant."

"I will remember that," Fastal promised.

Jade had feared they might have to resort to some kind of animal-drawn cart for transportation, but was relieved to find things were more up-to-date in Detalla. The rental place, conveniently located across the street from the transfer station, had no hovercraft, but there was an open-topped six-wheeled vehicle available with an enclosed flatbed for hauling cargo. It was motorized, seated the two of them and all their gear comfortably, and moved at speeds greater than a handful of kilometers per hour, so Jade had no great objections. Fastal paid an exorbitant fee to rent it for six days.

Detalla, the main settlement of Haldek, was a town of wood and stone, plaster and cement. Heavy industry had not yet developed on this colony world, and steel was too expensive to ship, so the Lemmantine colonists had made do with the lighter-weight technologies. The buildings were very solid, the designs very basic, as they'd been on most of the young worlds Jade had visited. Paint, however, was cheap, and the original settlers had used color to dispel the drabness from what otherwise would have been a very dull town. The ground floor of a building might be yellow, the upper floor red, and both levels might have purple trim along the windowsills. All combinations, garish and subtle, had gone into making Detalla a more interesting place to live.

But that was two years ago, before the Commancor legions invaded Haldek, before their small armored vehicles ground up the sidewalks, before their energy beams smashed through walls, and before their efficient little buzzbombers strafed the streets. Everywhere were the scars and pockmarks of battle. Rubble had since been swept from the streets, but the alleys were still full of broken glass, shattered boards, and crumbled bricks. Not a drop of new paint had been spread since that day, windows were boarded over, and a thick layer of dust covered everything.

The streets were paved, and wide enough to have seen considerable traffic in their day, but now they were broken and the traffic was minimal. In time, as the planet was absorbed into the Commancor Dominion, things would probably settle into a routine and people would return to their normal state of business. But for now a depression had settled on Haldek, the depression of a conquered people still stunned by their defeat and virtual enslavement. It was a hard lesson to learn—and Jade was still grateful she'd never had to.

The air was moist, and a warm soft wind was blowing as they went through their errands. The puddles in the streets and fresh clean air were the only evidence of the major storm that had raged for the three days before their arrival. The local newsstrips were full of tales of storm damage. Here, at least, it was hard to tell from war damage.

They drove west for several blocks, and suddenly Fastal stopped. Ahead of them was a large fenced-in area, most of it open ground, but with several hangars, barracks, and other large buildings. Jade recognized it as one of the standard configurations for a Commancor airfield.

"That used to be a beautiful park," Fastal commented.

"Times change," Jade said with a shrug.

They had to detour around the airfield, then continued west until they reached a river, where Fastal turned north onto a street that paralleled the bank. "Most of our large settlements are along the rivers," he explained. "We do not yet have a lot of steel to build railroads, so we rely on river commerce for our major transportation. There is always much activity along the docks."

Indeed there was activity on the river; it was one of the few places where people seemed to be *doing* anything rather than just existing. Even so, a lot of that activity was military. Nearly 20 percent of the craft tied up at the wharves were armored Commancor gunboats. Fastal must have noticed this fact, too, but he kept his views to himself.

They continued driving north as the river curved off to the west. Their next stop was the Haldek equivalent of a hardware and feed store. There they purchased everything they would need for moving furniture, for shoring up a ruined house while they moved the things, and for camping out inside it. The store's owner had known the Fornen family, and remembered Fastal as a young lad. While Jade walked through the store gathering supplies, Fastal and Scrhedol il Desnsr discussed the changes since their last meeting at Fastal's going-away fete.

"Your family was brave," the storekeeper said, taking a carefully casual look around to make certain they were alone in the building. "At the end they sent away all of those who had stood with them, and who the invaders might not be able to identify, so that some Lemmants of true honor would still live on Haldek, and someday restore her.

"The neighbors to the east of you, the Lughflins, betrayed your family in exchange for the right to have the land. They took nearly everything of value from your place; theirs is like a palace now, I understand." Il Desnsr wiped his brow and shook the sweat off his hand.

Fastal looked a little shocked but sympathetic at this movement, the equivalent of a human spitting on the floor at the mention of something foul. "I have not been there, of course—"

"Sorry to interrupt," Jade said, "but where are the plastic packing ties—you know, the strips you thread one end of through the hole in other end, so that the bumps hold it tightly around your bundle?"

"My pretty young Terran, they are four rows over, at the other end, near the bottom, in several sizes. Do you need help carrying them?" asked the merchant with some body language Jade assumed was supposed to be seductive.

"I'll manage, thanks. You go ahead and tell tales to Fastal. Are you a great-uncle of his, perhaps?"

The storekeeper made the gulping sound of amusement as Jade went off to get the ties. "A smart one, that. Too bad she is not Lemmantine."

"Are my cousins still here, the ones that survived?"

"The kids who'd been at school across the river are still there. Some of the teachers were relations on your mother's father's wife's side. They are forbidden the land and the home. Some of us saw that a few things— some of the goldware, the paintings, and the daggers and such—that the invaders didn't take were sent to them. We had no way to get them to you. It is forbidden to take things of value off-planet, except for crops and such sold through the government." Again il Desnsr sprayed sweat upon the ground, and this time Fastal did the same.

"There is little at the house. Some furniture is all. I am sorry."

Jade added some collapsible water cans and some steel wedges to the stack of supplies and pronounced it completed. "Total this up. We have a lot to do yet today."

The merchant looked over the things, which totaled

several hundred eus, and said, "That will be ten eus. On the Fornen-Dakk account, I would guess."

"What in hell do you mean?" began Jade.

"Of course," said Fastal, loud enough to cut her off. "Bill as usual. Jade Darcy, let us load our vehicle. We have a long drive."

As they began their trip, twenty minutes later, Jade asked Fastal what kind of farce that was. "I know there can't be any account for Fornen-Dakk. It doesn't legally exist anymore, and this stuff is worth twenty times that ten-eu charge. I don't trust people who are too accommodating—he might be selling us out to the Commancors right now."

"For many years our family traded with him. That prestige brought him much honor and other trade, for we were the highest-ranked family for many days' travel. He fought against the invasion with my family. Not only did my father send him away to save his life, but the fact that he is alive means that not one of my family, even when tortured, revealed his name to the slime that captured them. His honor demanded he do this today. Do you understand?"

They drove in silence for many kilometers.

Even Jade had to admit Haldek was a lovely world. The sun was hot and the humidity oppressive, but the gently rolling fields and farmland just outside Detalla were restful on the soul, as was the lower-than-usual gravity. Only the scarred hillsides and occasional bomb craters marred the effect of total tranquillity. Most of the craters were already being overgrown with the local grass; in only a few of them had the ground been so fused by heat that nothing would grow there for years.

Fastal rambled on like a cheap tour guide, talking about who had owned which parcel of land and relating pointless anecdotes from his childhood. Jade wasn't listening. Her eyes kept overwhelming her brain with images of Toranawa, another burned-out world two decades earlier, of people running in terror across open fields, while her ears echoed with the whistle of shells and the rumble of far-off explosions. Finally, to turn off the ghosts, she closed her eyes altogether and drifted into an uneasy sleep.

She awoke at twilight, when the quality of the road changed and her teeth were rattling in her jaw from all the shaking. It took but a second to recall where she was, and then she looked quickly around for any danger. None appeared. *You have no business sleeping that soundly,* she chastised herself. *You're deep in enemy territory. Every slight noise should trigger an alarm.* The fact that she'd had so little sleep in the past few days was, to her demanding mind, no excuse.

"I am sorry about the road," Fastal said beside her. "It used to be much better. It sustained much damage when the Commancors invaded the estate. We will be home in a couple of minutes."

The pothole-strewn road was lined with trees and bushes. Jade craned her neck in all directions, watching for an ambush, half expecting to see Commancor troops leaping from cover to surround their vehicle at any moment. But the dusky scene remained quiet; there was no one around but them to break the peace of the day.

Then they rounded a curve in the road and suddenly saw the house—or what was left of it—silhouetted against the red sunset. It had been big, three stories, forty or fifty rooms, rambling over a large parcel of once well-tended land. Even from a distance, though, it was obvious the building had suffered major damage; the exact toll became clearer the closer they drove to the front door.

Of the twenty-two windows in the facade, not a pane remained intact. Half the upper right-hand corner had been burned away, and smoke had stained the trim around the third-floor windows. The large front door hung half off its hinges like a drunkard leaning against the wall for support, and the interior beyond was dark and empty.

Fastal gave a cry of anguish and sped up to reach the house. The truck squealed to a stop just in front of the porch, and the young Lemmant leaped out to run up the shattered wooden steps. He tried desperately to open the front door, but it was wedged in place, and at last he gave up and sank to his knees, leaning his head against the wall and moaning softly.

Jade climbed out of the car and walked very deliberately up to the porch, avoiding the broken boards in the steps. She studied the tilted door for a moment, then lifted up on one side and managed to get it to swing partway open, rasping as it did so on the dusty porch. She did not go in, but stood silently beside the door, waiting for Fastal to recover.

Eventually he became aware of her presence. He stopped moaning and straightened up, then pulled himself with shaky dignity to his feet. "I am sorry. It is just . . . I knew intellectually that the house had been attacked and ruined, but to suddenly see it like this—it is very much a shock."

The discipline he took such pride in finally reasserted itself. "I am being a dreadful host. Welcome to Fornen-Dakk, my family estate—such as it is. Please enter and make yourself comfortable."

Still saying nothing, Jade pulled the blade from her right boot and stepped through the narrow opening into the dim interior beyond. She slid quickly aside so she was not silhouetted by the outside light, then waited patiently for her eyes to grow accustomed to the gloom. Her ears, meanwhile, were straining for any suspicious sound within the vast building.

There was nothing. Her ears told the story, and her eyes confirmed it shortly thereafter. The building was deserted. She walked cautiously ahead and peered into a couple of rooms off the entranceway, but everything was empty. Eventually she put her knife back in its sheath and relaxed.

Fastal had entered behind her and watched her go through her ritual. "No danger, then?" he asked when he saw her put the knife away.

"The ceiling might collapse," Jade said. "I'd be careful what I leaned against. But we're alone here, except for the inevitable rodents. Are there any lights?"

"I do not think so. The building had its own generator, and I doubt it has been well tended."

"Then we'll have to make our own." She reached

into her pack and produced a small lantern with a focusing mirror. Shining it around showed only bare walls, where once might have hung paintings or tapestries; some of the walls bore scorch marks or smoke stains, while others had large holes punched in them. The main hall and the immediately adjoining rooms, at least, had been stripped of furniture and carpeting, leaving the floor strewn with rubble, dust, and large chunks of plaster.

There was a set of wide stairs in front of them, as barren as the floor around them, leading up to a landing; the second flight doubled back over their heads to the next floor up. "Any other stairs?" Jade asked.

"Two more sets, toward the back."

Jade frowned. Even though the house looked and sounded safe, too many things could be lurking quietly on the third floor, waiting to creep down those back stairs the instant she was asleep. She couldn't be secure until she checked it all, and she couldn't do that effectively with the batteries in this lantern low after being stored in the dark for so long.

"I'm sleeping in the truck tonight," she announced. "We'll look this over more tomorrow." The vehicle, though open-topped, could not be approached without the attacker at least crossing some open ground.

Fastal put up no argument, and the two left the house again. The air outside was hot and muggy, but there was no threat of rain. The truck's seats weren't comfortable, but they reclined, and they would do until morning.

They went out to the truck and opened some containers with their provisions. Jade took her portable cooker out of her pack and prepared a prepacked and filling meal. They ate their food in silence. The Lemmant was lost in dismal contemplations of his family's death, and Jade refused to think about anything but the food that was currently in her mouth. She particularly didn't want to think about Megan Cafferty and what her presence on Cablans might mean. She didn't think about Megan Cafferty many times as she ate.

CHAPTER 8

Reconnaissance

Despite her general fatigue and the tensions of the day, Jade did not sleep well that first night on Haldek. Her brain had gone into what she called "field mode," and any slight noise was enough to rouse her—at least enough to determine whether it might be the sound of something hostile approaching. On top of that, Fastal made little puling noises as he slept, and was constantly—and noisily—shifting position. Jade didn't know whether that was standard for him, or whether seeing his family's home in this condition was disturbing his sleep. Whichever was the case, she couldn't get any decent rest while he was tossing in his seat, shaking the entire truck. She ended up merely getting a series of catnaps and resigned herself to not getting any sound sleep until this mission was over and she returned to Cablans—assuming things were normal there, too.

She woke her companion at first light. Both were stiff and sore from the awkward seats, but neither made a word of complaint. They ate a cold breakfast in the truck and then walked back to the house, which looked no more inviting in daylight than it had the night before.

The house was a ruin, a burned-out shell of a once-fine home that had come under too much Commancor attention. Daylight filtered in through cracks in boarded-up windows and holes in walls and ceilings. They spent an hour searching through the ground floor, which had been stripped of everything remotely valuable, and Jade could see the tension in Fastal as room

111

after room was found devoid of remembered objects. She kept alert for noises and movements, but there were none; the house was truly abandoned.

Having seen the rickety condition of the front staircase, Jade did not want to trust it with her weight, but one of the back staircases was in much more serviceable condition. It creaked loudly despite Jade's best efforts at stealth, but since the upper floors were as deserted as the bottom one it didn't matter. Here, though, the house seemed to have suffered less at the hands of its ravishers. Large murals on the walls were mostly free of smoke damage, heavy carpets had not been ripped up, and some articles of furniture had been left. This at least looked like a place where people might once have lived in some comfort.

Fastal had been stoically ready for the desolation on the ground floor, but seeing the traces of his past still lingering in the upper floors seemed to unnerve him as much as his initial view of the house. He stood in one room staring at the carpet, the mural, and an upholstered wooden chair standing sentinel in a corner; after more than a minute he went from his usual pale blue to a lilac-tinged white and began trembling so badly he could hardly stand. Taking pity on him, Jade guided him over to a corner where he could sit down on the rug and get over the worst of the seizure.

"I am sorry," he said when he could speak coherently again. "I know I am betraying my training, but the sentiment is so overwhelming. To see the destruction and to know what it cost my family . . . You must think I am a terrible weakling."

Jade said nothing, allowing him to regain some more of his composure.

"I was not here, of course," Fastal continued, "so I do not know precisely everything that happened. But reports did get back to Lemmanta, and I do know my family. Over the last two years I painstakingly pieced together a picture of what happened here. I do not know why I did it; it is not pleasant knowledge to have.

"When the invasion came, my family—even as seventh-rank nobility—felt honor-bound to defend their world rather than yield to the overwhelming odds against them. Fornen-Dakk became a rallying point for the defense forces, and my family were some of those in charge of what opposition the planet could muster.''

A house out in open countryside? Jade thought. *It's a miracle it's still standing.* But she said, "We haven't much time for memories, pleasant or unpleasant. Let's work while there's still light." *Especially when your memories are too much like mine. Only I really did see it, and smell it, and . . .* "Let's start by checking the closets, drawers, and such, okay?" *No reason for that, girl, not now. Put them away.*

Fastal and Jade spent the rest of the day crawling through the abandoned house, cataloguing what the Commancors and the Lughflins had deigned to leave behind. There was some furniture, most too bulky to carry, though a few pieces were manageable; Jade thought the style was ugly and brooding, but that was simply a matter of taste. There were some pieces of broken bric-a-brac, personal mementos of no intrinsic value but great sentimental importance.

Most of the drawers and closets had been emptied or become homes for what passed for mice on this planet. In one third-floor corner room, though, they found that the toy chest was full. The building blocks which most races with manual dexterity gave their children were enough in scale, and worn enough, to have been Jade's own. The simple items—dolls, ropes, toy buildings—all were too familiar. Jade quickly tied the box closed, carried it down the squeaking stairs, and loaded it on the truck.

"That was mine, and Ribli's, and Plecdal's, and Calla's, and many things here were my father's and mother's before us," said Fastal, as he sat in the middle of what had been his family's nursery. Jade stood in the doorway of the room, which was empty but for its built-in shelves and three small beds. The beds had obviously been repainted and rechipped by many children over the years; the former occupant, sitting in the center of the floor, hardly looked old enough to be out of this nursery yet.

"Fastal, do you want to take those little beds? They're pretty beat up."

"Beat up? There are five generations of living in those beds. My family brought them here all the way from Lemmanta. My maternal double-great-grandfather made these from the trunks of gcinfo saplings, trained to these shapes, harvested after five years, then cured into these frames. My double-great-grandchildren were to have slept on them . . . and maybe theirs as well."

Fastal rose and strode to the base of the nearest bed, grasping the footboard with a white-knuckle grip. "Each chunk out of them, here at the foot, is another piece of our history to pass on, for only the family, its life and past, is what we have to guide our future. Otherwise we would descend to beasts—as those Commancor bastards would have us do.

"Yes, we take the bed frames, at least one. And we take the headboard from the next room, and we send our first load back to Cablans, and maybe another, before we do anything more—because ten generations of this family will live somewhere, and Fornen-Dakk will live with them. In these beat-up pieces."

Fastal turned around slowly as though recording the ruined room with his eyes, then locked gazes with Jade. "My first lessons were in this room. And one of the first things I was taught was: 'Preserve the family, its works and memories, that your dreams may spring from solid ground and raise that spot for the next to build on.' My family's spot may be lower now, Jade Darcy, but I'll not see it flat."

"Just my back from hauling these things," Jade said as she wiped the sweat from her face again. "Let's get rid of all those mildewed mattresses, at least, and load them up. Yes, all of them, if I'm going to be stuck moving furniture for three days anyway. Oof. I hired on as a soldier, not a stevedore, remember?" she continued through clenched teeth as she tipped over the first heavy wooden frame to dislodge the ruined bedding.

"What is a stevedore?"

"Shut up and lift."

By the time they'd finished thoroughly searching the house, checking the power and the plumbing, making lists of everything the jackals had left, and loading up the truck for the first trip back to Detalla, the sun was beginning to set. Jade was dripping with sweat from the hot, muggy weather, even though she'd done very little actual work. More than anything she wanted her shower from home, but the haphazard nature of the plumbing left in this house—barely enough to keep the relatively human toilets in operation—made that impossible. She resigned herself to feeling grimy, to making do with sponge baths, and to the fact that all races smelled bad to one another. A little extra human-stink about her wouldn't make that much difference to anyone else here.

They ate dinner that evening sitting on the ground in the first floor dining room. Jade sat in a corner with her back against a wall, so that the two entrances to the room were in view at all times. Fastal, less paranoid or experienced, sat facing her. After rambling on at length over some childhood anecdotes, he suddenly grew very serious and quiet.

"You chided me for my lack of expertise," he said, "but I have worked long and hard on developing my plan. When it became obvious that the Council of the Families would not take action against the Commancors, I found a job on Cablans and studied the Haldek situation from a distance. I learned that Commander Horsson, who committed the atrocities against my family, has remained on Haldek, using this local region as a training ground for new assault troops. In four days there are war games scheduled to take place in the mountains behind this estate. I know that region intimately; I explored it well as a child growing up here. On that terrain I do believe we can isolate Commander Horsson from his troops so I can kill him."

Assassinating a commander in the middle of his army, Jade thought. *I was right the first time—this boy's bent on suicide. And for a lousy thousand eus I've agreed to let him take me with him.*

"Tell me about the area," said Jade, handing him a

battery-driven electronic pad. "Use this and make me a map. Start with this house in the center."

After an hour of work, Jade had what she wanted: a good basic diagram, with crude elevations, of the area. If the Commancors moved as expected—a chancy business—she and Fastal just might have good odds after all.

"We'll see how well your memory correlates to truth in the morning. For now, start your warm-ups."

"My what?"

"Start whatever movement exercise you need to do before major exertion to avoid strain."

"Why should I do that?"

"Because, little man, we're going to fight."

"Do not call me by such a name. Why should we fight, aside from your insults?"

"Because I've only seen you once with a knife in your hand, and then you were too drunk to hold on to it. I'm not going into a battle with an unknown quantity covering my back, if I can prevent it at all. So off the chair—we have work to do."

"I am paying you to take my orders, not—"

"Wrong. You're paying me to make this crazy scheme work, and this is one of the things I need to know before I can do that. However, if your vengeance isn't worth a few minutes' workout, let me know now, we'll finish loading furniture, and we'll go back home to Cablans."

Fastal rose quickly, said, "Come," and strode out of the dining room. Jade got up and followed him, smiling. Some people were just too easy to maneuver for their own good.

They stood out on what had been the front lawn. Jade took the blade from her left boot and handed it to Fastal. "Here, use this one, not your good one, for practice. Now, come at me."

"But you have no weapon of your own."

"If I need one, I'll have it. Come at me."

Fastal was still upset enough at her jibes that he charged straight at her. Jade easily dodged the charge. He made two more such charges, and Jade dodged them just as easily. On his fourth pass he made what he probably felt was a very clever feint and lunge. Jade stepped aside just as gracefully, and Fastal, off-balance, went sprawling on the ground.

"I thought you told me you'd had lessons," she said. "If you don't want to dishonor your teacher's memory, get up and let's do this for real."

He stood and looked at her more seriously. He did not charge this time, but closed the distance between them slowly until they were just a meter apart. Then he began a series of quick feints and jabs, testing her guard. When he saw an opening he leaped into it—only to find her grabbing his wrist and throwing him over her shoulder. He landed hard on his back and lay still for several minutes while the world settled down around him.

"A little better," Jade said. "There may be a few old ladies who'd be fooled by that move—or too arthritic to counter it. But if you want to fight Commancors, you'll have to do a lot better than that."

Fastal rose unsteadily, shook the dirt from his hair and the cobwebs from his mind, and started again. His movements became progressively less energetic, but more calculated. Jade watched him with analytical eyes, keeping her own movements to a minimum. She seldom retreated more than half a step, yet somehow his blade never came close to her.

After forty-five minutes they took a brief break, then returned for some work on what Jade had identified as some of Fastal's worst problems. His initial anger at himself for being so clumsy had dissolved as his respect for Jade's skills as a warrior had grown. After another hour of working he called a halt.

"Enough. I would need months of practice to truly learn all you have taught me this evening. You are a finer fighter than any I have seen, save a few of our Festival champions. Certainly I have never known a woman so fast and so skilled. It is an honor to learn from you."

"It's years of earning a living and keeping alive by such things," Jade told him. *Plus a computer implanted in my spine at great government expense,* she added silently, though there was no need to mention that to him. "You learn or you die. I intend to live a long time."

"If it depends on your skills as you have shown them tonight, Jade Darcy, and not on the gods of chance in their fickleness, you shall live to see great-grandchildren. So I wish it."

Jade turned and walked to a bucket of water they kept near the door for washing up. She made a big production out of cleansing her face. It wasn't that she was unfamiliar with praise; she received a lot of flattery, some of it as sincere. But Fastal had done more than that. If that expression on a Lemmant's face meant the same as on a human's, he had began to worship a hero. Jade had been the object of such admiration before; she had been nearly the oldest child in her family. But she no longer remembered how to respond to that without either crushing the child or encouraging the feeling.

The last thing I need is a damn Lemmant puppy dog following me around, assuming we make it home. Well, I'll let it stand, gentle him along. It'll make him listen to my orders better, and that might help us both survive.

By the time she was clean, she'd regained her mental balance. "Let's get some sleep. We have a dawn recon to do, a trip to Detalla, and more damn furniture to load."

"Of course, right away."

They slept inside the house that night. It was marginally safer than being out in the exposed vehicle, though Jade was still not convinced the building's structure was safe if a strong wind, or even a stiff breeze, were to come up. But as she gargled each breath of the still night air, she decided she was ready to risk one good breeze.

Jade set up the folding cot she'd brought and the light mummy bag, then looked at the hot mess and her filthy, too-warm jumpsuit with disdain. Fastal was stripped to a light undergarment covering his groin and midriff, and was clinging onto his bedding.

To hell with it. It's too muggy for modesty. She stripped off the jumpsuit, removing the weapons and keeping one of the knives with her inside the bag. The air felt good against her skin. She was thinking about staying on top of the bag when the sound of a throat clearing reminded her of the Lemmant. Suddenly conscious of the very humanoid male, she turned off the light and quickly climbed into the bag.

"May your night journeys bring wisdom and joy."

"Pleasant dreams yourself."

This night, Jade tuned out most of the noises her client made, but still stirred easily. She wasn't aware of grabbing the knife each time she was roused—but she was never aware of breathing, either. She rose when the light of the sun coming over the break in the wall forced them to, about an hour after dawn. She dressed before leaving the bag.

"Fastal, get up and dressed. We have recon to do before it gets any hotter." Jade shook the heavily sleeping Lemmant, and when he burrowed deeper in his covers, tipped over the cot and dumped him onto the floor.

"*Get up!* While we're in the field I expect you to be awake at my first whisper, understand? Do you think the Commancors will be any more delicate?"

Fastal apologized—for what he wasn't sure, but it seemed safest—and dressed hurriedly. Grabbing one of the bars made of dried fruit and jerked meat with crushed grain, and a pouch of juice, he followed Jade outside. She sent him back for his working knives, the ropes and lunch supplies, and those centuries-old and honored implements, entrenching tools, and they took off in the early-morning coolness.

They started out across the open ground. The first kilometer was meadowland; decades of plowing and the low grass it was seeded with made it flat and even, and the lighter-than-usual gravity gave Jade an extra bounce to her step that she greatly appreciated. Then they came to a stand of trees, and the going became slower. They walked along a narrow path, obviously seldom used. The brush arched over it, limbs lay across it, and often it was only a wider spot between the trees, not a true path at all.

The underbrush became thicker as they went, the forest denser, and the hikers had to lift their feet to avoid catching them in the vines that proliferated along the forest floor. The air was close and dripping wet—not quite a jungle, but filled with noisy life forms that screamed ahead of and behind them, while leaving them in a ball of relative quiet. Small lizardy things darted from the piles of decaying vegetation on the forest floor as Jade disturbed their hiding places. The leafy canopy filtered the light to an early-dusk dimness that even the very bright moons of Haldek wouldn't penetrate. The thought of possibly crossing this terrain in the dark was not appealing.

"Are there any unusual or dangerous animals or plants we'll have to watch out for?" Jade asked her guide.

"No animals large enough to attack us; those have long since been hunted out in this area," Festal replied. "Most others would simply run away. There are numerous snakes and insects, but none use venom. Sometimes you will find pits filled with one or the other of them. They are more a nuisance than a threat."

Jade didn't mind snakes; she'd had several as pets when she was little. But bugs . . . she put the thought from her mind. If they weren't a threat, she wouldn't worry about them.

The forest floor sloped upward—gently at first, then more steeply. The tangled growth on the forest floor was layer upon slippery layer of plants and vine roots competing for the small bit of sunlight and nutrition available on the thin soil of the hill. Even in the low gravity the exertion of lifting the legs to avoid the vines left Jade, in prime physical condition, panting slightly as they reached the crest.

The land dropped off sharply below them. They were overlooking a broad valley with some more sparsely forested land and a river running through it. Jade recognized the signs of severe annual flooding below them that would wash out the thicker brush they'd been going through, and make for such a graceful, open valley. The scene was all greens and yellows and browns, like a nineteenth-century naturalist's watercolors come to life.

"This is where the war games are to be, according to my information," Fastal said. "One side is to start from over there on the left; the other holds the river camp on the right. Commander Horsson will be stationed at the observation headquarters, but I do not know exactly where that will be."

Jade looked the area over, first with her naked eye and then with field glasses. She'd been in enough wargame situations to know that the layout Fastal described was a good one to test the soldier's training and equipment without the risk of serious injury. There were two possible places for the observation headquarters to be. The first was a large clearing, right on the river near a small bend, that would make a good campsite for the observers; a slight rounding made for good drainage and a good view of the area, and there was water right there. Almost directly below her, against the cliffs near the natural boundary line between the two divisions, was a grove of trees; it would also make a natural and logical observation post.

"There," she said, pointing at the second spot. "That's where we need him to be."

The Lemmant peered at the grove with his head cocked at a funny angle. "We can hope he'll accommodate us."

"We'll do more than hope," Jade commented. "We'll persuade him. And I don't know if you've thought of it, but we can't stand up here and watch the games. We'd be spotted for sure. And Commancors don't like being spied on."

"I have thought of that. Follow me."

Fastal moved along the rim of the ridge until he found a place where a narrow dirt trail descended steeply down the face of the cliff. Climbing cautiously downward, using rocks, tree roots, and any other natural projections as handholds, they came to a spot slightly wider than the rest of the path where some scraggly bushes partially blocked their descent. Fastal pushed the bushes aside to reveal the opening of a small cave.

"I used to play in here as a child," he said. "We can sit here unseen by those below and watch things happen up and down the entire valley."

Jade inspected the cave silently. It would be cramped—it had probably looked much bigger through a child's eyes—but the walls were solidly packed earth, with old broken supports that showed it to be a long-abandoned mine survey shaft that had partially caved in. The two of them could certainly stay here during the games and watch the goings-on. If Fastal's information was correct and Commander Horsson was in charge here, they could watch his security setup and make more detailed plans to catch him alone. She gave a curt nod and said, "How do we get down to the valley floor from here?"

Fastal pointed to where the trail continued past the cave ledge. "Down that way. The trail is not hard."

For a mountaingoat, Jade thought. "We'll leave most of our gear here for now, except the entrenching tools, work knives, and small folding saws. You take those, I'll pack the rest. Where's lunch?"

"But we just two hours ago broke our fast."

"By the time we reach that clearing we saw around the bend, you'll be ready for lunch. Trust me."

The trip down took an hour and half. Jade stopped continually to repair the goat track from the base of the cliff to the cave—not by widening and smoothing it, but by making it a series of small flat zones, ramps, and chutes that appeared as natural as the original but was much easier to travel. A fallen limb wasn't removed, but carefully lifted, and dug in so it wouldn't turn underfoot, and the area uphill of it filled with dirt that was removed carefully from under a bush so that no hole could be seen. After sweeping and scattering debris in the area, it looked as though a root had accidentally made a dam that filled with dirt during flood and slide; the fact that it just happened to make a good step for a climber was merest coincidence.

Large rocks were sometimes braced, sometimes tumbled downhill, sometimes dug behind to create a walkway totally hidden from observers below. Smaller rocks were dug in to provide firm footing. From the base of the cliffs, when they finally reached it, the hill looked undisturbed, even to the eyes of those who did the work.

"That's as fine a Ho Chi Minh trail as I've ever made," Jade proclaimed proudly.

"Pardon please my continual ignorance, but what is a Ho Chi Minh trail? I see what this is; I am wondering about the origins of the term."

"It's an old Terran term. I guess it was some general or someone who they named it after. It's a concealed trail you can move troops and supplies on. We'll be making one fast retreat from here. I don't want a sprained ankle getting us killed, or a suddenly improved road giving us away."

"Who would be giving us to whom?"

"Calling attention to us. Damned u-trans and its literalness."

They headed for the clearing Jade had seen around the bend. It took fifteen minutes to get there, and Jade called for lunch as soon as they arrived. Fastal sank to the ground with a grateful sigh, and both silently tore into their food. As the worst of their hunger eased, Jade began to examine the clearing with more care.

"Jade Darcy, what are you searching for? Can I be of any assistance?"

"I'm looking for small markings or flags, usually brown and green with gold, that Commancor scouts use to mark special sites. If they've scouted this area and chosen it for headquarters, there should be some."

Fastal rose, carrying the meat-stuffed leaves his race preferred for lunch, and began to walk around the clearing. In a few minutes he called out, "Is this an example of a scout's marking device?"

Jade walked over to the spot and examined the paint sprayed on the tree—or what was left of it. The storm of a few days ago had washed most of it away.

"That's it. And that symbol is the one for the generator. This is it, all right."

"What do we do now?"

"We unchoose the place. Don't ask what I mean—you'll see soon enough."

Jade walked around the clearing slowly, till she found a very tall tree with several large, dead-looking limbs. Like all the mature trees in the area, it was a hundred meters tall, and over four meters around the trunk.

"Fastal, wouldn't you say this tree is dying and about to fall over?"

"These are kodlut trees. They live a very long time, nearly forever. This one was struck by lightning, and insects have invaded it. It could stand for centuries yet, but another storm like the one of this week might bring it down if the ground was saturated enough, and it is weakened enough."

"It was, I promise you. Bring our packs over."

Jade walked around the tree a couple of times, sighting into the open area beyond it. When Fastal returned with the packs, she pulled out a small hatchet and started chipping at the trunk very near the base. The wood had been damaged in the area by the infestation, and gave way quickly. Soon Jade placed small wedges in the tree, took out the hammer she'd packed, and drove them in. She walked around the other side and began to saw at the trunk.

"Will not the Commancors be curious if they find the stump of a tree so recently harvested?"

Jade didn't answer.

"Do you want me to get you a bigger saw?"

Jade kept sawing till she had made a line across nearly 120 degrees of trunk. She then took the hatchet and made the line into a paper-thin notch. Returning to the other side of the tree, she drove in bigger wedges, then planed off a flat spot on a large root of the tree, angled toward her first cut. On this she placed the small hydraulic jack she'd used on the boulders. Laying the blade of the entrenching tool at the top of the jack, she began to pump the jack handle. It took several moves, pounding in the larger wedges, pumping, repositioning the jack, but finally the weakened tree, groaning and screaming like a hundred women in labor, shattered and fell into the clearing.

The giant tree rocked the earth when it hit. Fastal and Jade swayed and stumbled as ground moved beneath their feet. The air was filled with flying splinters and dust that made them both cough and close their eyes. The sound seemed to echo for minutes in the suddenly quiet forest, as all the animals grew still and waited to see if the noise signaled a threat to them.

After the dust settled and the natural noises resumed, Jade studied the trunk. Where there were toolmarks, she took rocks and splintered the surface of the stump and the trunk. Then she walked to the other side of the clearing to admire her handiwork.

The tree had been tall enough that it now bisected the clearing. Not exactly centered, it still meant, with the huge branches, that what had been the perfect clearing was now a two-day job for an organized crew to clean out—and with the scars dug into the grassy surface by the limbs and the machinery the crew would have to use, the meadow would be a bowl of mud with the slightest rain.

"You were right, Jade Darcy," Fastal said. "We unchose it."

Jade turned to look at Fastal for the first time since her tree surgery. The Lemmant was covered with dust, moist earth, and debris from the tree. There were pale rings around his eyes and where he had wiped his mouth. He looked as though he'd been in a fight with the demon of dirt, and lost.

She tried to stifle her chuckling, but that only seemed to make it worse. The strange choking noise puzzled Fastal, and as he started to ask about it, Jade let out an enormous sneeze.

The sound frightened a bird that had just felt safe in returning to the area, and it took off with a loud screech. Jade followed its flight over the river, wished again for a bath, then hit herself on the forehead.

"Idiot!"

"Jade Darcy, I assure you—"

"Not you, Fastal, me. Is that river toxic? Or contain any large predators?"

"We take pride in our ecological wisdom on Haldek. That is the—"

"All I want to know is, can we swim in it?"

"Everyone does. It is where my mother taught me. What are you doing?"

Jade had picked up her pack and started straight for the river. She ran to the edge, started to undress, decided that her clothes could use a bath themselves, dropped the pack, and waded straight in. With a loud cheer, Fastal followed.

Jade dunked a few times in the surprisingly cool water, and then stripped off her jumpsuit. She wrung it out and rinsed it till it appeared nearly clean, then carried it to a large rock and spread it out to dry. She waded deeper into the river, enjoying the sparkle of the clear water over the fine sand-and-gravel bottom and the sight of the tiny fish scurrying out of the way of her shadow and bow wave.

A color change alerted her to a drop-off, and, with the water nearly waist-deep, she dove for it in a shallow dive that kept her near the surface.

The current was strong but slow to a practiced swimmer like Jade. Glad for the chance to engage in some rhythmic full-body movement after all the chopping and sawing, Jade pulled in a vigorous crawl till she was fifty meters upstream, then rolled onto her back and started to float back. She heard an indistinct sound and came erect, treading water. The Lemmant had pulled even with her.

"You are a strong swimmer," Fastal said. "I didn't know you enjoyed it."

"I don't get much of a chance lately, but it's always been a favorite form of exercise. This clean, clear river reminds me of the one near my aunt's place when I was a girl. Race you."

They struck out at a good pace, and were soon swimming up and down the river. Finally starting to get winded, they raced back to the shore, neck and neck. Jade grabbed her soap and headed back to the water for a chance to get truly clean. The Lemmant was still at the edge of the water, and leaned out to help her in.

Jade had never seen a naked Lemmant, and was struck again by the cliché that the most alien things are those closest to you. Clothed, Fastal was easy to think of as human. From the waist up, his pouch-shaped belly and different muscles made him look like a flabby, blue-tinged human, despite his height and overall slenderness. The slight differences in musculature were masked by the dense subcutaneous fat all Lemmants had. Instead of the genitalia Jade would see on a human, however, Fastal had what looked like a small udder just below the spot where humans had belly buttons. Fastal looked at Jade, then turned suddenly away.

"What's the matter, never seen a Terran before?"

Probably hasn't, at least not nude.

"Not unclothed, and it is most unsettling," said Festal. He didn't look at Jade till the direction of her splashing told him she was in deeper water.

"What's so unsettling, as you put it?"

"Most of the time you look like a normal person. I can forget you are so alien. Like this, though, you appear—mutilated. I was told the Commancors amputated the genitals one lobe at a time, with lasers so no one died of blood loss, and . . ."

Fastal dove in the water and swam upstream.

Jade felt suddenly cold despite the sun and heat. She silently rinsed off the drying soap on her arms, hyperaware of the sounds of the forest and the thickness of the air. She scrubbed her hair and checked on her merc suit. It hadn't fully dried, but wasn't dripping, so Jade put it on and sat on the rock waiting for Fastal. When he arrived she just said, "Get dressed. We still have to do the path up from the cave and make a run to town."

Haldek wasn't as pretty anymore.

The rest of the day was spent in hard work and solemn silence. What little talk there was concerned their work. Each kept his or her own thoughts.

The sparring that night was different. Fastal battled with a fierceness he'd lacked the night before. Afterward they discussed the equipment and supplies they'd need to pack tomorrow before heading to the cave. Jade left her leotard-style underwear on and slept on top of her bag. Fastal had moved to his old room.

There is a resilience in youth that allows a night's sleep to restore a young spirit. The next morning was spent in packing the truck for one more trip to Detalla. The Greest was transferring the furniture for very little money, even though most of it was heading to Lemmanta, a two-station stop. Jade was more suspicious than ever of the Greest's motives, but knew she had no other choice at this point but to do what he seemed to want. It still infuriated her that he had manipulated her like this, but she concentrated on matters she could control, like packing up Fornen-Dakk, and tried to ignore his insufferable archness.

She comforted herself with the thought that while this was sweaty physical labor, it was far safer than attacking a Commancor leader in the middle of his troops—something that, despite all the planning, she had trouble believing she would do.

This day she listened to the stories Fastal told of his home and family. The tales were seldom interesting from a human viewpoint, yet they built a picture of a family Jade would have liked to know. They worked hard to develop their wealth. They tilled fields, bred animals, had jobs in town.

Over thirty members of the family had lived here. Fastal was of the latest generation. It was a proud and brave lineage, and they were kind-sounding people. Jade began to feel a shadow of Fastal's rage. More than he would ever guess, she felt a kinship. She found herself telling him of her own battles, and of the loss of friends, comrades-in-arms, to the Commancors. Even here—or especially here—she couldn't speak of her family yet. Somehow it was the faces of her brothers, her sisters, she saw when he mentioned his. She said nothing of this; she just hauled furniture and listened as around the ruin Fastal raised the ghosts of his heart.

In late afternoon they came to a piece of heavy furniture that Jade gave one brief shove against and flatly refused to carry out. But her shove had moved it just enough to reveal something hidden underneath it. It was a curved dagger in a jeweled sheath, similar in design to the ceremonial blade Fastal carried, only smaller, and with the same inlaid design in the handle. Fastal saw it and let out a great cry—but Jade couldn't tell whether it was a cry of happiness or anguish.

"This is my sister's knife," Fastal explained. "I do not know how it ended up here; perhaps it got kicked away during a fight. But it looks to be intact. Perhaps my sister's soul, as well as the blade, rides in the sheath."

He picked up the dagger, looked at it for a moment, then handed it to Jade. "Here. I would like you to have it."

Jade took a step back in surprise. "Me? Why?"

Fastal paused. "I do not know, precisely. I think you remind me somewhat of my sister. And yet, that surprises me because the two of you are in no way alike. She was always outgoing and talkative, you are reserved and silent. She was gentle and playful, you are rough and warlike. And yet you are both intelligent, both perceptive, both . . . vulnerable."

Jade flinched at that word, but Fastal continued on, oblivious to her reaction.

"At the ingesterie you could have taken my blade by force; as drunk as I was, I could not have put up much of a fight. Instead you talked to me of honor, as my sister would have done, and made me realize the consequences of my actions. I think Calla would have liked you, and would have approved of my giving you her knife."

Though Jade tried to refuse, Fastal kept insisting until eventually she took the dagger just to silence him. But as she tucked it into her belt she was glad that the differences in their respective physiologies kept him from correctly interpreting the flush that came to her face.

She walked over to move the next chest, cursing the dust that irritated her eyes and nose so badly.

CHAPTER 9

Commander Horsson

They'd packed the truck that night with one last load of furniture, mostly bulky but light items that wouldn't slow the vehicle down, "provided we live to escape in it," Jade kept muttering. Then they'd gathered together the supplies for the sortie.

Fastal questioned every item Jade packed: the plastic cable ties, the piano wire, the legs off the broken chair, even the amount of water. Jade finally exploded. "Look, you ignorant two-legged bovine, you hired me to get you in and out of this god-be-damned mess. Either shut your mouth, or I'll fucking well quit and spend the next week dancing on your grave—*if* they find enough of you to bury when the Commancors finish with you."

With peace and quiet restored, Jade finished packing in short order. She placed a small rucksack with the rest of her belongings in the truck, hesitated, then added the elaborate curved dagger Fastal had given her. *One more knife won't make any difference, and with that jeweled sheath it might give me away. And losing it would be a shame. It's too . . . valuable.*

Jade returned to the house and searched through it one more time for any possessions she might have forgotten. In the interest of efficiency she went immediately to the third floor and worked her way down. When she reached the ground-floor kitchen, she found Fastal trying to pry something out of the doorframe at shoulder level. In the twilight it was hard to make out what it was. She shone her flashlight on it and caught Fastal's face as he whipped around to see what she was doing. His eyes flared bright orange in the glare, then he shut them.

"What are you doing?" Jade asked. "Looking for treasure?"

"I wanted to take this for my home." Fastal pointed above the door to a carving he'd been trying to pry loose. "The dahgab is the demon of our house, our shield. This is the only one intact. It came from Lemmanta. It should go back there with me."

"It'll go back in pieces if you keep that up. Move over."

Jade examined the ugly carving of a mutated Jerusalem cricket and finally found the carefully puttied nailheads. She removed from her pack the diamond-dusted wire she always carried coiled in the pocket behind its clasp. Grasping the tiny handles, she pulled it taut and slid it behind the carving. In a few moments the piece loosened. Warning Fastal to be ready, she cut through the last tiny nail and it tumbled into his hands.

"Thank you. I was afraid I'd damage it."

"Stash it. Then, if you're done, moonrise is in a few minutes and we should get going."

Within moments they were on their way, each carrying a good-sized pack and extra water containers. Jade thankfully let the Lemmant take the lead when they reached the forest. Not wanting the trail to be found later, Jade hadn't marked the path through the brush, and only Fastal's lifelong familiarity with the place kept them from getting hopelessly lost in the darkness. It was still slow going, and it took them nearly three hours to reach the cave.

Jade was grateful to find no strange animals inside when they arrived. The beam from her flashlight showed the cave's low and narrow earthen walls as they extended deeply into the hillside. The collapse only blocked the descending shaft. The floor angled down toward the rear. She and Fastal planned to use the back part of the cave as a lavatory during their long stakeout, so they wouldn't have to emerge from hiding until they were ready.

Jade overruled Fastal's request for a rest period,

knowing that after the day's hard physical work they might not wake till morning. They would be under a strict code of silence then, and there were still things to do. Better to do them now, when noise wouldn't matter as much.

Jade set out the tarp and bag that would be her sleeping place far enough back from the entrance that she wasn't easily seen, but close enough that the night sounds from the valley were clear. As soon as Fastal had his place ready, she arranged the water, food, and weapons in easily accessible places, far enough away from each other that no accidental bangs and crashes would be made as they were used. Only after the cave was as secure a campsite as possible did she call a halt for dinner.

They had a cold dinner, then Jade arranged the tarp beneath her and lay down on top of it, away from the warmth-stealing ground. She'd crawl in after the temperature dropped, but now she enjoyed the coolness of the cave. The Lemmant, not as used to sleeping in the open, put most of his covers on top and got what sleep he could. He slept fitfully, knowing that tomorrow could be the most important day of his life, his last. Jade stayed awake, getting used to the normal sounds of the river and the different animals that lived here rather than in the open area of Fornen-Dakk. Finally she slept lightly, rousing when small animals passed too near the mouth of the cave, before her alien scent drove them off. Only when the temperature dropped did the motion cease, and Jade crawled inside her bag for some real rest.

She awoke early to the sounds of war, to the movements of troops and equipment through the valley below. Dawn had barely tinged the sky and no perceptible daylight was filtering past the bushes into the cave, but the two competing armies were already moving into their positions. Jade crept forward to the edge of the cave and looked out to see what was going on.

Troops were deploying in the semidarkness. Jade wished she had a pair of infrared binoculars instead of the birdwatcher type she'd bought here, but that would have been impossible to get through Customs. Even so, she could still tell a lot about what was going on below by the sounds and the hints of movement she could see in the growing morning light. She was suddenly struck by a sense of *déjà vu,* a flashback that was chillingly real. She could see human beings moving around down there, herself among them, and she could hear the sergeant's strong, powerful voice giving crisp orders of where they were to go and what their objectives were to be. She shivered at the memory.

Then she could sense Fastal crawling up behind her from inside the cave, and the present returned to her once more. The disquieting illusion was gone; in its place was the Haldek of today and the Commancor troops scattered across the broad valley before her.

She paid particular attention to the grove of trees at the base of the cliff. A group of five tents was being set up, all of different sizes, amid a great deal of overt activity. These were people who didn't care who saw them setting up, which said to Jade that they were immune to attack. This would be the neutral observation post, as she'd predicted; if Commander Horsson was to be found in any one particular place, it would be here.

She pointed and Fastal nodded, acknowledging she'd been right in her sabotage of a few days before. Jade wished she could have seen the commander's face when the "storm-damaged" tree was discovered, and hoped they accepted that obvious reason. With the enemy location confirmed, Jade backed away from the lip of the cave. "Not much will happen for another hour or so," she said in her quietest whisper. "They're still deploying. Let's have breakfast. Remember, they may send someone out to post a marker of neutrality on this bluff. We're well hidden, but any sound could give us away. Sign or write out anything you need to say."

They ate in silence, then returned to watching the games play out below them. Jade's timetable was somewhat off; the Commancor army was in position and ready much faster than she expected, recovering from the change in position sooner, and the battle was already under way by the time she and Fastal crawled back onto the ledge. A clinical part of Jade's mind was analyzing what she saw; data about the Commancors were always valuable. There were a number of races who might pay to learn what she was seeing here today.

Though Jade had never been an officer and had never had formal training in strategy and tactics, she'd absorbed a lot of practical knowledge from study and just by keeping her eyes and ears open. Battle plans actually varied little from race to race; they mostly depended on the battlefield terrain, weather conditions, numbers of troops on each side, how well each side was armed, and so forth. Different races had different psychologies of fighting, but those were mostly embellishments on the basic pattern and did not dictate the pattern itself.

Because the Commancor army was composed mostly of members of the subjugated races, the commanders placed less value on the lives of their troops. They made risky, often suicidal charges against their enemy's positions that many other races would have hesitated to make. That was one reason why the Commancor Dominion had expanded so widely; they could seldom be counted on to do the safe, conservative thing.

This much, though, was already known about the Commancors, and Jade saw little activity that surprised her. As Fastal had said, these were simple training maneuvers designed to put newer troops through their paces, not experimental tests of new weapons or tactics. Jade quickly grew bored, and took to watching the observation tents exclusively. Fastal was much more interested in the games, though he too paid close attention to the tents by the grove.

Late in the morning, Fastal suddenly stiffened. "There!" he whispered, binoculars firmly in place. "That is him. That is Commander Horsson. I have seen his picture. I know him."

Jade stared down where he pointed. Certainly there was someone important there, surrounded by a staff of aides—but she wondered how well the Lemmant could really tell one Commancor from another. Could it just be wishful thinking?

"You're sure?" was all she said aloud.

"I know him," Fastal affirmed.

Jade assessed the situation. Surrounded as he was, they could not easily get close enough to Horsson to use the knives they had with them. She could easily pick him off with a rifle at this distance—but she didn't have a rifle. Getting one would mean going down into the field and taking it from a soldier, which in turn meant risking being seen. And if Horsson was killed in so obvious a manner, her and Fastal's chances of escaping alive were virtually nil. "He's a tough target," she said.

"These games are scheduled to last five days," Fastal said. "They'll be camping down for the night. At that time he may have fewer people around him, and it will be easier for us to get near him unseen."

"I'd like to watch one night to be certain they're following standard routine. Those troops set up fast; that could mean they're good and have other surprises waiting for us."

"But if we wait, they will be even better established. They moved two of the tents after camp was set, and are still doing other things. They will be more organized and harder to surprise tomorrow. Also, I am not sure how much waiting up here I could take."

That at least made more sense. "In that case," Jade said, "I'll need a little more rest. Don't flinch like that. The first rule of good soldiering is 'Sleep whenever possible.' You keep watch to make sure he stays near those tents." And she went back into the cave for some more sleep.

Some inner alarm woke her at dusk, just as Fastal was climbing back into the cave to tell her they were serving dinner at the observation tents. "Now's the time to get a little closer," Jade told him. "We'll go as soon as we eat. If we can find our trail down in the dark."

"I have done it at night many times," he assured her.

Jade took off her belt and removed from inside it a

length of strong nylon cord. Fastal watched her curiously. "What's that for?" he asked.

"Strangling the sentries."

His face took on a curious expression. "The ordinary soldiers are not at fault for what was done to my family and my home. These weren't even here then. It is solely Commander Horsson's responsibility, and he alone must pay. I do not want you to kill anyone. Just get me in to face Horsson; I will kill him myself."

Jade looked at him open-mouthed. "You don't want to do anything the easy way, do you? Well, whether you like it or not, we're at war. People die in a war."

"This is an affair of honor between Horsson and myself."

"I'm not just thinking about getting in, but getting out afterward."

"That is not nearly as important."

"Maybe not to you, but it's high on my list."

"You took my money and agreed to do what I said."

"Within reason. But there's no one—*no one*—who can guarantee to get you close to Horsson without killing someone."

Fastal gave the matter long thought. "I can see the problem," he said at last. "But will you at least promise to try, and to kill only as a last resort?"

"I'll try," she said without enthusiasm, adding under her breath, "Amateurs!"

Jade forced Fastal to eat, drink his fill, and visit the rear of the cave. She reminded him of how distracting hunger, thirst, and a full bladder were, but it made little impact on the novice. He did what she told him because she made it inevitable, not because he wanted to. She wondered again at the wisdom of taking his cherry in a crowd of Commancor troops as she collapsed their water cans, dumped extra supplies down the rear shaft, and made a compact bundle of the rest of their belongings. This she placed just inside the cave mouth behind a small rock slide.

Jade followed Fastal down the slope with many reservations in her heart. She was not afraid of heights, but she did respect them. She and Fastal were facing a twofold task; first, to quickly negotiate the steep and narrow path to the valley floor, and second, to be as quiet as possible so they wouldn't alert the guards around the observation tents. Despite the improvements she'd made to the trail, the two parts were not entirely compatible; without clearly seeing where they were stepping, they often kicked loose gravel that fell to the ground below. Jade only hoped that the general noise of the war games covered their own slight sounds.

They made it to the valley floor just as true night fell. The air was, as usual, hot and muggy, and the sky was clear. Two moons shone, giving more light than Jade would have liked. The observation tents had lights of their own, making them easy to spot; Jade and Fastal kept to the shadows and crept closer through the grove of trees. The one thing working in their favor was that the Commancors didn't really expect any trouble. This was, after all, just a routine training exercise on a pacified planet.

They stopped at the edge of the shadows near the tents and watched. For a while, even after dark, there was a great deal of activity as messengers came and went, bearing news of the games or taking orders back to the commanders in the field. Fastal fidgeted, worried that they would never get a clear chance at Horsson. Jade waited patiently, knowing that a moment would come sooner or later and that she would have to be prepared for it when it arrived.

Eventually the activity around the tents slackened. Even Commancors had to sleep sometime. Two sentries remained on duty outside the tents—one a Commancor, the other a tall, bipedal creature from one of the subjugated races Jade wasn't familiar with. They saw Commander Horsson bid good night to his aides and retire to the smallest tent alone, presumably to sleep. The tent was at the far edge of the small clearing, and, in keeping with Commancor notions of privacy, the opening faced the woods more than the camp. As he entered, Horsson carried inside the lantern that had illuminated the outside. The larger generator-powered lights had been put out, leaving the opening just visible in the fading moonlight.

One of the moons was just setting, and the third would not rise for about an hour. They would never find a more ideal moment. Jade told Fastal to wait where he was while she took care of the sentries, and he signaled acknowledgment.

Jade crept through the shadows toward the first sentry, the non-Commancor, wondering whether Fastal would even know if she used her cord or not. Strangulation was the easiest and quietest way to take an opponent out of action—but luck was with her this time, and the cord wasn't even needed.

Reaching a spot along the sentry's route, Jade crouched in ambush. She picked up a rock, hefted it for a moment, and, liking its weight, held on to it. As the guard strolled by her, not expecting any trouble, Jade hit him hard along the side of the head with her rock and the soldier went down. Jade gave him another hit for good measure. The creature was still breathing, but unless he had unexpected stamina he would be unconscious for many hours to come. She took three cable ties from her purse and soon had him tied, his arms and legs around a small tree trunk, and a gag made out of his sleeve held firmly in his mouth.

Jade knelt and unslung the soldier's weapon from his shoulder. It was an energy rifle, a Commancor Ugazy-238. While Jade much preferred the projectile weapons she was most familiar with, she had trained on energy weapons and could use them when she had to. She held it for a while, getting used to its feel and weight in her hands, the shape of its curves, the way it sighted and fit against her shoulder. It was not her gun of choice, but it still made her feel infinitely better about her prospects for the immediate future.

This first sentry had been easy; tackling a Commancor one-on-one was a much riskier proposition. She had a rifle and could shoot him; energy weapons made little noise, so there was only a small chance of alerting the rest of the camp. But there was that damned promise she'd made to Fastal. She had to at least try to deal with him by other means first. The rifle would make a good backup if she needed it.

She discarded the rock; it would only weigh her

down. She needed speed and strength for this job. She couldn't let the Commancor have time to either get his own weapon out or give an alarm about her presence. Slinging her captured weapon over her back, she moved forward, preparing to strike.

Again, luck was with her. The Commancor leaned his rifle against a tree, turned his back to the camp, and reached both hands in front of him. Not expecting any trouble, he was going to take a piss.

Jade leaped out of the bushes, timing her strike so she'd have a clear blow against his throat. She hit him, but not quite as solidly as she'd wanted, because he turned his neck, startled, as she appeared. The blow would hurt him, but it would not prevent him from yelling an alarm. Commancors were sturdily built.

Much to her surprise and relief, he did not call out. Jade realized quickly what must have happened. The sentry was still only thinking of this as a training maneuver, and his job was mostly to keep stray animals out of the compound and make sure the recruits didn't wander in here by mistake. He must have thought one of the recruits had mistaken him for an enemy; he was mad, but not about to set up an alarm. Jade didn't want to let him have a second thought.

Jade landed gracefully, spun around, and delivered another blow to the throat. This one hit properly; she could hear the crack as she broke the Commancor's equivalent of vocal cords. He wouldn't be sending up any alarms now.

The waiting was over, and Jade was in her element. All the extraneous concerns and the tensions they created could be wiped from her thoughts. The battle state was often more relaxing to her than sleep; at least here she knew what she faced and precisely what her capabilities were.

Jade drove forward in a series of lightning movements, pushing her opponent constantly backward. The sentry was wheezing as he tried to regain his breath. Few people could fight a trained Commancor one-on-one and hope to win; even Jade, with all her training, would have had a hard time without her computer-augmented reflexes. She'd gained the initial advantage with her surprise attack; she had to continue pressing to prevent her enemy from recovering his balance and starting a counterattack of his own.

Step, step, slash, step, kick, forward, spin, step, forward, slash, forward, kick, spin. Jade's body became a relentless fighting machine, moving almost faster than the human eye could follow as she analyzed the Commancor's moves as well as her own to find the weak spot, the open place where her attack would be most successful at this moment—then constantly updating the analysis as the Commancor moved and she moved to press him backward.

If her opponent had been any less a fighter than a Commancor, the fight would have been over in a couple of seconds. But Commancors had reflexes on a par with her own computerized ones, and the fight was much more even than it should have been. As the sentry recovered from his surprise and his breathing difficulty he began fighting back. His rifle was leaning against the tree where he'd placed it, so he had to fight with his hands. The strong, sharp claws of a Commancor were weapon enough at such close quarters.

At first he settled for blocking the blows that Jade delivered with such devastating rapidity, and then tried to get in a few of his own. One swipe landed inside Jade's defenses before she could fully block it, and the sharp edges of two claws raked across her scalp. In making that extension, though, he opened his defenses, and Jade was quick to take advantage. Her left foot came up under the Commancor's outstretched arm, hitting him squarely in the body. He fell backward, off-balance, and Jade moved in even closer, arms swinging in a blur of motion.

One more hit, and her opponent was on his back. Jade showed him no mercy. She kicked again at his head, and heard a satisfying crack. The Commancor's body went limp, but Jade, adrenaline racing, had trouble slowing herself; she delivered two more kicks to the still body before she finally relaxed and took a breath.

She crouched and listened for a minute, waiting to see whether the struggle had been noticed elsewhere in the camp, but all was quiet. When she was sure she was still undetected, she gave the prearranged signal for Fastal to join her, then quickly tied up the Commancor and pulled him under a large, thorny berry bramble. He'd be less than comfortable there, and suffer from the scratches for days.

Fastal slipped out of the bushes beside her so quietly she barely heard him. *Maybe he's got more potential than I thought*, she reflected, but events were started and there was no time to consider the matter in depth. All they could do now was move and let the consequences take care of themselves.

Jade unslung her rifle and crept silently through the shadows toward Horsson's tent, with Fastal matching her stride for stride. They stopped at the edge of the tent, and Jade peered inside through a crack at the flap. Horsson was alone, lying on a cot and studying his portable computer terminal.

Jade paused for a few moments, trying to think how best to handle this. She could have picked Horsson off with a single shot, but that wasn't the way Fastal wanted to do it. After some fast deliberation she turned her rifle around butt end first and, taking a deep breath, rushed into the tent.

Horsson was as startled by her appearance as the sentry had been, but, reclining as he was, he was in even less of a position to combat her. Jade swung the butt of her rifle hard against his head, and he fell off his cot, senseless. He was still breathing, but he'd be an easy victim for her client's vengeance.

Fastal was behind her in the tent as she turned around. "He's all yours," Jade told him. "I've got one more job to do." She was out of the tent before the Lemmant could respond.

The murder of Commander Horsson would not go undiscovered for more than a couple of hours. If Jade and Fastal were to escape from Haldek alive, she would have to do something to keep their crime from becoming public knowledge too quickly.

The Commancor field generator was about fifty meters away, not even in a tent of its own. It was a big piece of equipment, about the size of a double-row, eight-seater outhouse, and Jade knew it would control all the power for the camp's lights, stoves . . . and long-range communications. Jade had seen its like many times before, and had disabled her share of them. It was nice to know the design hadn't changed dramatically in fifteen years.

There were two non-Commancor soldiers guarding the generator, not expecting the least bit of trouble. Jade's coming out of the darkness like a whirlwind was more than they could handle. Within five seconds both of them were unconscious on the ground and Jade was eyeing the generator with a grin on her face. Being suddenly in this situation made her feel like a girl again, doing a job in a way that made her father proud, and she had to consciously squelch the warm feelings that tried to arise. That was not a pleasant time, and it certainly wasn't worth getting nostalgic over.

She studied the generator briefly to make sure it was as she remembered, and looked around once more to fix the camp's layout in her mind. Then she backed away to the side of the commander's tent and stood beside the opening. Whispering the code word she and Fastal had established, she took careful aim with her energy rifle and pressed the trigger.

Sparks flew into the darkness, and there was a short crackling sound quickly followed by a loud explosion. Jade had turned her head away, and even so was nearly blinded by the sudden light of the fireball that erupted from the generator frame. The lights around the rest of the camp quit abruptly, to be replaced by moonlit darkness, and the air was filled with curses and confusion as the troops tried to figure out what had gone wrong.

Jade stepped through the tent flap, to find Fastal still standing inside. ''Ready to go?'' she asked him.

''I cannot do it,'' he whispered. ''Not this way.''

''What's wrong?'' she asked, exasperated.

''I wanted to confront him, to explain what he had done and why he had to die. For me to stab him while he is unconscious is dishonorable.''

''He probably knows more reasons than you do.

We've got to hurry. People will be here in a few seconds to report about the generator.''

"I cannot—"

"He deserves no mercy," Jade said. The wounds on her scalp suddenly started to hurt, and she tried to ignore them. "He invaded your world. He killed your father. He tortured your sister. He raped your mother. He brought war and destruction. He made the hills echo with death and the rivers flow with blood. He listened to your sister's screams and smiled as his soldiers disemboweled her, yanking out her entrails and chewing on them while she pleaded with him to stop, crying for mercy he refused to give. Then he cut out her eyes and her tongue, and he—''

She didn't need to go any further in her litany. Fastal had fallen on the body of his enemy and stabbed it two, three, four times, uttering harsh sounds and grunts as he did so. Finally he stopped, straightened, and stood up. "It is done," he whispered. "My family's honor is avenged.''

"Good. Let's get the fuck out of here.''

Fastal was moving slowly, like a man in a daze. Jade reached out and grabbed his hand, yanking him out of the tent with her. Already there were sounds of people approaching the tent from several directions, some of them with flashlights. She ran toward the nearest brush, pulling Fastal with her, and barely made it before the first of Horsson's aides reached the tent.

As the threat of discovery increased, Fastal finally came awake and realized the peril of their position. Taking the lead in the darkness, he guided Jade along the base of the cliffs until they found their precipitous trail once more.

"I hope you're as good going up in the dark as you were coming down," Jade said.

She hugged the rock wall as though it were an old lover as she climbed rapidly up the face. The dusty rock scraped at her clothes and dirt fell in her hair, but all she could think of was how exposed she was right now. All the Commancors below had to do was shine a flashlight up the cliffs to spot her, and then it would be an easy job for even a mediocre marksman to pick her off. A rifleman with an infrared scope wouldn't even need the light. At any moment she expected to feel the white-hot lancing of the energy beam from a Ugazy-238, and then maybe the air whistling by her as she plummeted from the cliff to her death. She was braced for the inevitable, but still she kept climbing.

They reached the level of the cave, and Fastal stopped. "We can hide in here until—"

"No," she said. "We leave now or we never will. Now get your fucking ass in gear." She pushed him on ahead of her—but gently, so he wouldn't fall. Not only would that alert the Commancors to their location, but it would leave her alone in unfamiliar territory. She picked up the pack she'd made earlier and pushed them both up the hill.

Down below she could tell from the sounds that the troops had learned their commander was dead, and chaos was reigning while the aides tried to sort out their position. Coming as unexpectedly as it did, they didn't know whether the murder had been done by one of their own force—an officer seeking to remove an obstacle to promotion, perhaps—or by an outsider, and so they could not concentrate their search in any one direction. That, more than anything, probably saved Jade and Fastal while they were climbing the face of the cliffs. It was many minutes before a strengthened perimeter guard was even established.

After what seemed subjectively like hours, Jade and Fastal reached the top of the cliff. Jade realized she was sweating, and not just from the clamminess of the air. But they weren't out of danger yet; there were still plenty of kilometers between here and the transfer station in Detalla.

They trotted through the dark forest, lifting their legs high to avoid tripping on the persistent vines. Very little of the sparse moonlight made its way through the branches, and the little that did made odd patterns of light and shadow on the forest floor. Jade had to trust to Fastal's sense of direction to get them back to their home base; left on her own she could have wandered for a long time before gaining her bearings, probably not until daylight—which might be too long.

The light gravity gave her a loping stride as she ran, helping her cover the ground quickly—until one spot where she came down did not support her weight, and she sank chest-deep into a pit that seemed to close in around her. The pit seemed alive, shifting and wriggling all over her body with a million tiny legs.

"Fastal, help!" she called—but not too loudly, lest any searching Commancors hear her.

The Lemmant turned and made his way back slowly to her, trying to make out in the darkness what had happened.

Things were crawling over her body and tiny feet, up her shoulders, onto the bare skin of her neck and face. "Help me, damn it. What the hell is this?"

"An insect pit. I warned you there were these, and snake pits."

"Well, get me the fuck out of here before they eat me alive!"

Fastal held out his hand, and Jade extended the barrel of her rifle while holding firm to the stock. The Lemmant pulled and Jade braced her feet against the side wall of the pit, and using their combined strengths they managed to pull her out of the hole. She was still covered head to toe with insects, some of which had already managed to get down inside her clothes. They didn't sting or bite, but Jade didn't care. She shook herself like a dog, then did a wild sort of dance to fling them off. That took care of most of them, and swatting at her face and hair brushed off most of the rest. The few that were still in her clothes she decided to ignore. It was more important to get away from here fast. "Let's go," she told Fastal, adding under her breath, "Bugs! Why couldn't it have been snakes?"

They made it through the woods without further mishap. Another moon was rising as they started across the meadow to their truck. Jade kept looking around as they ran, but there was no sign of pursuit. She knew from past experience that Commancors, though fierce fighters and excellent military organizers, tended to fall apart when faced with the unexpected. It might take them hours to reorganize themselves into an efficient group once more and start seeking the perpetrators of the crime. Jade hoped to be very far away by then.

They piled into the vehicle and sped off on the road to Detalla. Fastal drove while Jade rode shotgun, constantly scanning the ground around them and the air above for signs of pursuit that never materialized. Fastal never cast so much as a single glance backward at the skeletal remains of his family home. Jade wondered what the Lemmantine equivalent was for a pillar of salt.

If the Commancors suspected offworlders, they would immediately stake out the transfer station in Detalla. But it was obvious the crime could only have been committed by someone familiar with the region—or perhaps by a Commancor seeking the express route to promotion—and with the occupation so recent the new rulers would have plenty of local suspects. Still, Detalla was a logical place for fugitives to go, and word would be sent there as quickly as possible; Jade hoped it would take them a while longer to fix their generator and restore communications to the outside world.

She started to relax. At this point, any danger was more likely to be waiting for them in Detalla than coming at them along the road. She rested the rifle lightly in her lap and let her cramped muscles ease, then realized the gun was now more of a danger than an aid.

The news shouldn't hit town before we do, but the next two or more hours will be a bitch. If they can eliminate the locals and the camp personnel as suspects fast, we might not make it. She was trying to figure how long it would take to unload the furniture at the transfer station, return the vehicle and rented tools, get back to the station, and hope the Greest got them out of there before the Commancors started checking alibis at the gate. It was too long an interval for her to feel comfortable about it.

As they bounced down the road, Jade got an inspiration. "Is there someone real close to here you hate bad enough to sic the Commancors on?"

Fastal turned to her with the fire that had been missing from him since the kill. "The Lughflins, the traitors who sold out my family for the use of some land."

"Do they have any small kids at the place?"

"No one would marry the old man except Nenjila du Ballak, the barren spinster who died two years ago. No one would marry the son at all."

Jade grinned. "Where do they live?"

There was a small back road that led to the hills behind Fornen-Dakk where the Lughflins' land abutted Fastal's estate. Behind the neighbor's gatepost, wrapped in an old Fornen Dakk oil cloth tablecloth as though to preserve them, Jade planted the energy rifle, the extra knives they'd bought on Haldek, the jack—minus its identifying rental plate—and the ropes full of the cliff's dust.

"No one would believe the Lughflins capable of such a noble or valorous act," Fastal commented.

"Maybe not, but this should at least force them into some uneasy conversations with the local authorities—if the Lughflins live long enough to even talk."

The rest of the trip went smoothly. When Jade and Fastal dropped off the furniture, there was talk of a transfer delay; the Greest was playing games with scheduling again. But by the time they returned the vehicle and all the tools but the jack—which they reported as borrowed by the Lughflins for later return, a common Haldek custom—the delay seemed to have been straightened out. They were allowed right in and transferred immediately, and Jade, grateful for the luck, even thanked the Greest. She turned to say goodbye before heading home, but as she looked back at Fastal something itched at her mind.

He appeared normal, if perhaps a bit bleary-eyed. Jade had learned enough about his facial expressions to realize he was drifting emotionally; his big dream had been accomplished, and now he wasn't sure what to do next. As she stared at him, though, she couldn't shake the feeling that something was wrong.

"Fastal," she said suddenly, "where's your dagger?"

"I left it back in Horsson's body."

The world fell on Jade. "Shit! Why'd you do that?"

"I had to make a statement. Horsson died without knowing the true reason. I had to let everyone know that Fornen has been avenged."

"Motherfuck on toast! That knife can be traced. You might as well have taken out an ad. I had it all worked out. They could never have pinned it on us. Now you screwed that up!"

"I did the honorable thing."

All feeling of triumph left Jade's body. *God preserve us from the "honorable thing,"* she thought. *This imbecile is going to kill us both yet.*

Ignoring the message from the Greest coming over the small speaker in the entryway, something about how much he liked the cutwork edging, she turned her back on her client and started off for home.

Chapter 10

Megan Cafferty

"Val, I'm home! Start the tub and hold the messages," Jade yelled to the security mike on the gatepost, then walked up the last few steps to her door and touched her hand computer to the lock. As soon as she got through the steel door she dumped the duffel bag on the floor and headed back to the hydrotub she could hear filling in the bathroom. Each step felt like another climb up the exposed Haldek cliff. The strange floating feeling, mixed with exhilaration and the edges of tiredness, that was so common at the end of a battle won would desert her shortly, and there would only be enough energy left to lie down before sleep overwhelmed her. Knowing this, she skipped the impulse to stop by Rix's, to go work out, to do anything but take a long hot bath, listen to her mail, and be ready for sleep when the crash came.

"Jade, shall I retrieve the merc suit for cleaning, or leave it on the floor?" Val asked as Jade dropped the article in question and threw her underwear into the laundry.

"Leave it for now—there's live ammo in the pockets. I'll clean it out later. Shower, hot, and extra towels. I've air-dried enough for a while."

Val started the shower flowing at the pressure and temperature Jade preferred when requesting hot, and slid open the panel that held the oversized terry towels. Jade grabbed the fresh-smelling bundles, warmed by the fan exhaust ducts that ran through the cupboard from Val's mainframe in the basement, and hurried into the bathroom.

The shower first ran rust swirling down the drain as the water forced pounds of Haldek's soil from Jade's hair and body. Jade stood under the stream until the water had mostly cleared, then began the first shampoo. As the foam loosened dirt, oil, blood, and knots, the bruises and scalp cuts began to throb. The water turned from pale rust to pink as the dirt sluiced off and the blood flowed again from the small cuts she'd gotten from the Commancor sentry. Jade ignored these as she hurriedly scrubbed the rest of the dirt from her body.

"Shower off, Val."

Jade grabbed the first of the towels in the steamy room and started to lean over to dry her hair. The motion reminded her of the cuts, and she wrapped her body in the towel, grabbed the medical kit from under the sink, then straightened up and walked around the central sink and mirror island to reach the tub, now full and ready for her.

Jade dropped the towel from her body as she climbed the stairs, for once not minding the mess she was leaving. She eased into the tub, taking a moment to rearrange the footrests and lumbar supports to bear on the places that hurt the least. After she was comfortable and the air jets were activated, she cleaned up and bandaged the cuts.

Both cuts were less than an inch long; very little hair had to be trimmed to bandage them properly. The plastic fake skin she painted over them worked well and contained an antibiotic to keep out infection. Moving the part in her hair over an inch would conceal them from everyone except Jade—but every time she moved her head she'd feel them.

"I can't believe my fucking luck."

"What do you mean?" Val asked.

"Huh? Was I talking out loud again?"

"Yes, Jade. And that will get you killed someday."

"That will get me killed someday."

They said the last two sentences in unison. Jade threw back her head and roared with laughter, punctuated by "ouches" as the motion pulled on her hair and stretched her bruised ribs. No one on Cablans would have recognized this uncontrolled sound as hers. She seldom allowed such abandon.

"It will, honest to Greest. Anyway I was talking about the mission. This little sucker, I won't plague you with all the details, but this little sucker had the goddamnedest luck. We got in, got his stupid furniture *out*, got *us* out, all unharmed—well mostly," she said, easing her bruised back to be caressed by a different set of bubbles. "And he killed his target and I got a couple of subordinates that were in the way. It didn't go like clockwork, whatever that's supposed to be like, but when I think what could have been . . ."

"You were very lucky, Jade."

"Yeah." Jade settled into the tub, got the last bit of unbruised flesh settled on the seat, and then that eternal goad, duty, finally hit home. "Okay, Val, give me the messages. After a cup of—"

Jade cut off as a small mobile unit came up to the tub and elevated its tray, presenting her with a cup of her favorite herb tea. As the fragrance of the chamomile and hibiscus cleared the last of the dust from her nostrils, she said, "I'm suitably braced. Summarize and send 'em to me."

"Lorpet, the usual courtesy calls; no offer of new information, but asking for an assignment. Rix called; Cyclad Arik is fine. Cyclad herself phoned to say she was back at work; left her home number for you to call when you returned. Galentor called with an exhibition offer for twenty days from now—a Purrchrp fight to first real blood. There were also two messages from Megan Cafferty."

Jade quickly tapped the thermostat to raise the tub temperature, knowing that wouldn't help the kind of chill she felt now. "Play the Caffertys."

A very pleasant face appeared in the small screen near the ceiling on the wall facing Jade. The woman smiled, which crinkled her eyes and made it obvious most of those very faint wrinkles were from smiling. A full, young-sounding voice came forth. "Ms. Darcy, I was just informed you are on assignment. When you return, please contact me. I wish to hire your services.

I can be reached at the Palazzo Hotel, Regency Suite. Thank you.''

Val cut in, ''That one was left three days ago. This one is today's.''

''Ms. Darcy, please call as soon as you are free. I have been in negotiation with the Palovoi consortium here, and the talks have broken down completely. I don't know what happened. They've been very polite up till this time, but—''

Jade missed the rest of the message as she laughed, all three times Val played it. Exhaustion was allowing an edge of hysteria to creep into her mind. After leaving instructions, Jade went to bed for fifteen hours of solid, dreamless sleep.

Jade checked in with Rix as she was finishing breakfast and found that Hiss!arr's relatives were willing to cover her shift for another day or two. She left a greeting with Cyclad Arik's computer, then double-checked the schedule Val had arranged for her. Jade had forgotten to tell the computer she wasn't going in to Rix's until after the meeting with Cafferty, so in setting up the appointment Val had offered Cafferty the standard times for Jade's meetings: either at 1400, Jade's usual time for lunch, or 1800 hours, usually off-shift

''Val, contact the Palazzo, don't put me on line, and make the appointment for fourteen hundred at Rix's. Then call Rix and tell him I want table Green 11 for two Terrans at that hour in quadrant two, the other Terran to be facing east, and with a sonic but not optic privacy barrier—and I don't care what that does to his climate control.'' Jade rose from the table and started toward the exercise room, then turned and salvaged the remains of her breakfast from the cleaning arm Val had put out.

''No sense throwing it down the drain. That little scavenger will probably be around,'' Jade said as she walked to the door. When a check of the security cams showed the yard clear of any real danger, she opened the door, stepped onto the small rock patio in front of her home, and started to set the bowl down on the right-hand side. As she did, a click of nails on stone and a little snuffling noise alerted her to a sneak attack on her ankle.

The frizzlic had come from the opposite side and was between her feet. She froze, bent at nearly a ninety-degree angle, and began to giggle as the rough little tongue cleaned her ankle of an unnoticed milk spill.

The sound startled the little roly-poly critter, who backed up and chittered at Jade. Jade leaned down farther and looked back between her legs at the scolding animal.

"You little asshole, I won't hurt you. You just tickled me." She placed the bowl on the deck and got a face full of frizzlic as it ran forward for the treat. It made little contented noises as it ate the fortified cereal and milk Jade had brought it.

"Enough wasted time." Jade reentered the house and saw the kitchen screen still showed the porch. "Val, has more data come in on Cafferty? Where is it? Give me hard copy."

Val began printing the data for Jade, who ignored it until the frizzlic finished its treat, had climbed into the bowl to get the last bits, and had toppled it over on top of itself. It froze for an instant, then scurried away, carrying the bowl with it to the edge of the porch, where the dish finally fell off into the grass.

Jade got up and went out to retrieve the bowl. From the bushes she could hear the frizzlic scolding her, or the bowl, for such treachery. Smiling, Jade went back in and began reviewing the material on the woman she would meet in a few hours—the first human in five years to share a room with Jade Darcy.

Knives, slapshot, electric prod, alarm button for Val—Jade's checklist failed to bring the confidence it usually invoked. It was weird enough entering Rix's through the front door. Knowing that there would be another human in there, waiting for her, made it as alien as her first visit four and a half years ago.

The door opened as a group of reddish hounds exited Rix's Place, chattering away about their meal and their plans for some kind of dancing that evening. Bab-ankh, seeing Jade, held the door open. There being no logical reason to remain outside—fear not being a part of logic to Jade—she went on in.

Bab-ankh seemed to delight in showing off his rituals for his coworker, carefully signing off the table, gathering the rope that symbolized the start of the room, waving her forward, then bouncing in front of her to the table Jade had reserved.

As Jade had requested, Megan Cafferty's back was to the door. She seemed to be studying the menu readout as Jade approached. Hiss!arr, his brother, and Cyclad Arik were all close to the edge of quadrant two, and the praying mantis responded to Jade's stare with the scissorlike movement that signaled "All's well." Jade wasn't sure if she meant her health, the safety of the human, Cafferty, or both, but the gesture and obvious concern behind it warmed her.

Stop it. There's no reason to let down your guard. She could have you dead before Cyclad could move. You're not that kind of fucking fool.

Each step seemed tiny yet carried her too rapidly, as though she were walking along a conveyor belt speeding toward Cafferty's table. This shelter, made alien by another human's presence, swelled to battlefield proportions while the distance to her possible foe shrank. Little Bab-ankh, the animated powderpuff, seemed a sort of will-o'-the-wisp enticing her to danger. Her sweaty feet and palms were messages of a deep fear only she could detect and fervently denied, while her body thus betrayed her. Five years was too damn long. It wasn't half as long as she had hoped for. With the strong stride and calm manner she was famed for, she walked the forty meters to her appointment.

Jade followed Bab-ankh around the table and faced the woman who had shattered her fragile peace in this place.

The woman looked up at her approach. "Ms. Darcy? I'm Megan Cafferty."

Jade took the outstretched hand and shook it, surprised at the strength in it, but not the softness of the skin.

"I'm so glad to meet you," Cafferty continued. "I haven't seen another human in weeks, and while many of Cablans's residents are nice enough, they are still truly alien, and thus I've been alone in these crowds as I never am at home. And that's why I'm chattering so much, I suppose. Please, what will you have?"

Jade was glad for the torrent of words, and the excuse to read her menu. The u-trans was silent. This was her own English, or close enough to shut out translation. The silence of the device made Jade feel abandoned. The rest of the noise from Rix's Place was suddenly lost in the hiss and hum of the air wall that Rix activated. The privacy curtain obviously surprised Megan Cafferty. Grateful for the neutral topic, Jade explained.

"I wasn't sure how much of our discussion you wanted for sale tomorrow, so I asked for a privacy screen. No one on Cablans successfully reads human lips, so we can be private if that's what you prefer."

Cafferty's blue eyes seemed to fly through calculations as swiftly as Val, and settled on approval. "I appreciate the courtesy. I was hoping our business wouldn't have to wait for a more secluded place. Why don't we order, then get right to it?"

She must not fear committing a public murder. With her connections and my legal problems, I suppose she's right. Or she is who she says. But that's a chance I probably shouldn't take.

Jade signaled her assent by studying the menu. She quickly punched in her order, but Cafferty stopped her as she began to enter her credit code.

"This meal, whatever the outcome of our business discussion, is my treat. Please," she continued as she detected Jade's reluctance to be beholden to her: "It is so pleasant to have a woman, a human woman, to talk to instead of some report to read with dinner. It goes on my expense account, if you'd prefer."

"Fine with me. Whatever you like."

While Cafferty ordered, Jade took time to study her. The photographs hadn't captured the life in Megan Cafferty's face, or the force of her personality. *With your back turned, you'd know she entered a room. Confi-*

dent, but not overly vain. At least she isn't wearing some ridiculous evening dress. That business suit is real, not cyclable, and practical. She is willing to be businesslike without a lot of phony giggliness, and if she really only blathers like that occasionally, and if she is what she and the background check say she is, I might be able to deal with her. I might not have to kill her after all.

Jade carefully checked her weapons as if searching for the notepad she drew out of one pocket, and with mildly exaggerated care checked the software and set the little pad onto record.

"Do you have so many enemies, Ms. Darcy?"

Jade stiffened and placed her left hand on the small gun in her pocket. "I beg your pardon?" *I beg you to back off, 'cause killing you in Rix's might cost me my job, or at least my New Year bonus. And you don't want that.* Jade was only half aware of the sweat that had sprung up under her bangs.

"I'm not a child, or naive, and I realize at least some of those pockets you checked—for that pad?— are holding weapons. I wondered if I might be in danger from whatever you fear."

She hides her concerns well. This one may not be as stupid as she sounded on the phone. "I feared you, frankly. And I'm still not sure how much of a threat you are." *What the hell did I say that for? It's in the fire now.* Jade assumed a slightly more guarded pose, and tried to detect where her backups were.

Megan cocked her head to one side, then began to chuckle just hard enough to scramble her words. She gave up for a moment, holding up her hand palm forward to plead for time. Then she took a very deep breath and half-sang. "Don't shoot—I just want to show you this."

With two fingers, delicately on the barrel, and exaggerated care she withdrew the prettiest, deadliest, smallest dart gun Jade had seen since commando training—a weapon that, five years ago, in a less elegant state, was still a classified weapon.

"Do you know what this is, Ms. Darcy?"

With the same care, and nearly as wide a smile, Jade drew hers. "It's an upgraded one of these."

"I make them. That is, my company does. I won't ask you where you got yours."

Good, 'cause I wouldn't tell you.

"For one thing, you wouldn't tell me, and it doesn't matter on Cablans anyway. I wasn't too confident about your . . . benevolence either, Ms. Darcy. I find it reassuring that you are such a cautious woman. This might work out after all."

"It just might at that." Jade was surprised to find she meant it. The woman hadn't yelled "security leak," seemed genuine in her attitude, and was almost certainly the businesswoman, with a business problem, that she seemed. For the first time since Lorpet's call a week ago, Jade felt she might survive and even profit from this surprise visitor.

The food arrived, and conversation was limited to comments on it as they both devoted themselves to an appreciation of the chef's masterworks. It was a companionable silence.

When the meal, with attendant small talk, had been reduced to final cups of coffee, they both fell silent for several long seconds. Jade felt no inclination to volunteer anything. She was hoping the woman would get down to business.

"Ms. Darcy, over a year ago my research chemists discovered a drug in the leaves—the fallen leaves, in fact—of a common tree native to Palovok. Not only will this drug replace the current treatment for Parkinsonism, but unlike the implant surgery there are few side effects, and small doses appear to function as a type of prophylactic. It can be important. We want the rights to harvest the fallen leaves each autumn, and are willing to pay handsomely for the privilege. As you probably know, there has been almost no human-Palovoi contact, and that little has gone badly. I got permission to come here and negotiate only by diverting the special shipment of dirda melons from my space stations to Cablans this last quarter."

That explains the timing of that shipment, the high

price, and the eagerness of all the Palovoi this last run. This lady plans ahead—just not far enough.

". . . So then I attempted to negotiate this myself, and hit a dead end a few days ago. Lorpet, Galantor, Nywoliv, all agreed you were the only human ever to get along with them, and I should consult you. My so-called xenosociologists are baffled by the tapes I returned. I have only a few days to get this settled or I risk losing this season's harvest. Aside from the profits lost, there are too many people who could use this drug to risk that. Do you have any ideas on where I could start?"

Typical. Let those people with the initials after their names fuck it all up, then call in the Marines to set it right.

"Have you ever dealt with old-type Red Russkies?"

"Some, mostly those on the asteroid belts."

"Have you ever dealt with thirteen-year-old boys trying to gross out and drive off a girl they have a crush on?"

Megan smiled broadly. "I had two sons, and raised a few other boys along the way."

Jade nodded. "Then add a system where to mention parents is equal to throwing up at a formal dinner, on the Queen, in front of the Archbishop, but sex is as required a topic as the weather, and where anything other than the rankest insult is considered so ill-omened that you're only polite to your rankest enemy, because the gods are polite and responsible for all that is bad in the universe. Throw in a few other kinks, and you've got the Palovoi, who've been so polite to you—and you to them."

"Fuck!" said Megan Cafferty, her face suddenly pale.

"My thoughts exactly," said Jade, leaning back to see how this woman's mind would work this out.

After a minute, minute and a half, Cafferty ordered fresh coffee, then asked, "Who do I challenge, and who picks the weapons?"

"You couldn't challenge anyone. I could. I've got the weapons, and even so I only give it a fifty-fifty chance of working."

"What kind of odds if I try it on my own?"

"What was the very last thing the Palovoi said to you?"

"Have a nice day."

"Not a snowball's chance in hell."

"When do we start, and what do I owe you?"

This just might work out after all. "Tonight, and a deposit of"—*Hell, I'll go for it*—"five thousand eus against a thousand a day plus any expenses."

Cafferty pulled out her credit disk. "How long should this take?"

"With luck, less than a week."

"Ms. Darcy, if you can make it happen in three days, I'll throw in another twenty-five hundred bonus. For now, five thousand it is."

Cafferty slipped her card into the credit terminal on the table, paid for the meal, then credited Jade with the agreed amount. As Jade returned her own credited disk to her pocket, it seemed heavier. *If you keep paying like this, you can keep threatening me with your little dart gun. At least I'll die solvent.*

"I'll call you this evening to discuss this further, Ms. Cafferty, after I set up an appointment with the Palovoi team. Keep tomorrow clear, and wear something green."

"Green?"

"It's the color of birth, and very insulting."

"Green it is, and thank you."

"Don't thank me, just pay me."

Jade canceled the air curtain and walked away. Megan Cafferty stayed, ordered dessert, and tried to learn a little more about her new partner.

The next afternoon they met in the lobby of the Palazzo for one last quick briefing before the meeting, Jade in her scruffiest jungle daylight merc suit, Megan Cafferty in a dazzling emerald green satin dinner suit, with deep-green, nearly black blouse, hose, and shoes. The blouse had a Battenberg lace fichu that was cream with metallic gold threads forming the design. The oddly shaped, nearly round gold bag had what ap-

peared to be deep-green tourmalines on the clasp and
on a shamrock in the center.

"It's green all right, Cafferty. You can't get more
green than that."

"My husband was grand marshal of the St. Patrick's
Day parade just before he died. I wear it each year
since. It's the tackiest, dearest thing I own. He had the
bag made for me, too. I'm not sure you'll recognize
it, but it's the shape of Ireland, in gold, with a shamrock of antique emeralds. He did spoil me."

"I wouldn't mind that kind of spoiling myself, but
I'd take it in guns."

"He gave me those, too."

"Do you remember what we did, and redid, last
night? This is no time to get sentimental."

"You weak-armed, cheap-hearted employee scum.
You aren't worthy to lick the floor at the sound of his
name, much less give me any trouble for it."

"Perfect, Cafferty. Now can you keep that up for
three or more hours?"

"As I told you, I should have no problems. I once
forgot the lyrics to a Gilbert and Sullivan patter song
halfway through. I not only made up enough verses to
fill the score, they scanned, were right for the char-
acter, and were at full tempo."

Jade gave a deep sigh as Megan went on, "Those
are done so fast that . . . well, you've seen one of the
operettas, haven't you?"

"Cafferty, I told you last night I haven't had much
time to spend on the theater."

"I'm sorry, Ms. Darcy. It is an old habit for me to
think in terms of musical scores. I'll be fine, but I
might use some of the stuff in there. There's a lot of
songs about sex and mothers."

"The first is fine, but only do the mother stuff when
you're ready for a fight. Then run. They outnumber
us. Get it?"

"Got it."

"Then let's go. Follow me in after no less than five
or more than ten minutes; the room should be loud
enough by then." They walked across the lobby to the

meeting room they had reserved for their most important, and possibly last, meeting with the Palovoi.

It had taken every milligram of Jade's influence with Migul to make him intercede with the trade delegation and get them to agree to this session. Jade had spent the night going over strategies with Megan Cafferty, trying to explain how the meeting should go. But like the specimens in a dissection lab, the Palovoi would not have read the manual. Jade settled on an all-out assault from the beginning.

Jade gently opened the door, slipped in, and closed it behind her, then looked around. These were not the Palovoi who regularly visited Rix's, but that didn't bother her. With Palovoi, she preferred dealing with strangers; it was easier to be nasty.

She smiled sweetly, made a half-curtsy that caused the weapons to bulge in the pockets of her jumpsuit, and asked in a demure tone, "I apologize for the interruption. I do hope you'll forgive me, but you are here for the Cafferty meeting, right?"

The half-dozen Palovoi sat stunned. One of them shook her head in the way that meant assent.

"Then why in the names of all your ignorant, ugly, weak, overrated siblings, who look like perfection next to you, did you create such a goddam mess? None of you look bright enough to have done this deliberately; it had to have been planned by your mother."

A gasp was heard from several throats, and two of the younger members started to rise and reach for weapons. *That's far enough—now we can talk about it.* Jade let herself relax a bit and began to enjoy herself.

"I tried to let you handle this simple matter on your own. My cheapskate boss wants some worthless damn leaves, and you've got them. I figure you could send someone with half a yolk sac still hanging and get this done in one, two hours tops. But you backward, weak-legged, spindly-armed dependents, you tie up my boss for days, and don't even settle anything, and now I've got to come in and clean up the mess. I hate this shit, and only rude, blind imbeciles like you would get me stuck in it."

"Look, you two-limbed dandy," said the delegation's leader. "That rude white-topped human isn't worth a yolkless orphan to us. We know she's lying; no one wants glies leaves, they're poisonous and messy. She won't tell us what she really wants, and she's polite about it! You lowlife scum can deal with that sort of pirate{?} if you want, but don't expect us to. We won't waste the time."

It had been a long time since Jade had heard the beep that designated an approximate translation. The Palovoi were angry enough to use very obscure curse words. Despite their protests about wasting time, however, they were all still seated. Her reputation had bought her a listen.

"Poison, my ass. You'd all better head back to school. I like dirda melons." Jade ignored the stamping and low moans of applause this sentiment brought forth. "They taste okay. But that's it. Remember, not all biochemistries are alike. I think you all hypnotize yourselves or something; they don't get me drunk."

"They don't get us . . . drunk . . . exactly, either."

"Well, those leaves, glies leaves, after they've changed color, don't get us drunk, either. But the stuff that poisons you is treatment for a disease we get, a fatal one. We have other ways to treat it, but this looks better and maybe cheaper. That idiot of a boss of mine is too close-mouthed and paranoid to tell you, and will be real unhappy you know, but when I hear how greedy you've been—"

"Greedy! You human excuse for a nibbot worm. We hadn't bothered—"

"I'll see your four-limbed carcass cut to nine slimy little—"

Megan Cafferty walked in as the free-for-all hit a good twenty-decibel roar. "Darcy, you overpriced incompetent, why did you start without me?"

"Cafferty, you lazy excuse for a robber baron. These puling infants thought you wanted some nice dirt, or air, not those leaves, because the glies leaves are poisonous, and you're such a bungling nincompoop you never told them why you wanted them. You take my time, pay me less than I'm worth, make me associate with alley dregs like these, who probably don't have even one good trampoline to their name—and all because you couldn't bother to tell them what you wanted to buy and why? Enough of this and I won't work for an obstructionist exploiter of the working classes like you, no matter how much you bribe the Greest to make me.''

While Jade and Megan fought it out, the Palovoi cheered them on. As the insults, accusations, and counterclaims grew, so did the cheers. After ten minutes of bellowing, Jade turned to the Palovoi, pounded her fist into the table hard enough to crack the wood, and yelled, ''Enough! Do you want all the money for the leaves or do you want to go home failures? I haven't got all day.''

In less than one hour of some of the hardest haggling Megan had seen this side of a Baghdad bazaar, the terms were set. CafTech would provide the machinery but train Palovoi to run it, and within three seasons would have turned 90 percent of the harvesting over to them. The price was to remain stable for ten seasons, and included fertilizer imports to compensate for the loss of the leaves to their compost. Any leaves taken from wild sources had to be rotated by area to protect each area's nitrogen balance, and some supplements had to be brought in. The Palovoi would also receive a small royalty on the finished drugs from the leaves that was to go to the education fund for unclaimed infants.

The agreement was drawn up, signed, and electronically mailed to the Greest, who registered it and pronounced that he was ready to make any shipments pursuant to it at once, and bill CafTech.

Jade and Megan had turned to leave, goodbyes not being a Palovoi tradition, when one of the aliens yelled, ''It was great doing business with you.''

Jade turned and realized it was one of the hotheads that had jumped up when she made the insult about their mothers. For a moment she was at a loss—then Megan, in that glaring green satin suit, stepped in front of Jade, bowed low, and said, ''My father thanks you, my mother thanks you, my sister thanks you.'' Megan stepped back with each "thank you," till the last pushed Jade out the door. "And I thank you."

Megan slammed the door, grabbed Jade, and headed back down the hall. They were at least thirty meters away when the Palovoi boiled out of the room. They chose to pretend they couldn't hear the insults from behind them, and kept shouting at each other as Jade chased Megan toward the waiting elevator.

CHAPTER 11

Spirits in the Night

The two women stormed down the hall gesticulating and emoting. "Cafferty, did you want to start a race war, or are you on one of your damn musical things again?"

"I needed to do something when he insulted us, after giving me a runaround for weeks. Besides, George Cohan wrote a lot of good music for wars. This would be the first one he started, though. And damn it, he's Irish—or was Irish—and you said to wear green."

"I didn't say to pick a fight for real. I hope the older ones keep the hotheads from trying to fucking kill us. Of all the goddamn silly stunts to pull. . . ." The elevator door finally cut off the noise, and even the watching Palovoi were struck by the sense of calm that followed.

At the first lurch that signaled the start of the lift, Jade Darcy and Megan Cafferty both fell suddenly silent. Panting slightly, they checked the floor counter, then looked at each other.

"We did it, Cafferty. They'll settle the price tomorrow—you can do that on your own. The native harvesting setup can be done gradually, and you can move your people in as soon as you can get word to them." Jade looked back to the elevator door. "I'll go with you tomorrow, but it looks like I've fulfilled my part of the arrangement, and the bonus it—"

Jade turned and looked into the face of a madwoman. Megan Cafferty had placed nearly half of her lace fichu in her mouth, and seemed to be trying to force more in. Her face was bright scarlet with tinges of purple, her eyes were crossed, and she was rocking back and forth. The elevator came to her floor and she rushed out to her door, fumbling for the key. Ignoring Jade's frantic questioning, she darted into the room holding on to the door frame. As soon as Jade was inside, she slammed the door, hit the locking switch, and began to pull the Battenberg lace out of her mouth, while a sound equal to a scalded cat's yowl crossed with a donkey's bray erupted from her mouth.

"We did it! We did it!" Megan broke into an Irish step dance as she repeated the phrase over and over.

So help me, Jade thought, *I would have decked her in two more minutes!* "I thought you were going epileptic for a moment—or apoplectic, more like. Give a person some warning next time."

Megan danced over and, in tempo, grabbed Jade's wrists and began to swing them. "I didn't want to scream or laugh in the lift, 'cause elevator shafts carry noise—but Jade, me darling girl, it's dancing we should be doing now, and playing the pennywhistle, and lifting toast after toast in great abandon. *We did it!*"

Given the choice between breaking her own wrists, those of her employer—before she'd been paid—or doing a kind of polka around the furnishings of a hotel suite, Jade found herself to be a tolerable dancer.

The entry hall to the suite was practically a room all by itself, six meters by four, with a waxed hardwood parquet floor. It opened out into a huge parlor and dining area of over five hundred square meters. Several conversation areas were placed in the room, each defined by the large oriental-style rug on which the loveseats and chairs were clustered. Around these islands were wide aisles of polished hardwood, forming a mazelike path from the entries to the bedrooms, to the center hall entryway, past the bar and the dining room opposite it, and back to the other bedrooms beyond. Megan led Jade in a wild, whirling dance down each path, spinning past chinoiserie furniture and delicate screens, sliding past floor lamps, and cakewalking with high kicks behind the twelve-seat walnut table in the dining area.

A chime from the dumbwaiter brought Megan to a halt in the middle of a largely incomprehensible song about a McNamara's Band. She dropped Jade's wrists after launching her in one last turn and darted over to the dumbwaiter.

"I'd programmed the entry computer to send this up as soon as we came in the door. I figured one way or the other we'd need it." With loving care Megan Cafferty laid out a tray with two fluted glasses, a magnum of champagne in a bucket made of ice, and a small round bottle with a crown for a cap.

With a towel over the cork, a gentle twist, and a quiet pop, the cork came free. Megan replaced the magnum in the bucket, lifted the small bottle, and began to open it. "Do you like kir royales?"

Just what every carc needs—enough booze to short-circuit the world. More than one glass and I'm out of it. If she wants to uncover my identity, this could do it. She'd have been briefed about carcs and drinking. But I might get out of it. "I'm not sure what they are— I drink very little, and seldom can afford champagne or anything from Earth. What's in that little bottle?"

"My dear Ms. Darcy, in this crowned orb of a bottle is the essence of five hundred of summer's sweetest raspberries, condensed to a liquid of warm sunny days, heady perfumes, and all the giddiness of a summer-school romance. An ounce or so of this blended with the vivaciousness and complexities of Dom Pérignon's finest vintage sparkles, and we have a drink worthy of this celebration. Here you go. I envy you this, your first taste of a kir royale."

This is truly elegant bullshit, Jade thought. *I've seldom seen a trap sprung with as pretty a bait—the fruity color, the glorious fragrance. And if I refuse it with no good reason, she may guess the real one, or have it confirmed. How much harm can come from wine? Too much, maybe!* Jade took the glass, sniffed at it, and said, "Not while on the job, thanks."

"What are you talking about? I'm in the safest suite, in the best-secured hotel on Cablans. There are no threats against either of us at the moment, are there?"

Jade quickly calculated the odds against the Commancors' knowing it was she with Fastal on Haldek; how quickly they could learn Fastal's identity from his knife; and the odds that Megan had really made up this whole Palovoi deal to trap her. She gave it no better than 40 percent odds for the next day or so, and decided to try one more tack.

"It isn't that, Cafferty. I just don't drink much, as I said. This is a time to celebrate, and the drink smells very good, but I'll pass."

Megan set her own glass down on the dining table and sat at its head. "My husband had a computer-run, body-powered med implant for years before his death. Drinking distorted his body chemistry and fooled the computer's feedback mechanisms into giving the wrong dosages. Do you have a similar problem? I noticed the scars on your arms; some appear surgical. I don't mean to pry, or urge drugs on anyone who'd prefer not to take them; if you'd rather celebrate with hot fudge sundaes, I'll call for those." She reached over to the computer.

Damn, you're good, lady—laid, hooked, and sprung! But I'd rather risk an injury while drunk than have you think you've caught me. Jade raised her hand to stop Megan and said, "No need, you're right. We will need some food later, but for now, here's to our success." With a huge smile and the thought *How dangerous can some raspberry-flavored wine be?* she took her first sip of the kir royale.

For years Jade had eaten the same two dozen dishes she'd programmed for herself according to a pretty firm schedule, or field rations, or bits of alien nontoxic but foul concoctions whose ingestion was part of a race's contract rituals. She was unprepared for the tastes that send gourmands into delight, and make almost anyone a devotee at once. She stopped, stared at nothing for a moment, then very carefully took a second swallow. *I'm sure that now I'm prepared for it, it will only taste wonderful, not overwhelm me and my mouth, nose, and throat with . . .* She had no precise word for the pleasure, but took a second sip. "Greest save us all. It's even better when you pay attention to it."

"Yes. See why I said I envied you? It's always good,

but those first few tastes, with novelty to aid the sensation—they're as forgettable as your first piece of good sex.'' Megan gathered up the tray and headed for the parlor. ''Let's head in where it's more comfortable, start a fire, and enjoy this properly, my dear.''

Cafferty, you are either very shrewd, very bats, or more than a little of both. If you're only half the danger you seem to be, this may be worth the risks. Dammit! It has been five years, and if I remember not to trust her with more than I'd trust Lorpet—hell, than Galentor—I might enjoy this after all.

Jade took a large healthy swallow, nearly draining the delicate flute. ''Mix some more of these kir royales, slowly. I want to learn how to make them.''

Megan smiled knowingly and opened the little bottle. After half an hour of experimenting with differing ratios in search of the perfect kir royale, they discovered that the champagne was gone, but more than half of the Chambord was still in the bottle. Deciding quickly that such an inequity must be remedied, they ordered another bottle of champagne, fresh glasses, and some baked Camembert with ruvis nuts and sourdough bread.

''Cafferty, how'd you open this without it foamin' everywhere and soundin' like a mortar round? You coaxed that out like a spit shine on new leather.''

''It's simple—get that towel and I'll teach you. Wrap it around the neck of the bottle and loosen the wire cage. Then drape it over the cork and grasp the bottle near the neck. Now, turning the bottle slowly, ease the cork out into the fold of the towel with your thumbs. Slower—be patient—it wants to come out. Just think of it as a kitten being born from an old queen—slow, but surely being pushed out. There!''

With a gentle pop, the cork was released. Jade carefully unwound the towel and poured the champagne into the glasses Megan had already blessed with the Chambord. The wine foamed as it hit the thick, sugary liqueur, and Jade patiently waited for the first froth to settle before topping them off. The second pouring foamed less, and it only took seconds for Jade to place the fresh magnum in the ice bucket and settle back into the loveseat across from Megan's favorite over-stuffed chair. They both took slow grateful sips, then tried to remember what they were discussing before the arrival of the second bottle. The effects of the first bottle tended to prolong the process.

"Cafferty, you were going to tell me how you wound up on Cablans, of all places."

"You first, and my name is Megan—use it."

"Not till the job's done and I'm paid. Even if this is truce time. How the hell did the chairman of the board and chief executive officer of one of the five biggest human corporations in existence wind up chasing fucking Palovoi leaves on Cablans? Pardon my language."

"Even Palovoi leaves don't fuck, I think—with Palovoi, who knows? And what's wrong with English? You're not as prudish as you seem, are you?"

"Me? Prudish? Do you know how long a prudish commando would last? Besides, the question under fire, discussion, is 'How the fuck did you wind up here?' "

Megan turned sideways and curled her feet up under her in the chair. Jade was struck again that so much power of personality could be contained in what was basically a very small package. Megan looked into her glass as though for inspiration, then at Jade with eyes suddenly sober. Her gaze was as much a force as a wind to be tacked against while walking in a storm. Jade felt revealed before that gaze, but not threatened—except that all her lacks and flaws could be known by those eyes, and the judgment they'd make would be fair, but would take everything into account.

Megan shifted her eyes to the fireplace, where actual logs burned behind the glass doors, and told Jade her story. "I'm not chairman of the board and chief executive officer for CafTech."

Jade pulled herself erect from the arm of the couch that she'd been leaning against. "You aren't the same Megan Cafferty as in the *Who's Who* and all those books on big business? What the hell are you doing here, then?" *It is a trap. Damn wine—where's the back exit?* Jade began to struggle out of the too-soft couch.

"Wait. Sit down. I am that same woman, and where were you going, anyway? I just resigned—well, not exactly resigned; I gave up some of the titles so I could come here."

For once Jade's thoughts and words agreed as she asked, "What made you give up the power and money you spent all your life getting? No one walks away from that, ever. Who forced you out?"

"No one forced me. My son took over, but—look at me. I'm not young, but I'm too young to spend my life locked in conference rooms listening to old men and children fight about ad campaigns, and investment management, and production quotas. It was different when Liam was alive. We built the company and took joy in running it. We got as big as we dared—governments have a way of being nasty if you get bigger than they are—and moved it officially off-planet to see how big it could grow. Stopped it and sold off things when we realized that in a growing universe there was no longer any limit. So we went back to owning only those things we could run better than anyone else, and only those businesses we enjoyed. It's still the biggest Terran corporation in existence, and too big to give me any fun, so I bailed out."

"I still don't see why. What changed? How could you settle for being just a purchasing agent, or whatever you are now?"

"To explain that you'll have to hear my life story, and since you're nodding at me, hand me a fresh drink and I'll give you the libretto of a poor colleen who fell into good times.

"I was born and raised in New Jersey—that's on Earth, unless you're from New York; they deny that fact. Anyway, I was born to a middle-class family; Dad worked full-time, Mom part-time till we were all in high school, then started her own little parts store for semis and other trucks. Sold it fifteen years later for enough to let her and Dad travel the rest of their days. I was lucky enough to be forced to help Mom at the shop as I grew up. I got paid—most of that went to college savings, but I learned a lot about businesses, bookkeeping, day-to-day things that helped me more than many of my business professors later on.''

Jade took the plate Megan handed her and put some of the soft cheese and bread on it. ''I know what you mean. The time I spent learning to hunt large animals and track them, and to make a comfortable camp, was worth more than most books I've read on how to win a war in thirty days or less.''

''Precisely—thanks for the cheese. In high school I made good grades. figured I'd go to some college, become a professor, or doctor, or researcher, I changed weekly. Then I got my first not-for-Mom job, the summer before my senior year in high school. I was a typist for an investment firm. It was supposed to be part-time temp, but by fall I was a permanent part-time employee. I was saving toward college and doing real well, too. Then came the matter of the report.''

Jade heard the suddenly serious tone in Megan's voice and tried to concentrate through the sparkling mist that perfused her brain. *She's either about to break cover and try to arrest me, or tell me about the real pivotal thing in her life. I must remember this.*

''One day a very junior executive, fresh out of college, demanded I stop what I was doing and type his report,'' Megan continued. ''It was obviously his first for the firm; it didn't follow the company mandatory format. I would've typed it as is, but the kid came back and brought me a cup of coffee to make the job easier. I decided maybe he was all right after all, so I cleaned it up for him. With all the rewrite I had to do, I actually read it instead of just typing it. I noticed a problem. When I was done, I took him the report and showed him the flaw. He laughed in my face, and within six months the company lost over four million dollars because they did what he, and a few others, of course, said to do.

''That would have been the end of the story except for one thing. The conceited ass had told the entire plant about the loudmouth redheaded temp who said not to invest in the South American project because some general would take over the government and nationalize the factories, and didn't I know they hadn't done anything like that for decades? Well, when the industry was nationalized, I was called to the office of the comptroller. I was sure they'd caught me xeroxing my term papers on the company machine and I was about to be fired. I was seventeen years old, fifty kilos, with long flying red hair, dressed in the latest Rococo Revival style, all ruffles, prints, and froth, and I stood there for hours—all right, five minutes—while he finished talking to someone in Japan. Then he asked me to explain my accurate prediction.

"I did one thing smart. I admitted it was dumb luck, not psychic powers or inside information. It had been an accident. The semester before I'd had to do a report on a South American country or leader for one class, and a translation of a piece for my French class, and found the complete text of one of this general's speeches in a French magazine that hadn't been picked up for some reason by the American press. Quoting from that gave me the edge for an A in the civics class, and it was interesting to translate for French. In the speech, the general spoke of his impending takeover in the next election, which the interviewer seemed to accept as fact, and he spoke of the importance of self-governed and controlled industries. When I saw the report recommending buying plants in that country, I figured it was trouble.

"That old man just stared at me, asked me some very mysterious questions, and sent me home. A week later an application for a scholarship arrived. It was for a complete scholarship, through graduate school, if I was to get a double bachelor's—business and liberal arts—and a graduate degree in business, and work at that company for three years after graduation, and ten hours a week during the summer and all other school vacations. I graduated *cum laude*."

"What the hell could you do for a company ten hours a week, maybe that many weeks a year? It's worse than the weekend soldiers of the Interplanetary Peace Guard!"

"I spent them going over the company books, touring company plants, attending meetings, making notes, and reporting on it and asking questions of the comptroller later. I never called him anything but 'sir' or 'Mr. Hydaka,' but he became my second father.

"When he died, I had already earned my way up the executive ladder, and had almost everything in place to take over the company. The day before he died, he said he was looking forward to having me for an employer, because he knew I'd been well trained. By then I'd met my husband, and married him. Four years after that we merged the companies we controlled into CafTech.

"I stayed active in the company. We ran it together, each in charge of different divisions, but both in charge of the whole. We had our kids, one girl and two boys to start with, but a cousin orphaned a little one, and we took him in when he was three. With assorted best friends and strays, we put eleven kids through school. With the housekeepers I had, it was no strain on me, except my nerves.

"They're all grown now. CafTech is primarily run by one of my sons and one of our strays who became a daughter-in-law. All the kids do something—no wastrels in my crowd. I'm prouder of that than the company, sometimes—raising a company is easier than raising kids, as you'll probably find out someday."

Jade had returned to a relaxed pose on the couch, curled around a few of the large loose pillows like a well-armed impressionist Maja. She jumped at the suggestion, spilling pillows. "Not me! Never have 'em, don't want 'em or anyone who expects me to provide a world for them. I take care of me and that's enough. More than enough."

Megan and Jade reached for the fallen pillow, and both nearly fell to the floor. *We'd better get some food in us soon, and less of this tricky wine,* Jade thought.

"Well, I love my kids," Megan said, "even those who weren't out of me, and I'm proud of what they've become. I have a doctor, two engineers. One of my girls is married, has a houseful of kids, and runs a foundation for the arts. I don't know where she gets the energy. Altogether they turned out fine. What about you? You surprised me, you know, when I first saw you. With a name like Darcy I hadn't expected you to be Japanese. How did you get here?''

Jade stood up, slowly and with more of a wobble than she expected. "My father was French. But you still haven't explained why you gave up your business and came here. The champagne is nearly gone."

Megan started to reach for the terminal. "Don't order any more," Jade said. "We need dinner. Now. Get your shoes and coat. We'll go to Rix's. I'll call for a table."

With one problem or another—one of Megan's shoes was hiding in plain sight on the floor of the entryway, while the other was in the dining room, for example— it took nearly forty minutes to reach Rix's Place. They talked some more in the cab.

"After Liam died, it didn't seem as much fun anymore," Megan confided. "We were always goading each other with little challenges, little dares that kept the business fresh. Without those, it was just plain work. I was bored with the board—excuse me. I didn't need the money, I was set for life, but I wanted something to *do*, damm it!"

"The company decided to expand outward and contact new markets. There weren't any other companies dealing from Cablans, so it seemed like the perfect place to go. More than that, it seemed like the perfect place for *me* to go. After all, who can represent us better than the person who raised the company, right? I defined the position exactly the way I wanted it, then I appointed myself to it and stepped down from the board to take it. Working here will be a challenge— almost too much of a challenge, to judge by this first deal. But I'm going to stick it out. Oh, are we here? This doesn't look the way it did the other day."

From habit Jade had directed the cab to the alley entrance she always used. They stepped out, and she had dismissed the cab before she remembered Megan technically wasn't supposed to use the kitchen entry. *Damn raspberry stuff. I know better. Hell with it—the cook can only yell so loud, and his knives aren't that long.*

"Oh, the back way!" Megan exclaimed, comprehension suddenly dawning. "I love kitchens!"

"You've never seen one like this, I bet. Watch out for the chef, though, he's—"

"An absolute tyrant who waves knives at everybody. Don't look so shocked. I've run chains of restaurants, and hired more than one estate cook in my time. The best ones are all like that. It's the fumes from the fryers, I think. Shall we go in?"

"Right, it is drizzling, isn't it?" Jade said as she opened the door.

"Is it?" asked Megan as she slid past the loading dock. She started to point at something, and drops rolled off her sleeve. "I guess it is, and I've developed a fine attitude."

"Whatever. If we're quiet," said Jade as she led her client up to the swinging doors that opened to the kitchen proper, "we can slip past the cooks and they'll never know we're here." Jade hit the door and it hardly moved. Megan giggled, so she hit it what she thought was just a little harder and it flew open and crashed against the stops with a boom rivaling a blown steam line. All the normal sounds in the kitchen slammed to a stop except for the omnipresent nonsound of the ultrasonic dishwasher.

Sotto voce, Jade said, "Oh, shit."

Megan whispered, "Stand back. What's the chef's name?"

Jade whispered, "Landauris," and listened to her employer.

"Landauris, pardon this inexcusable intrusion, but after dining here the other evening I had to see the studio of the finest culinary artist I've experienced this side of the Cordon Bleu itself. What is this glorious creation being prepared here?" Megan effused as she examined a mixed-grill dish about to be burned on the open flame.

"Idiot! Turn them, turn them, and baste those chops again," said the six-armed humanoid as he swept past the suddenly bustling kitchen toward the two women. "They must glisten like rain-wet marble, not scorch like bad grease. Madam, welcome to my kitchen. Darcy! Introduce us!''

I don't believe this, thought Jade as the chef swept Megan over to the pastries counter to show off a sweet he was preparing for a special occasion that evening.

"Landauris, this is Megan Cafferty. Cafferty, Landauris.''

"You are the same that owns Le Salver on the L-5 station of Antares 7-299? But of course you are! You know fine cuisine when you see it.''

After a tour of the kitchen that took them to areas Jade hadn't seen in the five years she'd been there, Jade and Megan were finally escorted to a table with instructions not to order; Landauris would do it for them. As soon as they were seated a bottle of champagne arrived.

Jade took it by the neck and thought of throwing it down Bab-ankh's throat, but couldn't remember whether the skinny-legged blue fluffball had a throat. While she was trying to decide what to do with it, Megan slipped it out of her hands.

"Good vintage. Rix keeps a nice cellar. However, I need to make room if I'm going to put any of this bottle in me should I go?''

Jade stared at her, knowing that should have made sense, and finally realizing just how drunk she was. Before she could focus enough on that thought to panic her, Megan realized the problem.

"You really don't drink much, do you? Come and show me the way to the ladies' room.'' She stood and reached over to help Jade up out of her chair.

"I'll take you to the room, but there's never been a lady in it, said Jade, staggering to her feet. Her carc system was thrown out of whack by the alcohol, but still made corrections. Often they were overcorrections that demanded new neural messages, and the result was short spells that resembled cerebral palsy.

Megan steadied her, and after a useless attempt to shake off the help, Jade allowed Megan to hold her arm as they wove their way to the bathroom.

The large door labeled ''Excretion Facilities, Female, Internal, Privacy Mode'' was four meters tall

and double that wide, able to open to either side, and
so perfectly balanced that a few ounces of pressure
caused them to fold into the doorjamb. Within the
larger door, almost like a pet door, was one two meters high and wide that most species could enter. This
was the door Megan and Jade used.

Jade directed Megan to a section of the room that
had a system of running water over a trench. There
were folded walls to pull around it if privacy was desired, and a row of small, medium, large, and very
large U-shaped seats that could be pulled down from
the wall and adjusted according to height and distance
from the wall. Megan had seen such arrangements in
interracial habitats before and had no trouble adjusting
the furniture. While she waited for Jade and tried to
guess which of the many appliances were supposed to
be sinks for washing hands or other appendages, she
saw the murderer strike.

In a three-walled cubicle across the aisle and about
halfway to the left wall was an alien Megan had never
seen before. It resembled an overgrown, six-limbed,
curly-haired beaver over two meters tall if standing
erect. It was balanced on two large hind legs and a
fat, flat tail. Its upper body was arched over a trough
it was holding with both front appendages, while its
middle arms were grappling with its assailant.

On its back was a large sort of blob about a meter
long, with stumpy lower limbs but well-developed upper limbs. These were around the neck of the larger
beast, choking it. The large beaver seemed to be trying to squeeze the smaller one to disable it, but with
small success, judging from the terrible choking
sounds and the way the large creature was sinking
lower as Megan watched in horror.

"Jade! Code Blue! Red Alert! Murder! Help!"
yelled Megan as she ran to the creature's assistance.
Throwing herself on top of them, she tried to tear the
smaller creature's arms away from the other's neck.
That failing, as she slid off the bodies, she began to
try and pull the blob off the creature's back, still
screaming alarms.

"What the fuck! I'm coming! Goddamn fucking

suit.'' Jade cursed as her suddenly stubborn jumpsuit refused to untangle from around her ankles. In her drunkenness and suddenly supercharged state, it would be a several-minute mess. Jade pulled off her boots and the recalcitrant suit. Leaving her leotard unfastened at the crotch, she grabbed her gun and ran into the aisle, naked from the waist down, gun at the ready.

"No! Dear Greest in heaven, *no!* Stop that. I mean you, Megan. How fucking stupid are you? Let go of it. Now! It isn't murder, not unless it's yours.'' Jade pulled on the arms of the confused woman in the green satin suit till the message sunk in and she let go of the blob.

"Child stealer! Murderer! Help!'' yelled the larger alien as it turned and began to fight back, striking out at Jade with linked fists driven by both of the long, strong upper arms.

"Child stealer?'' echoed Megan. "Oh no, what did I do?'' She quickly moved out of the creature's way as Jade went into action.

Dodging the first roundhouse swing was simple for the carc, but it brought Jade into range of the fat tail. While Jade tried to restrain the flying fists, the giant beaver pivoted and slapped Jade's calves with the ten pounds of cartilage and muscle. Jade tried to dodge, but misjudged the response, and the blow landed while she was still off balance. It threw her toward the great steel sink the beast had been leaning over.

Jade twisted like a cat. Using the gyroscopic ability built into her, she oriented herself in midair and met the edge of the fixture with her feet instead of her head, then used the momentum to propel her back to the retreating, screaming customer. Quicker than Megan could follow, Jade ran across the cubicle, grasped the middle arms that had never for an instant loosened their grasp on the infant, and spun the being back into the room. She cursed the many shallow cuts she got from even this short contact with the shredded, curled scales that gave the Daimeitroo its soft, furry disguise.

"Is there a necessity for the assistance of another arbiter, Jade, or have you achieved adequate control of the situation?'' Cyclad Arik said, poking her head in the door.

At the sight of the giant mantisoid, the Daimeitroo stopped struggling and began to level her charge of attempted child-stealing at Megan.

"Cyclad, explain to her there was no attempt, it was a misunderstanding. Ms. Cafferty thought she was being attacked and tried to defend her. I'll explain to Ms. Cafferty."

Jade turned to scream at Megan and stopped at the sight of her. The bright green satin suit was somehow a clumsy costume, rumpled and torn by contact with the scales of the alien when Megan had tried to climb on its back. Her face was pale as a death mask, and her expression was that of deep shock and confusion. For the first time since they'd met, Jade realized Megan wasn't really that much taller than she was, and right now looked much smaller. Jade put a cap on her temper, and explained—in a much milder way than she otherwise would have—just what Megan's error had been.

"Look, you ignorant excuse for a grown-up, that's a Daimeitroo. They carry their eggs, and young, on their backs through what would be most of a gestation period and infancy for us. You tried to tear off its child, which might have killed both of them. You should have told me you were the one committing the murder; I would have let it kill you, as it would have as soon as it realized how easy that would be. You just paid that customer's bill for a month or more, and you owe it at least an apology and a trip to the doctor's. Now be still while I fix this mess you've gotten us into."

Megan closed her mouth without saying whatever she'd started to, and stood meekly by while Cyclad and Jade tried to sooth the Daimeitroo.

"Look, this human over here was unfamiliar with your race and was trying to help. She realizes her error and desires to make restitution. She will, of course, pay for any medical treatment you need, and has agreed to pay not just for tonight's meal, but for all that you wish to have in the Ingesterie—"

The Daimeitroo interrupted. "It is regrettable that

your backward little planet is allowed to send such pitifully ignorant individuals abroad to harass respectable races. If I were home, I would have you *sterilized!*'' The last word was pronounced with such a loud boom that the u-trans could barely be heard. ''There is little law in such a place as this, but what law there is recognizes the principles of *contra pacem,* and the Greest will assist my attorneys in receiving compensation for the damage this being has caused.''

The Daimeitroo began punching a code into its implant. ''I intend to name this creature, this establishment, its owners, and each of you as jointly and severally responsible for the dangerous actions I was subjected to by this barren loner. The right of all parents to be protected from thieves and trauma to their infants is as basic as the right of defense. Even the human law recognizes that—''

''Such a suit will never make it past the Greest to appeal on Daimeitran.'' Megan projected her voice in a way only stage people and attorneys seemed trained to do. It wasn't a shout, but cut through everything. ''In the first place, the precedents will reveal that in cases of *injuria absque damno,* the *mens rea* of the accused shall have weight in the verdict, provided the action was in itself such that any reasonable being might commit in the protection of self or others.''

''You have no assessment of any actual or consequential damages to myself, or my infant. The mental anguish alone is significant for myself, and what such a trauma may be to my child might not appear for years.''

''As regards the slanderous attack upon my reputation and value, I have raised three children of my own to maturity, plus several orphaned and abandoned infants—yes, abandoned!'' Megan paused in the sudden silence of the Daimeitroo's shock. ''It is a little-known mind illness of humans that allows them, sometimes, to abandon their healthy infants to strangers.''

''This I had heard of this, but assumed it was a mistranslation, or libel. I wouldn't dream that such a condition could exist within a civilized race. As the great jurist, Gilemers, said, 'It is within the bond of—' ''

'' 'Of the nurturing of offspring that you find the essence of all justice and law.' Yet as only half of our species is capable of such a bond, many discard their young as they would property, not essence of self.''

''Where did you learn of Gilemers?''

''Yes, Cafferty. Where did you learn of whoever it is?'' asked Jade.

''I am lucky enough to be the matriarch of the Caf Tech clan. My attorney selves are among the greatest in the human world, and have met your race in battle in many courts. They have been, at times, victors.''

''Even I have heard of this clan. Yet how come you to feloniously assault me in such a manner, committing battery upon myself and my child? Surely you cannot claim ignorance, and we all know that *ignorantia legis non excusat.*''

''Ignorance did lead me to my infraction, and needs provide, when combined with the reasonable and prudent being rule, my only defense. I have read of your race, but never seen even a holo of a Daimeitroo till this hour. Indeed, it is your attractive nuisance that has lead to the mental anguish I have suffered from your groundless accusations.''

''Under no circumstances can the normal performance of bodily functions within the prescribed place as custom allows be considered an attractive nuisance. The only claim to that may be this criminally negligent ingesterie that doesn't provide sufficient privacy screens for all patrons.''

''It is your child which is the attractive nuisance. I could not be expected, under the reasonable being rules of liability, to believe that such a large, strong, and healthy being was an infant still in bonding. Never have I seen such a well-developed and cared-for youngster.''

The Daimeitroo seemed a bit taken aback by this tactic.

''It's true,'' said Jade. ''I have seen several of your race, some with youngsters who walked part of the time, and none were as striking as yours.''

The alien added its upper arms to the grooming of the baby, and its tail fluttered a brief tattoo on the floor. "I must admit that I have reason to be proud of this young one. Yet such rash . . . misdemeanors cannot go unlitigated."

"I agree that proper notice must be made of such a problem, or perhaps the rule of condonation could be implemented."

"My u-trans failed to translate that. Please elaborate."

"Within human marital, that is, family or clan, law condonation is defined as the conditional forgiveness of an offense, such as adultery, that would otherwise result in divorce, upon agreement that such an offense shall not be repeated. Thus, that instance of the offense cannot be grounds for divorce litigation. Only a later commitment of the same offense, without signs of further condonation, or a separate class of offense, could provide grounds for legal action."

"It is clear that, by the *ratio legis* of condonation, I would receive your bond against further offenses of this class," said the Daimeitroo. "Does this mean I abrogate my right to compensation for damages for this initial violation of the offense, or merely that less formal arbitration may establish such a judgment?"

Megan finally smiled. "Such an agreement may be an informal or a registered formal part of the contract we draw up, depending on our tax and strategic needs. I believe an initial agreement, pending more formal negotiations, might include any such emergency treatment as is needed and indicated in the future for correction of the trauma, and, of course, meals for you and your nest at this establishment for the remainder of this week."

"It could take as much as a year for full health to be regained following such a trauma. My nest would suffer as a whole."

"Suppose we make it, say, thirty days, for now?" asked Jade.

"Pending final formal agreement, *in pais* of course. My attorneys can contact yours tomorrow," added Megan.

"Such a small offer—but as the opening for further discussion, I can accept, pending consultation with my nest."

Jade asked, "Do you need escort to your table?"

"No, my nest is waiting. I shall return tomorrow. *Fiat Justitia.*"

"When you make your reservation, mention the name Jade Darcy, and Bob-ankh will arrange our best tables for you."

With a parting growl the giant beaver dropped onto its back and middle legs and left the room.

"Cyclad, thank you for the help. You'd better let Rix know to bill any meals from the beaver the next month to Cafferty. I'll be out soon."

Cyclad went back out onto the floor. Jade turned back to Megan, who'd regained her color and composure. She'd removed the suit jacket, and pulled the blouse out of the skirt's waist band. This hid most of the damage from the scuffle, and she once more appeared in control of herself. Jade looked as serene, but the stress of the battle and the serious legal threat to Rix had her nerves frayed. Somewhere, somehow the energy had to explode.

"Cafferty, I must admit, you pulled that one out. All those meetings with lawyers paid off, I guess."

"Half of what a corporation head does is handle lawyers. Of course, the Diameitroo are a race of lawyers. They can be the worst. This will cost me a pretty penny before I'm done."

"Well, like I said, not bad. But Cafferty—" Jade's parade-ground voice suddenly filled the room and shook dust loose from the rafters. "I've seen some damn fool stunts in my day, but this ignorant bullshit takes the cake. I don't know for sure what you saw, but it probably appeared to be a choking, right?"

"Exactly. I thought the large mother was about to pass out, and—"

"She probably was, and that's how she was supposed to be. Those critters don't have assholes—literally. They vomit up their shit through a special pouch that comes out of their mouth. It's the most disgusting damn thing. When the child gets that size, it has a stomach, but shares food swallowed by its mother because it doesn't have a mouth yet—won't have one till it's nearly ready to be on its own. It has to choke the parent so that it can push its own pouch through the parent's throat, without the parent's stomach getting in the way. Choking is common and sometimes causes problems. We had to call the doc for one, once. Damned mess. Does this account for what you saw?''

"Yes, Jade, it does," said Megan, not quite concealing a giggle.

"What are you sniggering at?"

"I'm sorry, but I've seldom been read the riot act by a nearly naked and, if I may say so, very attractive woman in an alien bathroom before.''

Jade looked down. The stretch material of her leotard underwear had crept up to just under her breasts. Except for her breasts, the knives on her arms, and her shoulders, she was stark naked.

"Goddamn it! Why didn't somebody say something?'' yelled Jade as she darted back to the stall to get dressed. Megan's laughter followed her in, though she still was observant enough to notice the pattern of fine, hairline scars down Jade's spine and the back of her legs, and to wonder why that looked so familiar.

Jade's apparel was restored in minutes, and she could admit that she must have looked less than regal.

"What strikes me, Jade, is that I didn't consciously notice it until I mentioned it. I was so scared. I am sorry, I really thought there was danger.''

"Cafferty, I realize you can't know all hundred and some odd races we get through here, but learn to leave them alone, no matter what appears to be happening, until you've checked it out with someone, or they ask for help. Nine times out of ten, you'll be okay that way—and the tenth will be cleared up while you wait. Understand?''

Jade felt much more confident now that she was dressed. As the last of the panic mode left her system, she again was aware of her hunger, and of the meal that awaited them. Megan seconded the feeling, and, discussing the alien nature of things on Cablans and how they trapped greenhorns like Megan, they started out of the bathroom.

As they walked down the aisle toward the door, a huge tank, which cleared the sides by less than two centimeters, headed toward them.

"Cafferty, slide in here till it gets past."

They pulled into a large stall and Megan looked around. "All this one needs is closer stirrups and my gyne could use it tomorrow. I don't know what he'd do with that rope, though. He doesn't need to climb to the rafters."

"That's easy. He swings on it, screaming like Tarzan." Jade grasped the end and pulled it free from its friction clasp. Suddenly needing some action to release the rest of the tension from the fight, she leaped onto the table and began swinging in a great arc around the table and toward the other side of the area.

"It makes for quick exits, too," she called as she was carried into the aisle behind the tank. As she entered the aisle, she dropped into a crouch, looked down the aisle and around the corner, and back at Megan. She lifted her arm in a come-along gesture and called, "All clear."

"I was right. Jade Darcy, you're a carc." Megan clapped her hands with pleasure and tried to help Jade stand.

Jade heard the sentence reverberate in the big room. For a moment she was sure she'd imagined it, the way she'd dreamed the nightmare of discovery for the last seven years.

"A computer-augmented-reflex commando," Megan continued. "I'm right, aren't I? You have to be a carc."

I really hate to kill you, but what else is there? Jade turned, but Megan had already backed away.

"I have a carc as head of security," the older woman said. "He lost one leg and part of a hand, and they retired him. He's the best hand-to-hand combat machine I've ever seen. And he told me he doesn't drink, because of the side effects that confuse his computer and cause a sort of palsy. That's what you were doing."

Stop babbling, Jade thought. *Still, you can be dead, but like this you're too alive. Damn it, stop being friendly, and kind, and fun, and pretty, or to kill you won't be impossible, but might hurt. No, it can't hurt, but. . . .*

"I wasn't sure until just a minute ago. Then, in the fight, the way you turned in midair wasn't human, but familiar. I saw a carc graduation drill, and they all moved like that. And there's the scars down your back and legs. I didn't put it all together till you dropped off the rope and checked for enemy presence before signalling all-clear and standing up. A soldier does that. All of a sudden, it all clicked.

"I know they don't usually retire carcs early, but I won't ask how you got out. Injuries like that are hard to deal with, I know. They must have been internal, you look fine. Anyhow, I understand you better. But why did Landauris scare you so much? You're greased death and he's just a classically trained chef."

I can't decide, not like this, Jade thought. *A wrong choice, or that thing in the tank coming back, and I'll be a suspect.* "I can't talk about it. It's a major breach of security to discuss the process, or to let anyone not properly cleared know too much about carcs." *That much, at least, is true.* "If you want to protect whatever clearance you or your company's got, you'll forget you saw me. Speaking of Landauris, dinner should be ready."

"I understand. Secrets don't escape me. I do love solving puzzles, though, and you're an immense one. I'm glad to get the biggest piece down."

Dinner was exquisite, Megan said. Jade agreed, even though it tasted like sawdust under these circumstances. As time and food, added to stress, sobered her up, Jade felt as though down pillows had been placed around all her senses. What no alien had surmised in seven years, this woman had discerned in three days. The first piece of a puzzle she dared let no one live to complete. She'd been right to fear the appearance of another human. Keeping her involvement and identity hidden while removing this threat would be tricky. These things had to be done delicately.

After dinner Jade accompanied Megan back to the hotel and tried to plan the best way to remove the danger. The desk had several messages for Megan, including one from a diplomat even Jade had heard of.

That tears it. If I kill her, this place will be swarming with investigators galore, and I won't last a week. I've got to hold off, hope she keeps the secret at least long enough for me to figure out a way to set up someone else for the crime. I can't risk anything else.

Jade headed back to her place. As she entered, Val asked her if she wanted her messages.

"Might as well."

"Lorpet reports that you are mentioned in a memo to CafTech—not by name, only as a local expert. The utility company will be interrupting service for two minutes tomorrow; my battery backups tested fine for that. Two thousand five hundred eus were placed in your account within the hour from CafTech, followed by a second deposit of one thousand with a memo sent here saying it was to cover tomorrow's meeting. End of messages."

Well, she kept her word about the money, at least. Jade undressed very slowly, spilling her clothes into the laundry chute and falling into bed. As the restraints snapped over her arms she thought, *I don't want to kill her. She might almost have been a friend. But damn it, I'm tired of running. And she* knows!

Chapter 12

Threats and Pleas

Despite the effects of the alcohol, Jade had trouble sleeping that night. Over and over the thought repeated in her mind: *She knows. She knows I'm a carc.*

How long would it take Megan Cafferty to get a message to Earth? Cablans was as far away as one could get, and normally the interlocking communications might take three or four days at best—but Megan Cafferty had connections. By pulling strings, she might be able to do it in two. And the army would listen to her, too. They'd act instantly. They could get some people here in another two days, at the most. And then . . .

Four days. That was all she could count on, four days of freedom. After that, everything depended on the goodwill of a woman who was still a comparative stranger. CafTech did business with the army all the time; Megan had to please the military to keep those lucrative contracts flowing. Jade had made her a lot of money by saving the Palovoi deal, but would Cafferty consider it more valuable to let the army know there was a carc on Cablans? Or might she consider it her duty to tell them? It didn't even have to be a conscious act; a mere slip of the tongue in front of the wrong person could set the chain of events in motion.

Could she trust the goodwill and discretion of Megan Cafferty? Could she afford to believe in elves, Santa Claus, and the tooth fairy?

She did not have *the* nightmare that night, probably because she was so consumed with worry that she didn't fall deeply enough asleep. She did writhe all night in light sleep, chafing at the bonds that held her wrists and ankles firm, while vague, unsettled dreams floated through her soul and were gone before she could name them.

She awoke the next morning scarcely less tired than she'd gone to bed, but with new determination in her soul. She would brace herself for the worst, yes, but there was no point in panicking. She'd run this far, and there literally was noplace further. She'd run again if she had to—there were a couple of alternatives on her list—but not until then. Cablans was going to be her home as long as she could make it one. It was something she desperately needed—other than the army, she'd had no home for fifteen years.

But there were precautions she could and would take. She put Val on full round-the-clock alert to the extreme limits of her sensors; the polite little circle of light in front of her door was greatly expanded, and anyone approaching the apartment would be warned away or face the consequences. She took some of the money she'd earned on the Palovoi deal and paid Lorpet a premium to monitor all Cafferty's communications and report on any that related to Jade; in addition, Lorpet was to inform her immediately if any Terrans—or members of races who were Terran military allies—arrived on Cablans.

Her coworkers at Rix's were informed that some people who weren't friendly to her might come looking for her, and that they were to check with her before giving out any information; that was standard procedure anyway, but repeating it emphasized the danger.

Most important, Jade upgraded her standard armament. Except in the ingesterie itself, where discretion was the watchword, she was no longer content to carry just her two stash knives. She took her 4020 model Uzi with the fifteen-round clip out of her arsenal and, in addition to other, less common weapons hidden about her person, kept it fastened with a Velcron-3 strip to the right hip of her merc suit whenever she was in public—and she tried to be in public as little as possible.

Three days passed as Jade waited. She wasn't expecting anything to happen just yet, though there was always the possibility that someone could have been dispatched here from someplace nearer than Earth. But she remained alert, because she knew that when something did happen it was bound to be the unexpected.

She took the individualized cabs between her apartment and the ingesterie, despite the added expense, because they subjected her to less outside contact than the public transports. Still, there was a stretch of almost a hundred meters between the street and her house and a long back alley from the street to Rix's back door; if anything unpleasant happened, it would probably be in these places where she was least protected. She knew this, and even so she was surprised.

She was coming down the alley to start a night shift at the ingesterie, passing the T intersection where other businesses' loading docks demanded a wide turning spot with two arms. It was raining heavily, as usual for a Cablans evening at this time of year, and she was hurrying to get inside. The sound of the downpour obscured any incidental noises that might have been made in the alley, and the heavy droplets blurred her vision. The ground was slick and the footing treacherous, and Jade knew this was a perfect spot for an ambush. She kept her right hand beside the Uzi strapped to her leg.

Movement on her left; movement on her right. Even as Jade grabbed her weapon and ripped it from its Velcron strip, her peripheral vision told her there was a third person coming up from behind her as well. There was a bright flash of some energy weapon, and the puddle of water at her feet hissed into a sudden cloud of steam.

Jade froze at the warning shot with her gun halfway lifted into position. They had missed on purpose the first time, and she didn't want to give them cause to try a second shot. Very slowly she changed her grip on the gun, holding it away from her gingerly with just the thumb and forefinger of her right hand. If they wanted her undivided attention, they would get it.

The three stepped closer out of the shadows, and Jade was stunned to see they were not Terrans, but Commancors. Each had a 481-Zendari energy pistol aimed directly at her, making any attempt at fighting pure suicide. But they showed no inclination to shoot immediately, giving Jade some slim margin for hope.

"You are being called Jade Darcy?" asked the one on her left.

"I am."

"You need not stand in so ludicrous a pose. You may holster your weapon."

"Thank you," Jade said with surprise. Moving with exaggerated slowness she refastened the Uzi to her hip, wondering exactly what her attackers were up to.

The Commancor on her right stepped forward and held out something, while the one who'd spoken before asked, "Do you recognize this?"

Even in the alley's dim light and the driving rain, Jade knew what it was: Fastal ip Fornen's family dagger. "Yes," she said slowly. "It's a knife."

"Very particular knife. Do you know who owns it?"

"Should I? A knife is a knife, after all."

"You traveled with its owner, Lemmant called Fastal ip Fornen. Does that name mean nothing to you?"

Jade remembered a certain bigot she'd served with in boot camp, and tried to copy his manner and phrasing. "All these shit-ass alien names sound the same, like someone's trying to talk around a mouthful of broccoli. If you say that's his knife, I'll believe you. What difference does it make?"

"This knife killed high-ranking Commancor officer on Dominion territory. Such behavior does not go unpunished. It sets bad precedent."

"I can see you have a problem, yes." Why were they toying with her this way? They knew she was involved. Why didn't they just kill her?

"This Lemmant you traveled with—where is he now?"

She decided to keep the bigot's voice. "How the fuck should I know? He probably went back to Lemmanta. It's not my business to keep track of every alien I meet."

"Your business. Yes, we know about your business. He paid you to accompany him to Haldek?"

"Do you think I travel with asswipe aliens just for the thrill of it?"

"Is nothing bad about being mercenary. Is honorable profession for lesser races within Dominion. True mercenary bears no stigma for his acts; such burden lies with his commander. You have acted beyond reproach. May tonight bring you success."

And with that the three attackers backed away, each in the direction from which he'd initially come. The end of the interview came so abruptly that Jade was left standing in the rain uncertain what to do next. If she pulled her gun again she could probably kill one of them before the other two got her—and what would be the point of that? They'd left her alone; they'd absolved her of guilt in Horsson's death. She couldn't ask for more, could she?

She found to her disgust that her hands were shaking. *Dammit, this is stupid! I can't let them see me like this, especially not them. Not Commancors. They can't see me trembling like some whimpering schoolgirl.*

The twenty-eight-year-old mercenary stood in the rain clenching her hands into fists to control the worst of the shaking, so tightly that her fingernails cut into the flesh of her palms. The rain soaked her cheeks, disguising any tears that might have strayed from her eyes. She took long, slow breaths of air that eventually steadied her nerves, and when she could again will her legs to move she walked the rest of the way to the back door of Rix's.

Safely inside on familiar ground, she pressed her hand terminal to an exterior line and called Val. "Get hold of Fastal ip Fornen, if he hasn't already left Cablans," she said. "Tell him the Commancors are looking for him. Tell him to get his ass out of here, somewhere they can't trace him." Though where that might be, she had no idea. There wasn't anywhere the Commancors didn't go, and for a crime like this they'd track him down even on Lemmanta itself. *Why did he have to leave that fucking knife there?* she asked herself yet again.

She was next to useless on her shift that night. She

walked around in a fog, and nothing short of mayhem would have attracted her attention. Fortunately for all concerned it was a quiet night at Rix's, with patrons more interested in eating and talking than making trouble for one another.

She found herself strangely wanting to unburden herself to Cyclad Arik, as though bringing the large mantisoid into her confidence would somehow make the problems evaporate. But Cyclad wasn't on duty tonight, and the other arbiters were relative strangers. Suddenly, after years of existing in a vacuum, Jade realized just how alone she was. It was a life she'd chosen out of necessity, and most of the time she didn't mind it, but tonight . . . tonight she would have liked someone else there. Almost anyone—even slimy Lorpet would be an improvement over the deafening silence around her.

The shift dragged unbearably on, but even it came to an end and Jade had to face the gauntlet leading back to her empty house. She should have felt relieved—the threat from the Commancors was over, and all she had to worry about was the army—but still her soul was leaden as she left the cab and walked through the drizzly dawn toward the door of her flat.

There was a movement in the bushes, and Jade had the Uzi out in her hand faster than even she would have believed possible. Only her exhaustive training and a whispered codeword last used on Haldek kept her from firing before she heard the hoarse plea: "Jade Darcy, it is I, Fastal ip Fornen. I must speak with you."

Jade looked quickly around. The Commancors had spared her once, but if they saw her associating with Fastal again they wouldn't be as lenient. "Let me get safely inside my apartment first," she told him. "Then you come in. Make sure no one sees you."

She accessed her door and stepped inside, then held it open for Fastal to slip in behind her. Only then did she dare relax and let out the breath she'd been holding. "What are you still doing here?" she demanded. "I warned you to get the hell away."

"I cannot. The Greest demands twenty-five thousand eus as a transfer fee. I do not have that much money.''

Twenty-five thousand? It didn't cost that much to ship a ton of iron halfway across the known universe. What kind of game was the Greest trying to play? What "pattern" was he trying to fit their lives into?

"What did you come to me for?" she asked harshly.

"I need your help to escape from the Commancors."

"I thought you once told me it wasn't so important if you got away, as long as your mission was a success."

Fastal paused for a moment to find the proper words. "If I had died while fulfilling my mission, that would have been a noble and an honorable death. But to be hunted down like this . . . the Commancors have no concept of honor."

"I could have told you that a long time ago."

Fastal straightened his body even stiffer than it was. "I am not a criminal. I will not die a criminal's death."

"I don't make moral judgments," Jade said. "In my business I can't afford to. Tell it to the Commancors."

"You must help me."

"How? Do you want to hire me as your bodyguard for the rest of your life? That's what it'll take with the Commancors after you. They won't stop until you're dead—and they'll go right through a horde of bodyguards if they have to. If I take a long-term assignment, I want one with a little better job security."

"If you could just lend me the money to get to Lemmanta—"

"I haven't got that kind of money, either. Besides, I'm the mercenary. You're supposed to pay me. That's how the system works."

Fastal paused again. "I know you have scorned my ideals—but surely you must have some code you live by, some set of principles, some honor."

"Sure, a mercenary's honor," Jade said. "I don't desert my comrades in the field. I don't kill innocent civilians if I can avoid it. I don't change sides in the middle of a job, and I give fair value for the money. That pretty much sums it up.''

"But—"

"You paid my fee and I did what you asked. I went with you to Haldek, I helped you avenge your family, and I helped you escape alive. I gave you the benefit of my expert advice, most of which you tried to ignore; I even did my best to work under the constraints you imposed, and believe me that wasn't easy. I didn't take your money and then run out on you when things got tough.''

"But that is just what you are doing now.''

"No!'' Jade shouted. "This is another matter entirely. I arranged it so the murder couldn't be traced to us. The timing of our visit would have been highly suspicious, but there'd have been enough doubt that they might not have come after us. You were the one who chose to leave your family dagger there for anyone to see. If you'd even mentioned it to me at the time I'd have gone back and taken it away. You brought this entirely upon yourself, and I'm not responsible for the consequences. You can deal with those on your own.''

Fastal sat down, shaking his head in a very human gesture. "Your idea of honor is very constricted,'' he said. "Honor means much more than this. It is a promise you make to yourself, not to someone else. You promise yourself that the ideals you live by are worth more than words, more than pieces of paper. You say that your values are worth defending, possibly even worth dying for. You respond to the honor in others and come to their aid in noble causes. This is what it means to be honorable in a Lemmant—or a human.''

"My values are my life, staying alive, and saying that's worth dying for is a silly paradox. I need to earn money to get some revenge of my own—and no, it's none of your business, but you should at least understand it. *That* is a promise I made to myself, and by God I intend to keep it.

"I was raised to take care of others—men, babies, elders—like all women. Everyone and every rule came before me and my life and my needs. But I woke up and burned that shit from my soul. Now, like every *intelligent* person, I've got room for me, my goals, and my reasons—period. I've got no room or time for your fucking honor. Mine'll do."

"But the more you limit your honor, the more you limit yourself. Is that all you are worth to yourself? Is the purpose of living merely to keep on living?"

"That seems to be your biggest concern at the moment. That's why you're here, isn't it?"

Jade could see Fastal's neck muscles stiffen. "I am prepared to die for this cause. I always have been. I would prefer not to, and I will take what steps I can to avoid it without compromising my principles. But you . . ."

He shook his head again. "You who have so little honor also have so little life. You say you value it so highly and yet you cheapen it by all you do. You put a price on everything. That is why you cannot have honor, because honor has no price. When you die it will make not a ripple in the universal ocean of life, because your life stood for nothing and so has no value. Only the principles we cling to will outlive us, and make our lives of some consequence."

Jade clapped slowly and sarcastically. "A fine speech. I'll have them put it on your tombstone, if you people use tombstones. But I think I've been offended enough for one day. If you don't have anything useful to say, I'd suggest you get out of here and try to find someplace to hide."

Fastal stood and walked slowly to the door. Just before reaching it he turned and looked at her again. "Thank you, Jade Darcy."

"For what?" she asked, puzzled.

"For helping me remember what I am and what I am about. In my fear I lost sight of those things. You have restored them, and I am grateful.

"I am going now, most likely to die. But at least I shall have a reason, and those reasons will resound on Lemmanta. What will you have when it comes to your turn?

"I am sorry for you, Jade Darcy."

"Save the pity for yourself!" Jade yelled as the door closed behind him. "You'll need it more than I will."

She started into her exercise room. "Set up the target range, Val. I need to shoot something."

CHAPTER 13

Responsibilities

The alarm woke Jade with a sudden shock. She sat up, or tried to; her arms and legs were still pinioned to the bed. "Dammit, Val, I'm awake. Let me up."

The restraints vanished immediately, and Jade swung herself off the bed. Though she normally slept in the nude, the past few nights she had taken to wearing two-piece pajamas whose bottoms included sturdy slippers; she was not going to be caught unprepared in an emergency.

Her Uzi was on a table beside the bed. She was grabbing it even as she said, "Show me on the screen, Val."

The wallscreen lit up to show the scene of the lighted area in front of the door. No one was there, and at first Jade was perplexed about what had set off the alarm. Then she caught a flurry of motion in the lower left-hand portion of the screen and realized instantly what was happening.

"Door, Val," she said, racing forward.

The door slid open as she reached it, gun in firing position. The shapes beyond were indistinct in the growing dusk, but Jade already had a good idea of their position from the screen. She squeezed off four quick shots without pausing, and was rewarded with a pained howl that quickly died along with the creature making it.

Lying on the ground just beyond the walkway was a very dead dasko, its trim body nearly torn in pieces by the force of the Uzi's bullets. Lying beside it was the body of its victim, a frizzlic. A frizzlic with a white triangular mark on its forehead. *Her* frizzlic.

Keeping her gun at the ready in case there was anyone else lurking out here, she knelt beside the frizzlic's body and examined it. At first she was afraid it was dead, but then she could see its sides moving slowly with each labored breath it took. A wave of relief swept over her, but she knew the relief would be short-lived if she didn't act quickly.

"Call the nearest veterinarian, Val," she said to her computer.

"There are no veterinarians on Cablans; no one will admit to being an 'animal' and there is no ranching."

Holding the gun in her right hand, Jade gently picked up the wounded creature with her left and hugged it tightly against her body. The blood smeared against her pajamas, but she didn't even notice. "Then how about someone who specializes in small mammalian creatures?" she asked, reentering the apartment with her bleeding bundle securely in her arms.

"Checking. There are three. The nearest one practices at Octal 4 Hospital.'

Jade was quite familiar with Octal 4—it specialized in mammalians, was only six blocks away, and had patched her up before. "Call them and let them know I'm bringing in a patient in a few minutes—a badly chewed-up frizzlic."

"Shall I call you a cab?" Val asked as the frizzlic whimpered in Jade's arms. Jade started to stroke it, and it caught her fingers in its teeth, chewing at them gently.

Jade shook her head. "Takes too long. I can run over there faster."

She looked at the Uzi she was still holding in her right hand. Hospitals usually took a dim view of people walking in with automatic weapons. Getting rid of it would let her hold the frizzlic better. Tossing the gun onto the bed, she cradled the frizzlic more securely in both arms and raced out the door.

The hospital was a source of frustration to Jade, as hospitals had always been. There was the filing of forms, the irrelevant information, and the waiting to see a doctor who meant well, but who freely confessed he'd never treated a frizzlic before. He checked the internal organs and said they all seemed to be functioning normally. He stopped the bleeding and sewed up the wounds, but admitted that was the least of the problem.

"The indigenous animal life is prey to many local infections," he explained. "These have little or no effect on the offworlders who come here, and we have specific cures for those they do affect. But we're shooting in the dark when it comes to curing the native species. All I can do is give you a range of general antibiotics that *should* have some effectiveness. If one does not work, try another."

The hospital refused to waste a bed on a dumb animal, but the doctor took some measure of pity and loaded Jade down with a wide assortment of pills, liquids, ointments, and creams, along with detailed instructions and warnings about the use of each. With the frizzlic wrapped in a hospital blanket and looking little better than when she'd first brought him in, Jade took a private cab back to her house.

"Drawer open, Val—any drawer."

Val slid open the deep ammo drawer closest to Jade's bed. Still holding the frizzlic in one hand, Jade tossed the boxes of ammo on the bed with her other. She called for fresh linens and, layering towels and sheets, quickly made a soft nest.

She laid the frizzlic inside the drawer. The animal whimpered as Jade turned away, and Jade hesitated, looking indecisively from the drawer to the pack of medicines she'd put down across the room. Uttering a loud "Motherfuck!" she flew across, scooped up the pack, and only then realized one of Val's remotes could have fetched it.

"Val, get me some tepid water, some bandages, and cotton batting, and turn on the heat in here—he needs it warmer."

Jade got the frizzlic to drink, but foods and the medications came right back up. She lost track of the number of towels and sheets she changed, the bandages cleaned and replaced. It felt as though a hot thin wire were laced through her shoulder muscles, and her body ached as though she were back in basic training. But every time she left its side the tiny animal began to whimper, and, unable to tolerate the sound, Jade remained next to it till it finally seemed to sort of sleep.

She stretched, headed into the bathroom, and climbed under the hot shower, watching the frizzlic through Val's monitors. There seemed to be no change. Once clean, she asked Val how the time was going. Val replied, ''You're due at Rix's in one hour.''

The job had totally slipped her mind in the anxiety. She was tempted to call in and tell Disson she couldn't make it—but she had missed so much time lately with Fastal's assignment, and several other arbiters had been off too, making the backup schedule nonexistent. She couldn't miss any more time without seriously disrupting the workload and possibly getting herself fired. She shuddered at the prospect of having to accept employment at Galentor's. At the same time, she knew she couldn't leave the frizzlic unattended, or she'd come home to a tiny corpse.

Cyclad Arik was off-duty today, so Jade called her—and encountered an unexpected problem. ''Yes, Jade Darcy, I am familiar with the indigenous life form given the common associational name 'frizzlic.' ''

''Could you help me out, then? One got wounded in front of my house.'' *Thank God, I'll even be on time.*

''I am, of course, indebted to you by a substantial amount, and expect to make restitution however I may. It is not, however, within my pattern of dining to eat scavenged food. If you require this creature to be disposed of, I—''

''No. I don't want it eaten, I'm trying to heal it. I need someone to nurse it for me while I work.''

The screen showed Cyclad bobbing, as she often did when confused. ''Then it is *your* dinner? Why not just trap a healthy one? I find a web and noose work well.''

''No, you see, it's . . . it's . . . hard to explain.''

''A religious imperative, perhaps? I could learn the ritual—''

"Never mind, I just realized what I can do," Jade lied. "I'll see you tomorrow."

"Goodbye then, Jade Darcy."

In her frustration Jade slapped the console to turn it off, and hit the credit-readout key instead. The last activity came up on the screen—the thousand-eu deposit from CafTech.

"Val," she said, "call Megan Cafferty. Maybe she knows what I can do."

Within minutes Megan's face lit up on the screen. "Jade? This is unexpected. I was just getting up. What can I do for you?"

"Megan, I . . . I . . ." The words were hard to say. Maybe she could find another approach. "What do you know about animals?"

Megan looked at her curiously. "Is this a trick question?"

"You see, there's this creature, a frizzlic, a little animal that lives wild around here, and sometimes I feed it, and it was attacked and now it's hurt, and I have to go to work, and I . . . I . . . I need your help." There, it was out at last.

"You have a pet," Megan said with a bemused smile. "I didn't know that."

"It's not a pet, it just comes around sometimes. But it's badly hurt and I have to be at work. Can you h-help?"

Megan gave her a warm, friendly smile that made her cheeks look even fuller than usual. "As a child, mother, and grandmother I have handled eight cats, three dogs, four horses, five hamsters, a boa constrictor, an iguana, a guinea pig, a parrot, four parakeets, and uncounted hordes of mice and schools of goldfish—not to mention all the children and grandchildren, the most expensive pets of all. I doubt this frizzlic of yours can throw me any curves I haven't seen before. When do you need me over there?"

"I have to leave in half an hour."

"I'll be right over. Where do you live?"

Jade hesitated. It hadn't occurred to her before that she would have to let Megan Cafferty into her home—and not only that, she'd have to leave Megan alone there for hours. She had very few visitors here, and she never let anyone in while she was away. Did she trust Megan Cafferty that much? *Could* she trust her that much?

The frizzlic woke up and began to whimper.

"Intersection of Tritian and 42," she said. "Area 396, building four."

"I'll see you shortly," Megan promised. "Hold on."

Jade dressed and ate absently, while her mind raced in circles on other tracks. She had actually invited Megan Cafferty, another human, a human who knew she was a carc, into her house, where she could pry into the rest of Jade's most intimate secrets. She felt like a virgin on her wedding night, about to be violated in ways she could not foresee, dreading it yet bowing to the inevitable.

It was with horrid relief that she finally let Megan in. The older woman entered and nearly tripped as she encountered the stronger gravitational field inside. "A bit heavier than I'm used to," she said.

"I like it at one point one gees," Jade said. "Keeps the muscles in tone."

Megan made no immediate reply. She dropped her red-silk-lined black cape over a chair, looked quickly around the room, and said, "It's you, all right. Very spartan. That must be your frizzlic."

"Not *my* frizzlic, just . . . well, never mind. That's your patient. Here are the medications the doctor gave me, and all the instructions. I have to leave now. I've instructed Val, my computer, to give you anything you need for yourself or the frizzlic."

"Then I'll be fine. Go on to work. Your frizzlic couldn't be in better hands."

"It's not my goddamn frizzlic!" Jade shouted as she hurried from the door.

If her previous shift at work had been foggy, this one was positively opaque. A riot could have broken out at the table beside her and she would scarcely have moved except to get out of its way. Regular patrons who greeted her either were ignored or received absentminded salutations. Jade's thoughts were kilometers away, with a quivering little lump of flesh lying on a blanket in a drawer of her house; and when she wasn't thinking about the frizzlic, she was wondering whether Megan Cafferty was snooping through her home or asking Val personal questions, trying to dig into the secrets of Jade's past.

At every break she called home for status reports, only to be told that things were about the same. If the frizzlic was not improving, at least its condition wasn't deteriorating, either. Still, Jade fretted. She was lucky enough to have a quiet shift again; she could not have survived an active one.

After work she raced home, grateful the schedule had her off for the next several days. She entered the door to find Megan sitting on the floor, feeding the frizzlic some grayish liquid with a small spoon.

The older woman was looking like a slightly weary grandmother as she sat in one of Jade's chairs holding the frizzlic in her lap and stroking it tenderly. The frizzlic actually turned its head as Jade entered the room.

"I think we've passed the crisis point," Megan said in tired triumph. "He's still a sick little baby, but he's holding down water, food, and medication. If the antibiotics don't kill him now, I think he stands a chance."

"I tried holding him and feeding him, and he only seemed to get worse. What did you do that was special?"

"I don't know if it was special," Megan said, "but I sang to him."

"Sang?"

"Music hath charms, you know. But you'll have to take over in that department now, my throat's giving out. I'm out of practice, I'm afraid."

"I—I don't sing."

"Nonsense. Everyone sings. Some just do it better than others."

"I don't know any good songs."

"You mean to tell me you've lived, what, twenty-five years without learning any songs? I can't believe that."

Jade searched her memory. She remembered some anthems and marches and barracks ballads, none of which seemed appropriate to the situation. "There was one old lullaby my mother used to sing to me. I believe it was called 'Nothing's Gonna Harm You'—that's the first line, at least."

Megan smiled. "I know it. It's beautiful, though I never thought of it as a lullaby. Believe it or not, it's originally from a rather grisly opera. Your mother has great taste in the classics. Go ahead, sing it."

With a thin, shaky voice Jade started crooning the old melody, very self-conscious in front of a trained singer like Megan. Her voice picked up strength as she went along, though she had to hum in a few spots where she forgot the words. It had been so long since she'd ever thought of the song, yet the tender, nurturing of its lyrics came back quickly to her mind. When she finished, the whole room seemed warmer, and silence descended for a moment.

"Good enough to heal a frizzlic," Megan finally said, "but I wouldn't suggest quitting your job just yet." She took a closer look at Jade as she took up the sleeping bundle of fur. "If you don't mind my saying so, you look terrible. How long has it been since you slept?"

Jade did a quick calculation and suddenly realized she'd been up for almost thirty consecutive hours. "Honey, you need some rest yourself," Megan told her firmly. "If there's one thing I've learned, it's that you can't pour healing energy into anything if you haven't got the energy yourself in the first place. I'll be fine for another few hours. You go get some sleep. Is your bed in the next room? Your computer wouldn't open that door for me."

So, she had been snooping. Jade felt a sudden chill as her fears were confirmed. "Why were you trying to get in there?"

"I went to use your lav, and the door was right in front of me as I came out. I was just curious to see what your bedroom was like, that's all."

"It's not my bedroom, it's just . . . well, personal. I sleep out here."

Megan looked around. "Where?"

"Val converts the table into a bed."

"Doesn't look very comfortable."

"It's okay for me."

Megan shrugged. "If you want to sleep there for a few hours while I tend the frizzlic, that'll be fine."

Jade hesitated, but before she could make a decision, Val interrupted with another call. "Jade, urgent message coming in."

Jade immediately tensed. "Who's it from?"

"Someone named Cord du Dassenji. I have no record of her in my memory.

The name sounded vaguely familiar, but it took Jade a few seconds to place it. Cord du Dassenji was the Lemmant who worked in the kitchen at the ingesterie. With a feeling of horrible premonition, Jade said, "Put the call through, Val."

A moment later the Lemmant's features filled the screen. "Greetings, Arbiter Darcy. I have most tragic news for you. The young man Fastal ip Fornen—do you remember, the one who caused the trouble at the ingesterie several weeks ago?—this fellow is dead, murdered."

Jade's fists clenched so tightly the knuckles turned white. "Oh?" was all she said.

"The health authorities called me when they found the body because I am the only other Lemmant currently residing on Cablans, so they thought I would know best what to do for him. They said he was murdered, probably by Commancors. They refused to let me see the body, because he had been tortured, but they said he had been beaten and nearly every bone was broken and his skin . . . his skin . . ."

"No need to go into detail," Jade said quietly. "I know what Commancors can do to bodies."

Cord du Dassenji took a few moments to regain her composure before she could continue. "I know vaguely of his family; Fornen is one of the minor noble houses. I am making arrangements to have his body shipped back to Lemmanta later today; the Greest actually agreed to do it for no charge. The pyre should be attended by important people."

"What . . . ?" Jade had to clear her throat before she could continue. "What made you think I was interested in any of this?"

"I was allowed to go into his apartment to prepare his effects. He did not have many possessions, but your name appeared prominently in his notes, so I thought I would call you. Did you know him?"

When Jade did not reply, but just continued to stare at the screen, Cord du Dassenji said, "Well, I have many preparations yet to make. I am very sorry to have disturbed you with such unpleasant news." She signed off, leaving Jade staring blankly at the empty screen.

From behind her where she'd been putting the frizzlic to bed, Megan said quietly, "A friend of yours?"

"No!" Jade whirled angrily, her face flushed and her jaw set. "A client, nothing more—a particularly stupid client who wouldn't listen to sensible advice. The world is well rid of him."

"I see," Megan said as quietly as before. "That's why you're so happy now."

Jade rushed up to her and grabbed her by the shoulders. "What the fuck do you know about it?" she yelled. "What the fuck do you know about anything? Damn it, I should kill you now, should have killed you the other night."

Megan looked straight into Jade's eyes and refused to back away even a step. "Why would you do a damn fool thing like that?"

"You know! You know I'm a carc." As though the admission had somehow freed her limbs, Jade let go of the other's shoulders and began to pace about the room, always watching Megan.

In a very quiet voice Megan slowly said, "Why should that . . . you weren't wanted for something?"

Jade stopped suddenly.

"That's it, or close enough. Isn't it?" Megan continued. "There's someone, or something, after a lone young female carc, and if I spread word of your presence, you'll be in some kind of trouble."

Jade's continued silence prompted Megan to push. "Is that it? You're hiding from something?"

"That's close enough, Cafferty. After seven years I can't afford a leak—not this time, not now."

"Well, killing me isn't smart or easy." Megan's hand was suddenly full of the small needle gun she'd shown Jade at their first meeting. Jade had hers in place just as fast. For a long moment they stood, face-to-face, and neither moved or spoke.

"Jade, killing me will bring the forces of CafTech, and of the government officials who depend on my campaign contributions, onto this backwater so fast even you couldn't hide from them for long. It wouldn't take them much effort to figure who was missing, and who she was. You'd lose exactly what you're trying to keep, this hole in the shadow. The spotlight that would glare on Cablans would find you. If you don't kill me, we might still work out a deal for your safety. You're a businesswoman, just like I am. Shall we negotiate?"

"What the hell can you offer me? Promises? Sweetness and light? It's my life you're negotiating. My fucking life, not some damn leaves."

"It's *our* lives. If you're in danger, I'm dead. Right?" Jade nodded. "Now we know the stakes. Let me see if I understand the starting positions."

Megan shifted her weapon slightly, and Jade dove behind her table. When Jade peeked around the edge, after aiming at Megan, she saw Megan's pistol still aimed at her. Megan continued.

"You need to be assured that I will keep your identity as a carc hidden—and your name I assume"—Jade lifted up slightly so Megan could see her nod—"so that no human, or at least no one from a Terran-allied planet, becomes aware of it. You need the kind of jobs I can offer you, but your safety comes first. The only way you can let me leave here tonight is if I can give you a guarantee you can believe that I will keep your secret."

"And you, Cafferty, have every reason to lie to me to get out of here and then blow the whistle on me."

"That, I think, is the first point we need to discuss. Of course I'll lie to save my life, but only when the truth won't work. In this case, I shouldn't need to lie. I have every reason to get out of here alive, but no real reason to blow the whistle on you. I'm not even a hundred percent sure where the whistle should be aimed, and I don't need to know. The less I know about that part of your past, the safer I'll be, right? Right." Megan took a slow, deep breath.

"Point one: I've never heard of a carc being wanted for any crime, but I could have missed it. The point is, I don't believe you did anything that I would feel honor bound to turn you in for: treason, terrorism, child killing. It wasn't anything like that, right? OK. Then, point two: anything that long in the past isn't relevent to what we are, here and now. I don't ask every contractor for a life history, just references on her work. Your work is fine so far, and your recommendations are good. That's all I need to know. Your past is your business. As long as it doesn't threaten me or my business, I don't give a flying fuck about it."

Jade looked startled at the obscenity, and Megan said, "Marines aren't the only people who cuss. Wait till you inspect a few space construction sites some time." Her smile didn't appear to have an impact on Jade, and it quickly faded.

"Point three: you are useful to me. You've help me earn several million eus already with this deal, and can probably help me earn more. There is no one else available to me, that I know of, who can provide me with these services. Here on Cablans you have a monopoly on the informed, bright, respected human consultant market. *Turning you in is cutting my own throat!*"

Jade jumped at the sudden bellow, then held up her free hand and spoke. "So far that makes sense. But all that applied before now. Before these." Jade raised her pistols lightly, then returned her aim to Megan's midriff. Megan's gun hand hadn't wavered. "You now have plenty of reason to remove a threat to you."

"Jade, there's even more reason for me to remove the threat and maintain the business associate. I can't promise to forget what I know. I can promise to keep

it secret. So far I haven't told your name to anyone
back home, and there hasn't been time to mention
you're a carc. I'll keep it that way. You can be carried
on the books as a secret informant and industrial spy.
We've got dozens in one division or another—it won't
look odd. Everyone here knows your name, and if it
hasn't caused comment in all these years, it shouldn't
now. I won't help the process.

"I can't promise I won't ever reveal you, but I will
promise this: I will not investigate you on Earth or
elsewhere, or mention you by name or description off
this planet, or discuss you with anyone else who may
come here who might even remotely carry the information back, as long as you don't betray me, or my
company, or any family or employee of mine. As long
as you play straight with me, do right by me, I will
pay you a fair amount for your work, and will ignore
what isn't my business. I hope someday you will tell
me what this all about, but I won't demand it. Is that
a deal?"

"Let me think a moment." Jade stood up slowly
and sat on the bench. Her pistol was still pointed in
Megan's direction, but was no longer aimed directly
at her belly. Megan stepped back to the chair she'd sat
in while nursing the frizzlic, turned it around to face
Jade, and sat down. For several minutes silence
reigned, broken only by the rasp of a snoring frizzlic.

Damn, she's right about the danger of her death,
Jade thought. *I realized that myself, but how the hell
can I trust her, of all people. She's too sharp and too
well connected. So she hasn't betrayed me yet, big
deal; the silence from Lorpet's spies told me that. The
K'luune run the bloody fax system; they can still monitor all her outside communications, so that flank would
be covered, at least here. Her rep for honesty is good,
but that could be just P.R. bullshit. She pays well,
though. This week, this job, added more to my accounts than three, four, nearly six months of savings.
But if she opens her mouth. I'm dead.*

*Wait, as long as she's here I'd still have those four
days. Lorpet's too greedy not to go for the bonus I
offered; he won't let mention of my name, or any de-*

scription of me, go unnoticed—and I doubt she has a code for this except a rescue code, and none of the data brokers will let forty-eight hours go before they tell me about another human—not if I offer a reward on it. Hell, I'll have to sift through reports on every humanoid that comes in.

"Cafferty, you want me to believe you'll ignore my little medical abnormality, keep my identity hidden even from your people at CafTech, and if you decide anything else will warn me first, because you think I'm too valuable to the company."

Megan smiled with half her mouth, a very cynical expression on her usually grandmotherly face. "Yes, you're important to the business. If that's all you want to see. Also I truly believe your long dead past is none of my business. It's your history from the day we met until now that matters. I don't have the time to waste on all my colleagues' peccadillos. If you hadn't pulled this stunt tonight, I might never have thought to mention your identity to anyone, perhaps for years. I certainly would never have investigated you beyond the inquiry I made here."

She makes sense, she may mean it. I need the money, and there is Lorpet and all his kin. As long as she's on Cablans, I might at least make it safe enough to build up a better bank account at her expense before I have to move on her. She'll pay for a lot longer run than I could make before. I still would feel safer with her dead, but she's right about the mess that would make. Fuck it all, the bitch could be right and I may be safer with her alive. At least while she's here where I can watch her.

The sound of an incoming call pulled Jade from her thoughts, so suddenly she turned her gun for a second on the speaker. With blurring speed she covered Megan again, to discover that Megan had made the same move but not quite recovered. In the split second of hesitation before Jade could decide to fire, Megan looked at Jade, and very slowly returned her weapon to her purse.

A bewildered Jade called out, "Val, who is it?"

"It's Lorpet, Jade."

The bitch has turned me in already, that's what this whole farce is about. Let her see this, so she'll know what a stupid thing she did, trusting her charm to buy her out of her mess. "Put it on both screens, Val."

Jade and Megan could both see the sluglike K'luune as he began his usual prolonged abasement. "Most gracious and respected Jade Darcy. This unworthy creature regrets this intrusion into your vitally important time by one with so little value and of such—"

"Cut the crap, what is it?" *That will cost me, but who's got time for his shit now?*

After a few extra blinks Lorpet said, "It has come to this one's imperfect attention that the being you so recently traveled with on some certainly monumental purpose has met his demise at the hands of the Commancors. It was this inadequate person's thought that the illustrious Ms. Darcy would want this known. I'm certain the details of such a death are beneath your interest, but this—"

"Lorpet, for once you're right. Cut it, Val." Before she was done speaking, the connection was broken.

The image of Fastal swimming beside her in the river on Haldek filled Jade's mind, overlaid with that of his mutilated body lying in a gutter. A snort from the frizzlic made the image fade, but not disappear, and made Jade aware of the weapon she still pointed toward the unarmed Megan. *Hell, if I can't handle an unarmed civilian. . . .* Jade put her own weapon in her pocket holster.

"Why don't you tell me about it?" Megan asked quietly.

I've come close to killing you not five minutes ago, lady, and you sound like you really care. You are strange, Jade thought, even as her body responded to Megan's gentle, caring manner. She found herself sitting across from Megan telling of the adventure on Haldek, the subsequent Commancor threats, and her encounter with Fastal—and she found herself unable to present Fastal's views on honor with the scorn she felt. The conversation came out sounding more balanced than she really remembered it. The older woman listened without comment, but her eyes never left

Jade's face, as though searching each word for hidden meanings.

"If this was such a suicidal mission," she said when Jade ended her tale, "why did you agree to it in the first place?"

Jade took a deep breath, wondering what to say. She didn't want to tell Megan she'd panicked at her arrival. That would make her sound weak. So Jade gave her what she wanted to believe was the secondary reason.

"I was born and grew up on Toranawa," she said.

It took a second as Megan did the mental calculation. Then she reacted with shock. "But that was . . . you must have been just a kid."

"I was thirteen," Jade said. "Old enough to escape with my male relatives into the jungles and serve with the freedom fighters when the Commancors came. I spent two years as a guerrilla, learning hit-and-run tactics. Then the commandos made their famous raid and rescued me, taking me back to Earth. That was when I decided to be a carc. I had to wait three years as a ward of the court, completing my education, before they let me enlist. Then, by the time I went through basic, had the operations, and finished the Special Training, the war with the Commancors was over and I wasn't allowed to fight them. I couldn't punish them for what they did to my world and my family."

"So you saw this as a chance to get back at them at last."

"It was a business deal. That made it attractive, but I wasn't going to kill myself for revenge. I've spent too much effort trying to stay alive. I did everything right. Fastal's the one who screwed it up, leaving his knife back there—nearly killed us both. I did everything I agreed to do. I didn't owe him anything more."

Megan sat silently for several seconds, still staring at her. Finally she spoke. "Jade, if you won't listen to anyone on moral grounds about the subject of honor, maybe I can find another way. You pride yourself on being an independent businesswoman. I've had some success in that area myself. Let me speak to you as one businesswoman to another. You can't build a business just by doing minimal effort. Living up to the terms of your contracts is necessary, but not sufficient. If you won't give that little bit extra, you'll lose out to your competitors who will.

"Take our agreement. There was nothing in there about my tending sick frizzlics. Even if you won't accept the fact that I did it out of friendship, think of it as a business investment. I'm investing extra time and energy in you now. Maybe nothing will ever come of it, but maybe you'll decide you like doing business with me, and you'll work a little harder next time. No one ever got ahead by doing *only* what he had to. No one. That I guarantee you."

"I did more than I had to. I gave him lots of advice, which he ignored. I warned him the Commancors were looking for him; I didn't have to do that."

"Do you expect applause?"

"I expect not to get dumped on. *He* was the one who left his dagger with the body, knowing it could be traced back to him. What happened was the direct result of his action, his deliberate choice. I am not responsible for his stupidity."

Megan sighed. "Early in my career I worked as an office manager. One of the men working under me was an alcoholic. I knew it, but the drinking didn't affect his job too badly, so I figured it was his business. Our company had an alcoholism-recovery program; I made sure he knew about it by the subtle method of leaving the brochures on his desk every month. He didn't take advantage of it, but that wasn't my problem. If he wanted to poison himself and ruin his liver, why should I stop him? He was an adult with free will, right?

"One day he didn't come in to work. I figured he was hungover again and didn't think too much of it. About midday, his wife called. He'd been drinking the night before, then had gone out driving and crashed the car. It killed him. I didn't shed many tears for him—but I did cry for the three innocent people in the car he hit, who were also killed.

"If I had taken some action earlier, if I had *made* it my responsibility to straighten it out, those people might have lived. No, I didn't kill them. No court would ever convict me. But I sure as hell didn't help them any, did I? There were steps I could have taken, pressures I could have applied, to push him into that program. Maybe it wouldn't have worked and the crash would have happened anyway. But at least I would know I had tried.

"We're responsible to all the young, and the good, and the right in our midst. If we wrongly hurt them, we must correct it. If we know they've suffered, we must try to prevent a further wrong. That's our duty to the world around us and the world yet to evolve."

She paused for breath, then continued, "What kind of contract did you have with the frizzlic?"

The question caught Jade by surprise. "Huh?"

"Did you and the frizzlic make a deal—he would be funny and adorable if you would feed him and take care of him? Of course not. You had no responsibility to him whatsoever. Yet here you've spent money, time, and energy to keep him going when you could easily have walked away and been freed of this nuisance who's always pestering you for food. Sometimes responsibilities come on you without your asking for them, without your wanting them. It's part of being human, Jade. You take the good and pour yourself into it. If you have honor, faith, goodness, you will fill it and it will fill you. You're part of a larger system, and your own selfish considerations aren't the only ones that matter.

"Whether it was something you wanted for your life or not, you took on the responsibility of caring for this frizzlic. Fastal was another intelligent being, someone who'd been through a tough ordeal with you. Don't you think you owed him the same consideration you'd give a frizzlic?"

Jade shook her head. "I did nothing wrong."

"You did damn little right."

"Who gave you the right to judge me?"

"Nobody—but then, I'm not the jury you're pleading before. Val, I need a mirror."

The wall screen obligingly turned reflective.

"There's the court you have to convince," Megan

said. "Tell *her* how innocent you are. Tell *her* you're not responsible for Fastal's death. Tell *her* you did everything you could."

Jade tried to look away, but Megan refused to let her. Relentlessly she pointed at and watched the mirror. As though by a giant's hand, Jade's head was forced to turn and look at herself for long silent moments.

"There's the woman who controls your fate," Megan said. "Plead for *her* mercy. If you're lucky, she may give you only a light sentence."

Jade heard again Fastal's voice telling her family stories, talking to her of honor. She stared into the mirror at the gaunt face, at the dark eyes staring vindictively back at her. That wasn't her reflection standing next to Megan's, but that of some stranger, some woman who hated her and all she did, a woman with no mercy in her heart, no tolerance for error, no compassion. Plead with her? What was the use? She could just as soon drink a boulder. She held to that cold thought, and remembered making that bargain with her soul when she fled the remnants of her family to wind up here. Jade renewed the promise of isolation she'd made herself and accepted that as a soldier's lot. With a sense of loss but some faint stirring of pride Jade lifted her chin and turned to reply to Megan.

That motion of her head brought into view the knife, the jeweled dagger Fastal had given her, lying innocently on top of the bureau. Suddenly, for Jade, the room was filled with the sound of screams—the throat-rending screams of a young girl being tortured; of her genitalia being stripped away in pain before she ever learned the pleasure of them; of her skin, unwrinkled and unscarred, being scraped off her; of all the screams the civilian child had made because she refused to talk, and so had saved that silly Haldek merchant and all the other rebels from the Commancors—had saved the lives of strangers and comrades.

And as Megan stood silently by, there were other screams, too. Screams from her brothers and her uncle; screams from long-dead comrades on Toranawa; even screams she'd never heard from Miclavra as he died at the hands of some nameless Commancor. All those screams that mind and memory had blocked from her ears spoke to her clearly from the jeweled dagger.

And echoing through the screams in Jade's mind, reinforced by fatigue and the emotional pressure of the moment, was her father's voice, talking to her about loyalty to comrades and the importance of the cause above the individual. *"Liberté, egalité, fraternité. But above all, fraternité.* This is the concept on which justice is based. Without it, you are only trash. And we are not trash—we are d'Orsai."

And the strange Jade in the mirror scowled at her unforgivingly.

"No!" Jade screamed, falling to her knees, eyes averted from the mirror. "I won't look."

"You don't have to," Megan said more softly, kneeling beside Jade on the floor and putting her arms around her shoulders. "You already know what your judge looks like."

Jade pulled away from this offer of comfort. "Don't. I haven't earned your sympathy. What I did—no, what I didn't do wasn't right, it wasn't d'Or . . . it wasn't Darcy."

Megan patiently rewrapped her arms around the trembling mercenary. In her lowest, gentlest voice she said, "This is one of the lessons I learned all those years ago. Sins of omission require a very special pardon, usually the hardest to get. Mine cost me several thousand dollars and a year in analysis, and it's still more a probation than a full pardon. But I can look my judge in the eyes every day without flinching, now. That's a major triumph."

Jade held still in Megan's arms for several minutes. Then, slowly, she leaned away and looked into Megan's face. "In the alley, the Commancors told me I'd acted beyond reproach. I should have known it right then. When a Commancor compliments you, you must be doing something wrong."

She sat up straighter, cross-legged on the floor, her breathing even once more. "I received my sentence. I know what I have to do. I'll take your deal for now.

When you decide what to do about me, what you know about me, tell me. Meanwhile, can you take care of the frizzlic for me, possibly—no, *probably* forever?''

''I let myself in for that one, didn't I?'' Megan said. ''All right, yes, I can take on that kind of responsibility.''

''Good,'' said Jade. ''Take him with you now, please. I've got a funeral to attend.''

CHAPTER 14

Funerary Rights

Jade spent the next two days putting her affairs in order, making a new will, and trying to plan what to do if she got back to Cablans from Lemmanta. She chafed at this time of inaction once she'd decided what she had to do, but she didn't want to arrive on Lemmanta too early for the funeral.

Now, the time for action having finally arrived, Jade stopped across the street from the Pale House to get a quick meal. As she consumed the ersatz burrito, she reviewed what Val had told her about Lemmantine funeral rites.

"Funerals are of extreme importance on Lemmanta. They signal major changes in status within the family, and possibly for the family within the community. Participation within the funeral itself is not open to the general public, or even the entire network of friends. There are precisely 241 relatives, honored guests, and friends allowed. No more or less. The rites take two days, ending at a feast before the funeral pyre at which everyone speaks.

"Most speeches are short, two to three minutes, but the major speeches, particularly that of the one asked to light the pyre, may take hours. The honor of lighting the pyre is often given to the highest-ranking visitor, rather than the closest relative, although in some cases that may vary. After the last speech, the pyre is lighted, and all disperse except for three witnesses who remain to feed the flames until only fine ash is left. Then they sweep up a token amount and place it within a special chamber at the family home. There, mingled with those of the ancestors, it is said the spirit rests and adds strength to the home and family.

"In the case of the poor—"

"Val, what happens if there is a dishonorable death?"

"The body is buried, and when decayed, usually at fifty years or so, the area is dug up. The soil is burned to remove the taint, and then scattered."

"That's enough."

Jade rose, leaving half her meal, and walked across to the Pale House. At the entry she stepped up to the screen and demanded immediate transfer to Lemmanta. The travelers, teamsters, and merchants waiting laughed at her, until the announcement came.

"Jade Darcy, proceed to door three for immediate transfer to Lemmanta. The trip will be our gift."

In the stunned silence of the crowd, she strode like a commander on a parade ground. The door opened as she approached, and closed after her. Before she could reach the other side, the lurch of transfer occurred. The other door opened immediately.

Jade had asked Cord du Dassenji about the funeral, and received the time and place. Since Fastal was of a noble family, the funeral was in the capital, the same city as the transfer station. The funeral had started the day before, and Jade figured the banquet would begin soon. She was almost right.

The cab took her to the large hall reserved for such events, and the driver told her he'd wait for her to come back, because they wouldn't let her in. "This is a big one. I am surprised, because Fornen is only low-ranked nobility. But this had to do with Haldek, so all the Council of Families is here, the speeches are going out on the radio, and—"

"Shut up. I'll get in." Jade overpaid the cabbie, who waited anyway, and sailed down the ramp to the door, ignoring the crowds waiting on either side of the ramp and listening to the speeches by loudspeaker. A pair of large men stood in front of the door. As she approached they stood straighter.

"I'm sorry, but there is a service today," one said. "No one is admitted."

"Oh, really?" said Jade as she took out his kneecap and straight-armed his partner in the genitalia hard enough to break the light protective cup he wore. She opened the door and walked in.

The hall was larger than Rix's, an immense gray oval with six-meter-high ceilings at the door that soared to fifty meters before the pyre. The room had concentric ovals of tables that were filled with people in a rainbow of colors, sashes, crests, and head-dresses. In front of the pyre was a podium, and at it an elderly Lemmant with yellowed hair and wrinkled deep-blue skin was holding forth about the importance of youthful training in the arts of civilization. He stopped as Jade walked forward, jumped onto the first table, leaped from there to the second, and marched, as if on a parade ground, to the dais.

As she approached she saw the pyre. Clothed in all the finest garb, the body didn't look like Fastal. Jade knew the pieces had to be stuffed inside the clothes. There was a wax mask of his face obviously taken from an old photograph, for it looked more like the little kids seated in front of her than the Fastal she knew. As she came to the dais she saw two daggers stuck in the podium. One she recognized as Fastal's; she'd heard that it had been left in the body. The other she didn't know.

"By what right do you dishonor this proceeding?" harrumphed the man who had been speaking.

Jade pulled forth the dagger Fastal had given her and thrust it deep into the scarred wood that formed the top of the stand. She then pulled out the other knives. One she flipped to the table. The people seated at it started to move away, but before they could more than stir the knife was pinned to the table top, quivering as though in response to the emotions in the room. Fastal's own knife she held in fighting position as she turned to the speaker.

"There can be no honor in this place as long as it's filled with Lemmants," began Jade. The audience were not wearing u-transes, but the computer system that broadcast the speeches translated Jade's words for them. The room filled with murmuring, and several people began to rise. "I went to Haldek with Fastal ip Fornen. He taught me of honor. That's how I know there can be none in this room."

Jade stared at the old man. He met her eyes, then signaled to the rest to be seated.

"I shall wait outside," he said. "Then the number will be correct." The hall was silent. Many showed shock as the dignified man retrieved his knife, saluted Fastal's pyre, and walked out of the room.

Jade took the time to let her nerves settle, and carefully placed Fastal's blade back in the stand. She took a deep breath, and realized she hadn't come here to pick a fight with the whole planet—not really. There was, however, a duty she had to perform. She stepped to one side of the podium and, though it made her spine tingle and itch to turn her back on so large and hostile a crowd, she faced the ruin that had been Fastal, her employer, and spoke to him.

"You were right. There is something you own beyond the body, above survival. I still don't know if I'd call it honor. At least it wouldn't be honor the way you meant it. You seemed to think there was some great principle, some measuring glass that all creatures' souls were poured into, and if they had honor, they would fill it, and if not, they were as no thing and seen no more.

"I'm not sure about that, but you were right about what we owe each other, and I owed you better than this."

Jade took her hand from her side and touched the dagger Fastal had given her the night before they moved to the cave.

"When you gave me this, you said I reminded you of your sister. Your sister who had withstood Commancor torture without giving away—that's right, you don't know the phrase—without betraying her friends. I turned away and cursed the dust we'd stirred up finding it. Now I tell you, I am proud of this gift. It is a gift filled with honor. It is the blade of the girl of the only family on this planet who knew what honor was.

"You knew. You didn't know how to use it, or how to ignore it. You only knew that when a great wrong is done a people, it must be avenged. And not avenged on innocents—that is why you had me disarm instead of kill the sentries—but on those that committed the wrong.

"Here and now I understand, I understand what you tried to tell me then that I couldn't hear. That such wrongs cannot be allowed to stand. That when innocents are slaughtered and tortured as you wouldn't a dumb beast, when people are torn from all that they love for the greed of a few, when children and old people, babes and friends, are slaughtered and no one stops the killers, no one removes from them the power to kill again, then those innocent lives are truly lost. And lost again with each breath the murderer takes from that day forward.

"Those lives can never be regained, but they can be put to rest when people of honor retake the things that were lost, stop the beasts from their rampages, and send aloft in letters of flame and blood the message that here, now, and from this day until all time has passed, this shall be a place ruled by honor, not strength, and where beasts shall roam no more.

"Where you were wrong, Fastal, was in believing your people were people of honor. For they stood and watched the beast ravage your family, and they cowered. They hid and told the beast that it was proper for him to torture, and maim, and cheat, as long as it was others. As long as the beast troubled only the distant, and not them.

"You thought they were different than me."

Jade turned and looked at the still silent faces around the room.

"They weren't. I knew you would die, and I hid. I knew the Commancors would strip your skin from you with astringent-coated knives so you couldn't bleed to death too soon, and I turned away. I knew that each bone would be broken in your body, that your genitals would be burned off with caustic one lobe at a time, that not till the last would they burst your eyes with their thumbs—not until they had shown you your mutilated body in their mirror. I knew this and I did not even give you a way to die quickly and cheat their torture.

"I was no better than these who claim to mourn you. But for one thing. They raised you to believe in honor. They told you that such a thing shouldn't be, that they would never allow such a deed to happen if there was breath and means to try to stop it, even if the trying only caused their own death. For to do so was dishonorable, and they were honorable people.

"In this I was better. I didn't lie to you.

"They will make speeches to you today. They may weep over you. They will go on leaving Haldek, and your family, and your death, unavenged.

"For these are not honorable people, They are ones who would play with the words, and deny the reality."

Jade reached into her right hip pocket and drew forth a small one-shot, high-energy laser. Aiming at the piles of oil-soaked kindling at the base, she fired, and the pyre roared into flame.

"At least an honest woman, who learned too late that honor was worth all you said, will be the one to perform this last duty for you. You deserve better, but I am the best one here."

Jade removed the knives from the podium and threw Fastal's onto the pyre. "No one shall ever dishonor your blade. No coward shall carry it." She put her own into the scabbard and walked slowly from the hall, waiting for the challenge she was sure would come. Eyes followed her as she walked—silent eyes, accusing eyes.

The stillness was finally broken by the sound of her opening the door. She stepped out and saw the two door guards had been taken away. At the curb, the old man she had replaced on the podium stood next to the open cab door. Jade got in, and mumbled, "The transfer station, please."

The radio hissed and crackled the sounds of the pyre. There were no other sounds from it during the trip. Jade put the fare on the seat next to the driver, who hadn't bothered to turn around once, and walked to the door of the transfer room she had left.

Only later did she wonder that it was open and empty. She walked to the other side, and exited back on Cablans, where it was the same day. Only as she sat in the cab on her way back home did she realize tears were streaming down her cheeks—as they had been since she lit the pyre.

CHAPTER 15

Jade's War

Jade returned home with adrenaline still pumping through her system. She couldn't afford to lose that edge of anger; it would have to carry her through some unpleasant tasks. The first item on her list was to call the ingesterie and hand in her resignation. The odds against her returning to work there were so enormous that it wouldn't be fair to leave them hanging.

Her call came in at one of the rare times when Disson Peng-Amur was in repose—"vegetating," as Kokoti often referred to it. Cyclad Arik answered the call and spoke to Jade. She was shocked to hear of Jade's resignation. "Is it that you are transferring your habitation to some world other than Cablans?" she asked.

"Not exactly," Jade said. She still felt awkward talking to the large mantisoid. "It's just that I'm going somewhere and I don't . . . I don't think I'll be able to return."

Cyclad Arik cocked her head at a strange angle. "Is it that you will not be given permission to return, or that you will not be physically capable of returning?"

"If I come back at all, it'll probably be in a box," Jade growled.

"I believe I comprehend," said Cyclad. Then, after a long pause, she added, "Is it both permissible and possible for another being to accompany you upon this venture?"

"What do you mean?"

"I interpolate the meaning in your statements to

represent the potential of great peril on your undertaking. I am meanwhile indebted to your actions of several weeks ago to the preservation of my life. It is my desideration that my companionship and assistance in your undertaking may enable you to emerge successfully on the other side of the action without the necessity of your immediate demise, thereby exhibiting to you the gratitude I possess which is so otherwise impossible to express through mere verbal communication.''

"But this is a suicide mission.''

"Perhaps my presence within the nexus of events will obviate the need for your untimely extinguishment.''

"Another person won't make any difference, except we'll both die instead of just me.''

"Argument is pointless, Jade Darcy. My mentality is irretrievably committed to this proposition. As I am presupposing that your venture will occur on some planet other than the one which we are now occupying, I shall betake myself with due haste to the transfer station, there to foregather with you in preparation for our departure. May the fortune of Favorable Endeavors accompany our ambulations.'' And the screen switched off before Jade could protest further.

Jade could only stare at the blank screen, dumbfounded. Cyclad Arik was willing to accompany her into certain death. Not only willing, but insistent. Someone was prepared to lay down her life for Jade—a concept as alien to her as the mantisoid herself.

"I was never very friendly to her,'' she muttered. "I hardly spoke, except for business. I saved her life, but big deal, that was part of my job. Why would she risk her life for me? What's in it for her?'' The darkened screen, though, would not answer any of her questions.

Her next call was to the transfer station, where she got the voice of the usual computerized dispatcher. "I want passage for two beings, Cyclad Arik and Jade Darcy, to Haldek,'' she said.

"What is the purpose of the visit?''

"Death and destruction." *Why lie to the blood-thirsty four-dimensional SOB?"*

"One moment." Jade was sure that Greest was deciding on such an unusual request personally, and she was prepared to do battle even with him if necessary to gain passage.

The computer came back on line. "Round-trip fare has been set at the rate of one energy unit per passenger."

For the second time in five minutes, Jade found herself staring at the screen. She'd been prepared to empty her entire bank account if needed to finance the trip. Starting a war was seldom a cheap proposition.

You transparent bastard, she thought at the Greest. *If I didn't need you right now, I'd really show you what I think of your fucking "patterns."*

But there was still more to do and very little time to do it. Going into the next room she opened up her arsenal and studied the wide array of weapons at her disposal. She strapped on several belts, bandoliers, and holsters of different sizes. She packed more grenades and flares into the pockets of her clothes, and slid her arm through the shoulder strap of a minibazooka. She tried to envision the sort of weapons a praying mantis could handle, and failed utterly, so she packed an assortment of spares in a duffel bag and took it with her.

Plagued by the strange feeling she was forgetting something, she scanned the room until she saw the dagger Fastal had given her, the one that belonged to his sister. She had set it down on the countertop when she came in, before making her calls. If anything symbolized her mission, it was that. Picking it up, she tucked the scabbard inside her belt, its jeweled and carved handle standing up proudly next to her guns. *Now* she was ready to go.

She stopped at the doorway and took one long last look around the room. "I probably won't make it back, Val. You know what to do."

"The instructions are all in order." There was, of course, no hint of emotion in the computer's voice.

Jade tried to find words of goodbye for the one true

companion she'd had these last few years, but it was impossible. *Doesn't matter anyway,* she thought. *It's just a computer.* She left the house without another word, and the door slid silently shut behind her.

Jade met Cyclad Arik outside the transfer station, and the two were quickly ushered into the transfer chamber that would take them to Haldek. Barely were they inside when the floor gave the familiar lurch signaling their journey had begun.

Jade stared across at Cyclad. She wanted desperately to ask her why she was coming along on this fool's mission, but she didn't want to listen to the speech Cyclad would give her. There'd been enough speeches in the past few days.

"I brought some extra weapons for you," Jade said, indicating the bag.

"I am experiencing great gratitude. The sole form of armament my hasty departure permitted me to bring was my Sarton-A."

Jade was impressed. The Sarton-A was an energy weapon of undoubted power. Few people bothered to carry them, because they could fire only a few shots—but those few hit with the impact of a cannon.

"I prefer projectile weapons myself," she said. "I like something that packs some recoil and makes some noise, something that lets me know I'm shooting it. Besides, the shells are safer; I've seen what happens when a spare energy pack goes off in someone's pocket. Have you ever worked any of these?"

Cyclad inspected the array of weapons Jade laid out before her. "I regret that not a one of them has come within the purview of my experience."

Jade looked at the other's "hands"—actually manipulators at the ends of those incredibly long and impossibly jointed arms—and realized it would be impossible for Cyclad to hold the guns and press the triggers at the same time. She sighed and wrapped them back up in the bag.

"Here—at least I can give you some grenades and some flares. You can do a hell of a lot with them." She gave a quick description of their use, and Cyclad listened attentively. Then she stowed her minibazooka in her duffel bag for the moment. These first few seconds were crucial, and she'd have to move unencumbered.

The floor gave another lurch, signaling their arrival. The battle was now to begin. Jade's hands were steady, her body calm and poised. This was what she'd prepared for all her life. She had found her destiny at last.

"The first step is Customs," she whispered to Cyclad. "Take this duffel bag and follow me out."

Uzi in hand, Jade stood before the door blanking her mind and putting her body in the care of her computer-augmented reflexes. As the door slid open, she leaped through, prepared to fire. Something moved just to the right ahead of her; two shots and it went down. Another movement off to the left; she whirled and pumped three shots into it before the soldier could unholster his weapon. Leaping over the inspection table, she ran to the office on the right where the Commancor lieutenant was stationed. He had started to pull his gun when he heard the commotion outside, but Jade was still more prepared. Her gun spat twice, and the Commancor crumpled.

Two soldiers and the officer. There'd been three last time. Worried about where the other one might be hiding, Jade did a tuck-and-roll out of the office, coming up with gun at the ready—only to see Cyclad across the room. One of her long serrated forearms had locked round the Rozhin's throat as he took aim at Jade and, with a simple contraction, beheaded him.

"My sense of etiquette would not allow me to leave all the work to you," Cyclad said. "I did, of course, form the hasty supposition that he was among the enemy."

"Good guess. Let's get out of here in case anyone heard the shots. Take that side door."

They went through an empty storeroom, Cyclad still carrying the duffel bag, and peered out a door that led to the street. It was dusk in Detalla, and the lengthening shadows would do wonders to hide their movements.

As they waited for the street to clear, Cyclad said, "Perhaps this would be the propitious moment to enlighten me about the objectives of our current exercise."

"We're going to drive all the Commancor forces off Haldek and free it for the Lemmants again."

"A rather formidable task."

"Sorry you came along?"

"No," said Cyclad. "Just grateful there is the pair of us. Have you a specific strategy in mind?"

"I'm making it up as I go along. But I've done this sort of thing before with a band of fifty guerrillas behind me. It shouldn't be too much harder by ourselves. Come on."

The street in front of them was momentarily deserted, and the two invaders dashed out across the way to the safety of some shadows on the other side. From there they found an alley leading in the direction Jade wanted to go.

"Are we ambulating toward a particular destination?" Cyclad asked.

"The airfield. On sparsely settled colony worlds, the Commancors like to move their troops around on air transport. If they weren't alerted by those few shots, we can catch their carriers on the ground—and if we knock them out, Detalla will be cut off. It'll be a couple more hours before they could airlift in any new troops. A pair of determined people can do all sorts of things in a couple of hours."

They crept along the darkened back alleyways of Detalla until they came to the Commancor airfield Jade had seen on her first trip here with Fastal. It was surrounded by a sturdy wire fence. "Think you can climb over that?" Jade asked.

"I can do far better," Cyclad said. Standing totally erect and reaching upward, her elbow cleared the top of the fence. Bringing her forearm down and contracting her arm once more, she snapped the wires as though they were paper.

"I'm glad you're on my side," Jade whispered as she walked through the gap.

The Commancors had occupied Haldek for two

years, and after the initial resistance they had met no substantial opposition. Horsson's murder was an isolated incident, now taken care of. As a result, security was very lax here at the air base; there were only four sentries to walk the entire perimeter, leaving stretches unguarded for up to twenty minutes at a time. Making things even simpler was the fact that some of the lights were out around the grounds.

"They're almost inviting someone to attack them," Jade said, adding bitterly, "I wish they'd been this obliging on Toranawa."

They easily avoided the patrols and skulked across some open ground to the first hangar. The wooden door had a simple padlock on it, which Cyclad's strength again made short work of. They slipped inside to find a jackpot—a dozen of the large troop transports sitting peacefully on the ground, waiting to be sabotaged.

Cyclad looked at her supply of grenades. "We'll have enough of these to—"

Jade smiled and shook her head. "A guerrilla has to learn minimal effort for maximal effect. Those carriers have to be lightweight to haul all the troops. They're made of magnesium alloys. They burn, once you get them started. It's a beautiful sight. These flares are hot enough to ignite them, if you set them properly. When they're parked this close together, all you need is one flare every third transport—the ones in between will catch fire from their neighbors. Here, I'll show you."

Jade crept aboard the nearest transport and set the flare down in the front, just under the control panel. "The flare's on a two-second timer, so you have time to look away before it lights up. It takes a few minutes before it sets off the carrier, so you also have plenty of time to move on to the next few before the first one goes up."

She showed Cyclad how to set the fuse, and the two left the transport just as the flare started to burn. They sprinted through the building to their next target. "Here," Jade said, "you try this one."

Cyclad worked much more slowly than Jade, both

because she was less sure what she was doing and because her manipulators were not used to such delicate controls. But she was a quick study, and got the settings exactly right the first time. The flare was sputtering nicely behind them as they left the transport.

"You learn fast," Jade congratulated her.

"I possess the advantage of a superlative instructor."

"Let's split up, then. You take this next one and I'll take the one at the far end and work back."

Jade was just finishing her second and Cyclad was finishing her next one when the first one in line burst into flame with a magnificent *whoosh* and a blast of hot air that ripped through the hangar. Flames leaped ten meters into the air to lick at the ceiling of the building, and fiery pieces of metal went flying in all directions.

"It's time to leave," Jade yelled over the fire's roar. "We can't do anything more in here except get killed."

They got out of the building just moments before the first of the Commancor troops arrived to investigate what was wrong. The flares were setting off chain reactions, and the heat within the hangar quickly became unbearable for any living creature. Jade knew from past experience that the standard Commancor automatic fire defenses seldom worked against this intense a blaze.

Taking refuge against the back wall of a building a few dozen meters away, Jade assessed the situation. "Next step is to knock out communications. That's probably in that tall building way down there at the other end. Why don't you go down there and lob in a grenade? Then meet me over there by the fence."

"To what endeavor will you apply yourself in the interim?"

Jade smiled. "Just miscellaneous mischief."

They went their separate ways, and as chaos increased at the brightly lit end of the field, Jade worked her way up from one building to another, peering in windows until she found the one she knew had to be there—fuel storage. She tossed a flare inside and ran away at top speed—and even so, the concussion from the blast knocked her off her feet. She rolled as best she could carrying all her armaments, got ungracefully to her feet, and kept on running.

Soldiers came running by. Without even stopping, Jade swung her Uzi around and fired off an entire clip. She didn't bother counting how many of the enemy fell; she just kept running to make sure none of them could get a clear shot at her. But the troops seemed too disorganized to consider fighting back against an enemy that struck out of the darkness.

There was an explosion up at the far end of the field, closely followed by a second. Jade reached the rendezvous spot and waited, using the time to change clips in her Uzi. She hated just sitting here and waiting when there was so much yet to do and she was so vulnerable. She felt helpless if she wasn't on the move. But she had to wait for Cyclad.

Moments later she saw the angular form of the large mantis coming toward her. "Good work," she said. "But why did you use two grenades?"

"It was a large edifice."

"If you take out the first floor, the others usually come down, too," Jade said. "Waste not, want not. Our grenades aren't infinite." She looked around. "They must have their arsenal somewhere around here, but we don't have time to look. We'll have to restock some other time."

They broke through the fence again and started racing off to the west. They wasted no breath in talking; Jade simply took the lead and Cyclad Arik followed obediently after her. Jade ran at top speed, but the mantis's legs were so long she kept up at an easy lope. The light from the burning transports and fuel dump lit the sky for this whole section of the city; the fires cast dancing shadows as they flickered, providing plenty of cover for the two saboteurs.

They reached the river, and Jade brought them to a halt. "To what new form of mayhem is your temperament now inclined?" Cyclad asked.

"Fastal told me that most commerce takes place up and down these rivers," Jade said, wiping the sweat from her forehead. Haldek was hotter than she remembered. "We've taken away their air transport and some communications. Now we'll make the river a little harder, too."

She looked over the piers analytically. There were plenty of vessels moored here, but many of them were merchant ships, good only for trading. She wanted to disable the Commancors, not the Lemmantine colonists; she would not strike at civilian targets if she could help it.

"That one over there. You can tell by the armor plating on its hull, it's a military river craft. If we can sink a few of those it'll really have an impact."

Studying the ship more closely, she saw there was an open hatch about three meters on a side on the top deck, for either cargo, troops, or weapons. "I was never very accurate at throwing things," she admitted. "A grenade is useless against that armor plating, but if we can drop one through that hatch it'll tear the boat apart from the inside. How's your aim?"

In response, Cyclad took the grenade, pushed the setting button, and threw it in a high arc more than forty meters. It fell squarely through the hatch opening, and a moment later there was a flash of light and a rumbling roar. The ship shuddered, and shortly a cloud of black smoke started rising up from inside.

"That does it," Jade said. "You're pitching for my team. Come on—there's more where that came from."

Jade pointed at the crews leaving their own ships to go help the burning one. Not yet realizing it was enemy action instead of an accident, they left two barges unguarded. A quick detour, three grenades, and Cyclad's pitching arm put an end to that misconception.

They moved down the wharf amid growing chaos, until Jade decided their talents were needed elsewhere. "The trick is to keep moving, never let them know where you'll strike next," she explained. "Not only does that keep them from predicting your moves and setting a trap for you, but it works psychologically. They're never sure where you'll be, so they're constantly jittery. Even the troops you don't go near get nervous. They fire at shadows, at friends, kill off commanders they don't like. Most important, they make mistakes.

"It also hides your numbers. Right now they're probably convinced there are at least ten or twenty of us, if not a whole battalion. Keep them off balance, keep them guessing, that's how you play the game."

The three burning boats Jade and Cyclad left behind them were enough to light the whole pier. Civilians came to launch their boats and move them out of danger. The tangle of boats and lines soon filled the river and blocked nearly everyone's escape.

Some of those with ships next to the first one tried to cut it loose and launch it into the current, away from the rest. Taking this for sabotage, the Dominion's mercenary troops began shooting at the civilians. Some of the Lemmants fled, while others pulled open their sea chests, dug out weapons hidden years ago, and returned to the battle.

The fighting raged for hours. As word spread, Dominion soldiers in the area rushed to the pier, but were nearly matched by the number of Lemmants joining their comrades. The sun was up before the whole thing was over. The pier, the ships moored there, and four warehouses were totally lost—but only Lemmants walked away from the scene.

Unaware of all they'd started, Jade and Cyclad raced out into one street, almost directly into the path of an oncoming tank. Jade saw her mistake immediately and turned to run back, but her foot slipped on the wet ground and she fell to her knees. Before she could get up, the driver of the armored vehicle was aiming his big energy cannon at her.

By this time Cyclad Arik had planted her feet firmly and aimed her Sarton-A. The energy beam seared straight through the heavy armor plating, probably killing the occupants instantly. The beam must have also touched the tank's energy pack, for the whole machine suddenly exploded in a ball of incandescent fury, shattering windows up and down the street. Pieces of hot metal rained down, a small one landed on Jade's shoulder, and she quickly shook it off.

"Thanks," Jade said as she and Cyclad ran back into the alley. "I think we're even now, if you'd prefer to go home."

"The enjoyment is only now commencing," Cyclad said firmly.

"I don't know what I did to earn it," said Jade, "but I'm glad you're here." She took a deep breath as she considered their situation.

"We've made a good start this way," she said, "but from now on I think we'd be better off splitting up. We can do twice as much damage in two directions at once, confusing the enemy still further."

"I have not previously participated in a conflict of a military nature," Cyclad said. "Do guidelines exist for a combatant's comportment?"

"You destroy enemy property, anything that might be useful to him, and you kill enemy troops. Anyone in a Dominion uniform is an enemy. Anyone who tries to harm you is an enemy. Anyone else is a civilian, and you try to leave civilians alone. Anything else, wing it."

"Wing it?" Cyclad twitched a muscle on her back that was a vestigal wing.

"Improvise," Jade corrected.

"Have you envisioned an overall strategy?"

"Yes, a pincer movement. You start here on the west side and push everything eastward. I'll circle around to the east and start pushing westward. We'll catch the enemy in a crossfire between us somewhere in the center of the city."

"I acknowledge the plan. May fortune favor you." Cyclad gave Jade back her duffel bag and moved off to start implementing the strategy.

Jade stared at her for a moment before turning to the east to begin her own phase. *Of course,* she thought, *that presupposes we each have at least a couple of squads to back us up. But why should I discourage her?*

She set about creating her own particular brand of havoc. The streets were bare of civilians by now. Most didn't know what was going on, but they knew *something* was happening and did not want to be caught in the middle of it. This made life simpler for Jade; if something moved, it was the enemy and she could shoot at it with a clear conscience.

The Commancor troops were finally starting to organize, prepared to strike back against this unknown force that had so disrupted their orderly existence. The Dominion's soldiers fired many shots, mostly at shadows. They didn't know how many were ranged against them, but they refused to go down without a fight.

Jade debated the wisdom of taking a sniper position on a convenient rooftop and holding it against all comers; short of demolishing the building, she could make it almost impossible for them to take her. But sniping was more a defensive move, a delaying tactic to buy time for her side to do something—and she had no "side." She was here on an assault mission; she would not die backed into some corner.

Hour after hour she wove through the east side of the city like an avenging fury, hitting in as random a manner as possible, destroying all in her path, taking care she couldn't be anticipated and cut off. She sent another warehouse up in flames with her minibazooka and cut down random bands of soldiers who came into her sights; with her computer-augmented reflexes she could usually shoot them before they could react to her. She got cuts, scrapes, bruises, even a stray burn from an energy gun, but she felt nothing. Like an addict transfigured by his drug of choice, she was beyond the normal world of pain and hesitation. She felt as though her heart were pumping straight adrenaline through her veins, without benefit of blood. The universe became an enormous whole known as the war, and even the enemy troops were integral to this mystic experience. Killing and destruction were not just part of existence, they were the *essence* of existence.

There seemed to be no gap between the days on Toranawa, on Panaguar, on Haldek. Any other existence was a washed-out dream. In this full-color reality, only the next target mattered. Again and again,

Jade chose and demolished; the enemy followed and protected—too late with too little.

The silence from the other side of the city was ominous, and in the one pocket of conscious thought she had she hoped Cyclad was all right. That half of the war would be quieter; the Dominion troops used the noiseless energy weapons almost exclusively, while Cyclad had started only with some grenades and her Sarton-A. Jade wasn't worried about leaving her companion underarmed; she knew Cyclad was smart enough to scrounge energy weapons from her fallen foes. The Commancors' weapons would actually be easier for her to hold and fire than Jade's rifles; the only question was whether luck would hold long enough for her to scavenge what she needed.

Jade pushed inward toward the center of town, as she'd told Cyclad she'd do, but the maneuver was not working strategically. Without the manpower to help her, she could not force the Commancor lines to pull back. The most she could do was cause a temporary tear in the line, which mended itself almost as soon as she went through it, like poking a needle through an amoeba. The only effect her tactic had was to get herself surrounded by the enemy, who were very intent on purging her from their system.

Time and effort began taking their toll. Even in a berserker state, Jade could not keep going indefinitely. By the time the larger moon set, her muscles were starting to rebel, refusing to meet the demands her fighting placed upon them. She comforted herself with the thought that the fatigue was only temporary. Soon this would all be over; her tired body would duck a trifle too slowly and an enemy's gun would find her. Then her troubles would be done. Her only regret was that she wouldn't get back to Earth and take the revenge on Barker that she'd long ago promised herself.

A loud booming shook the city, penetrating even the haze that was clouding Jade's weary mind. The shouts of battle suddenly intensified, and the noise from the normally quiet energy guns intensified to a humming so loud the buildings shuddered. Could the Commancors have brought in reinforcements to deal with the two-person invasion? It was a flattering thought, but as Jade checked the computer in the back of her left hand she saw that there hadn't been enough time yet to fly in the troops and guns from the outer regions. Unless they'd coincidentally been on their way when she started. . . .

What does it matter? she thought. *Who cares if there's five hundred or five thousand of them out there? All it takes is one to kill me. Ah, but he's going to have to be a lucky bastard!*

She rounded a corner and suddenly stopped dead. There were two armies squared off in the predawn darkness, firing at each other across a small plaza. One army was in the familiar uniform of the Dominion; many of the people in the other were in a uniform Jade didn't recognize. But she recognized the race: Lemmants. The Lemmants were fighting to reclaim Haldek.

This development so astonished her that for a moment she stood in the open just watching the battle before her. Then an energy beam came flaring past her, and common sense reasserted itself. She leaped back to her left, behind the building she had just emerged from.

Her world was now turned upside down, but she couldn't let that affect her actions. The Lemmants might be fighting here, but so were the Commancors, and the Lemmants' record was a poor one. She had allies now, but she could still be killed if she made the wrong moves. Overconfidence, she knew, led to the worst mistakes.

She peered out again to assess the situation. She was much closer to the Commancor's lines than to the Lemmant's. She took a flare from her belt, set it, and tossed it behind the Dominion soldiers, illuminating them from behind so they'd make good targets for Lemmantine guns. Then, taking the last of her grenades, she lobbed it directly into a mass of Commancor troops. She might not have Cyclad's uncanny accuracy, but such finesse wasn't needed now. The grenade exploded with a gratifying devastation, and she followed it up with a volley of shots that had equally lethal results. This attack from a new direction demoralized the surviving Dominion troops, and they scattered for safety in all directions. Few of them made it; most were cut down either by Jade or by the Lemmantine fighters.

Sensing victory, the Lemmants surged across the plaza and secured it for themselves. Jade seriously debated whether she should reveal herself to them or remain hidden to continue her own private vendetta. But this break had restored her to thinking on a rational basis. Her own resources were limited, and fading rapidly. The Lemmants were fresh. They could take up the fight now where she was leaving off, and probably do a better job. She didn't want to die if she didn't have to.

And that thought came as such a divine revelation to her that she repeated it in her mind like a battle cry. She didn't want to die. She didn't *have* to die. The Lemmants were fighting here, and Fastal's ghost would rest easy. She no longer had to sacrifice herself to appease him.

She looked around frantically for something to use as a truce flag. White was the universal color for truce—not because it had been used on Earth, but because it could be seen by creatures sensitive to a wide spectrum of electromagnetic radiation and because it was usually easy to find. Halfway down the street she saw a window with white curtains hanging in it and raced to it. Smashing the window, she grabbed the fabric, probably startling the house's inhabitants, if they hadn't fled in terror by now. The curtain rod came down with it, and she took that as a staff on which to mount her flag.

She went back to the plaza, stuck out her improvised flag, began waving it, and, when she was confident it had been seen and noted, stepped out into view of the Lemmants.

The army was not sure what to make of her at first. She was not a Commancor, but it was widely known that Commancors hired mercenaries. She was not in uniform, but would that mean anything to them? They knew that *someone* had helped them in their recent battle, but would they guess it was she?

To improve their recognition, Jade reached slowly to her waist, pulled the Fornen dagger from her belt, and held it up in her left hand while still holding the flag in her right. Even from a distance the soldiers could recognize that Lemmantine symbol of a noble family, and they relaxed noticeably. Jade let out a deep breath and advanced more quickly, assured she wouldn't be shot by the side that was nominally hers.

One Lemmant came forward to meet her, wearing a fancier uniform than most of the others—obviously an officer. "I am Dar ip Appineal," he introduced himself. "I believe I recognize you. You are the person who shamed an entire world by speaking so eloquently at the Fornen funeral."

"If you came all this way for an apology," Jade said, "you won't get it."

"It is we who must apologize—and thank you for reminding us of the honor we abandoned in our slide toward comfort and complacency. Your speech was reported by our journalists and broadcast around our world. You reminded us of what we stand for. You are a hero to all of Lemmanta—and soon all of Haldek, I hope."

"Me?" Jade felt her face flushing. "I'm no hero. I'm the fuck-up who left the real hero to die. I'm just carrying on the fight Fastal wanted. Build statues to him, if you build any at all. I don't want to spend eternity covered with pigeon shit."

"But to come here all alone and fight against impossible odds—"

"Not all alone," Jade said, shaking her head. "Another person named Cyclad Arik came with me. There's another hero for you. She came here to a fight that was none of her concern, simply because . . . well, I'm not really sure why. Find her if she's still alive, and make sure she stays that way. If anyone from your army accidentally kills her, I'll tear his guts out personally."

"But you as well came here to a fight that was none of your concern."

"No. I was paid to do a job, and I left it incomplete. I was . . . I was honor-bound to finish it right. Have you established any safe zones yet? If I don't get some sleep soon, I think I'll pass out. You don't want your troops to see a hero faint, do you?"

CHAPTER 16

Knight's Move

Jade slept for fourteen solid hours, and woke stiff and sore. She was startled to see Cyclad Arik standing over her in battle posture, then realized that was how the creature slept. Cyclad, too, had survived this folly. Jade closed her eyes and let out a deep prayer of gratitude to all the gods of war, of many races, she'd ever heard of. Sometimes things did work out right.

Cyclad, assured that Jade was now in safe hands, returned to Cablans the next day. Jade stayed on Haldek a week, traveling with the Lemmantine army. Dar ip Appineal turned out to be one of the generals in charge of the Lemmantine invasion forces, and he continually asked for her advice. Jade was a line soldier, a captain at best; she wasn't used to giving her opinions on policy matters like a general, and found herself very uncomfortable in the role. Ip Appineal would not let her go near the front lines, though, so she saw no further fighting.

When the Lemmants decided to get into the war, they did it in a big way—they had moved ten battalions onto Haldek, all for the price of fifty eus per battalion. That was more than enough to overwhelm the Dominion forces stationed in Detalla, especially after Jade and Cyclad had appreciably diminished their fighting capacity and destroyed their organization. With the Lemmants in control of the transfer station, prepared for a fight, the Commancor Dominion would have a hard time reinforcing their garrison on this out-of-the-way colony world.

Some of the Commancor outposts decided on do-or-die heroics to defend their territory. The Lemmants, fighting with zealous fervor, overwhelmed and overran them. Other outposts, seeing the fate of their colleagues, decided to surrender at once and save themselves the casualties. In under a week the Lemmants had retaken the colony world they had so ignominiously lost two years earlier.

When Jade saw how the tide of battle was turning, she realized her job here was done. Fastal's homeland was recaptured, and his soul, if indeed he had one, would rest easily now. Let the Lemmants work out the rest of their guilt on their own; she'd done all the atoning she wanted to do for a while.

When communications and travel had stabilized a bit, Jade received a request to visit ip Appineal's tent. She brushed herself off and headed over, exchanging greetings with the troops, who all knew about the warrior woman with the name of a stone.

Jade entered the tent, and a young soldier bellowed the type of inarticulate sound that means "Ten-*hut*" in any army. Before Jade could tell the shavetail to stop, an old Lemmant called, "At ease," and turned to face her. It was the man Jade had met on the podium at the funeral, the one who'd left so she could speak.

General ip Appineal stepped forward. "Jade, please meet Racswilr ip Fornen. Fornen ip Fornen, Ms. Jade Darcy."

Jade stood still as Fastal's great-grandfather walked up to her. "You may want these now," he said, handing her a small sealed gold box. "His ashes belong with you, too."

"But . . . I thought they went to your family's home."

"Some. Some go to each of the family homes." He reached out to touch his great-granddaughter's dagger, which Jade still wore at her waist, and continued, "You proved yourself worthy of this. This gift and your courage have made you Jade da Fornen, if you would not be dishonored by such a title . . . granddaughter."

Jade looked at this brave and gracious man and said,

"I will proudly be known as part of your family—as long as I don't have to become a farmer on Haldek. There's just too many bugs."

"Granddaughter Jade, I don't like the bugs, either." The laugh they shared was only the first of many that night.

The night before the surrender treaty was due to be signed, Jade stole a vehicle and drove back to Detalla. The guard there recognized her and allowed her through without any trouble, and she transferred back to Cablans with neither fuss nor ceremony. She left the hectic bustle of the transfer station itself and walked furiously next door to the Pale House. "Identify, please," the computer requested.

"You know damn well who I am, and if you don't open up this second I'll blow your fucking door off."

The door slid open without further comment, and Jade stormed inside. This time the Greest was manifesting himself as two large round balloons, a pink one on the ground and a green one floating up by the ceiling almost directly above it. The interior of the Pale House was as barren as ever.

"You shitheaded, slime-faced, turd-eating murdering bastard, you killed Fastal ip Fornen!"

"Pleasant salutations to yourself as well, Jade Darcy.'

"Cut the bullshit. I'm not letting you off the hook that easily. I don't care to play your stupid word games today. I want you to answer some charges."

"Very well, though your lack of accuracy is appalling. We have neither head nor face as you would understand it, we do not digest excrement, we are neither legitimate nor illegitimate, and it was a group of Commancors who killed Fastal ip Fornen. Your charges are erroneous on all counts."

"I told you I'm not playing games. The Commancors killed him because you made it impossible for him to get away from them, charging him a fortune to leave Cablans."

"Our fees are set according to precise patterns far beyond your ability to comprehend—"

"Oh, I can comprehend them, all right. You're a bloodthirsty asshole. You love a good fight. You love watching people die. It was impossible for Fastal to get away, so he died—but when I went to Haldek with murder in my heart and guns on my back, it was just petty change. You charged less for the whole Lemmantine army to transfer over to Haldek than you wanted to charge Fastal simply to save his life."

"A small difference," the Greest said. "Scarcely worth noting."

"Jesus H. fucking Christ. Doesn't it matter to you that hundreds, thousands, even millions of innocent people die because of these games you play?"

"When a gardener prunes a topiary bush, or a bonsai tree, each snip he makes condemns that twig, composed of thousands or millions of cells, to lingering death. Yet he does this because he knows that the pattern as a whole—"

"Fuck the pattern as a whole! We're not talking about brainless plant cells, we're talking about intelligent beings. You wanted a war between Lemmanta and the Dominion, didn't you?"

"The optimum pattern did seem to require one, yes."

Jade was taken slightly aback by the Greest's uncharacteristically blunt response. "Why?"

"Imagine a plant—say, a vine—growing out of control. At first it can be beautiful, and the gardener encourages its growth. Then it threatens to overwhelm the wall it is climbing, so the gardener prunes it back a little to keep it within manageable limits."

Jade's eyes went wide. "Are you telling me you want to stop the Dominion's expansion?"

"You are approaching the pattern from a very limited perspective."

"But that doesn't make any sense. If you wanted to stop the Commancors, all you'd have to do is stop transporting them places. You took them to Haldek in the first place; it's your fault they expanded."

"The wise gardener does not prune a bush by poisoning its roots, but by guiding its branches in the appropriate direction."

Jade paused to consider the matter further. "You wanted the Commancors stopped, but you didn't want to just do it yourself, because that would make them mad at you. So you got them to invade Haldek, expecting the Lemmants to fight back and beat them. But the Lemmants disappointed you by not fighting. So when Fastal came to you with his idea, you figured it was a good way to stir up more trouble, is that it?"

"Still only a primitive appreciation of the overall pattern, but perhaps considering your limited three-dimensional perspective it is the best we can expect."

"So you used Fastal and you used me, and you got your little war. The Dominion's been pushed off Haldek. Does that make you happy?"

"Does it make you happy that red exists? Or would you rather it be green?"

"Dammit, I will not be used as a pawn in your stinking games!"

"We sense you have a dissatisfaction with our gardening metaphor. Several times you have referred to games and playing. Very well, we shall attempt to translate to the new analog. You say you dislike the role of a pawn, a reference to the popular Terran game of chess. Within that same analogy, we might inform you that you are not considered a pawn, but a knight."

"A knight?"

"Yes. You would refuse to move straight forward in any case, and you may upon occasion move through or around other pieces. Your movements are certainly far from orthodox."

"Are you trying to tell me I'm important to you?"

"The whole pattern . . . pardon, the whole game is important. All the pieces on the board play their individual roles. If some pieces become unavailable, the strategist improvises with others. Do not flatter yourself that you are indispensable."

Jade walked around the bare room, considering this new information. "But if you're playing a game, who are you playing *against*? And who's winning?"

The Greest paused. It was a very long pause, for the Greest. "Two dragons fight over the lost pearl. Which one is victorious?"

"Shit! Well, what does a gardener do when his hedge clippers turn on him? What happens if I pump a few rounds of bullets into these pieces of you here?"

"We are not especially vulnerable to anything that occurs within a three-dimensional cross section."

"Then you don't mind if I try it?"

"Not if you don't mind living with the consequences of that action."

Despite her rage, the menace in that reply made Jade consider her position sensibly. The Greest was the ultimate authority on Cablans because he controlled the very reason for Cablans's existence—the transfer station. So far the Greest had never minded her talking back to him—but if he ever did decide to punish her, he could make life hellish in a million different ways, both blatant and subtle. She hated him and everything he stood for, and the way he manipulated her and everyone else on his cosmic chessboard—but she'd already fought one impossible battle this week. There were absolutely no percentages in challenging the Greest, and she couldn't even claim she was doing it in a good cause. It was simply her anger talking, and the loss of self-esteem from how easily he'd maneuvered her into doing what he wanted.

"What do I do about Megan Cafferty?" she asked, changing the subject abruptly.

"What do you do about the sun?"

"I use its light, I block it out, and sometimes I dream about blowing it up. Now what the fuck should I do about Megan Cafferty?"

"Patience. Waiting is."

"I hope you strangle in your own vines," Jade said as she turned and stomped out of the Pale House.

She returned home, and the door opened at her touch. The lights were on inside, cheery and waiting. "Welcome home, Jade," Val said. "I've kept everything ready for you."

"Of course you have. That's the way you're programmed. You couldn't do anything else."

Jade took off her guns and bandoliers. With the slow deliberation of a new priest removing his vestments after his first mass, she stored everything neatly away in her arsenal, each item in its own special place. The last items she removed were the gold box with Fastal's ashes and the Fornen dagger she'd carried proudly in her belt. Those were things she could not hide away in a cabinet. They had to be out where she could see them and constantly remind herself of the lesson Fastal had taught her.

"Val," she said, "I need to mount these on a wall—over there, I think."

Three tiny pegs obediently manifested themselves in just the right positions to balance the curved dagger impressively, and a small shelf protruded below them to hold the box. Jade placed the items there and stood back to look at them. The arrangement looked beautiful, and she realized the wall had needed it. Now her decor was something more than the Greest's.

She sat down in a chair and tried to relax. The house was very quiet. Breathing slowly, she could hear the sound of the blood rushing through the veins in her ears. She looked around. Val had done an admirable job. Everything was neatly in place. But the ceiling was lower, the walls were closer, the house was smaller than she remembered it. Somehow this did not feel like the place she had left.

"Hell, I can't go cold turkey," she said at last. "I'll go nuts. Val, call Disson for me."

In just a moment one face of the ingesterie's chief security officer filled her screen. "Disson, this is Jade. I know I resigned last week, but I didn't think I'd be coming back, and—"

"Cyclad Arik has explained the entire situation to me," Disson interrupted. "Fortunately—or unfortunately, however you view it—you are not one of those employees who can be adequately replaced on short notice. If you'd like your job back, it is available."

"Thanks, Disson. It'll feel good to be back. Uh, what about the next shift?"

"That had been fully scheduled—but Nal/Arp has been on duty every day this week, and could use the rest. You can fill in at spot assignments until I work you back into the regular lineup.''

Jade's next call was to Megan Cafferty, who was delighted—and not a little relieved—to see her again. "Good news," she said. "Our little friend has weathered the crisis, thanks to your quick action and our mutual dedication. He'll be back snuffling around your house as soon as I bring him by.''

"Uh, why don't you just keep him? You've done so much for him—''

"Oh no. I'm a pet sitter, not a pet owner. This is one responsibility I won't let you dodge. When will be convenient for me to bring him over?''

"I'm working the next shift. I'll be home about twenty-five thirty.''

"The middle of the night? All right, I'll be there then. But I'll expect a good story about Haldek.''

"Val, start the tub, not too hot.'' Jade walked slowly into the bathroom, shedding her clothes and throwing them with practiced ease into the hampers. The tub was half full and barely steaming even with the cool temperature Jade preferred in her place. She started to climb into the tub when she spotted the tiny carving the Furgato exec had given her weeks and a lifetime ago. It looked vulnerable and naked on the ledge.

Jade walked to the cupboard that contained what little odds and ends she'd tolerate in her minimalist existence, and found an old brass magazine for a derringer destroyed in a fire fight many years ago. A moment's rubbing with an old cloth removed the grime, but left a soft patina intact. Satisfied, Jade put the five centimeter square, one centimeter high brass magazine on the ledge of the tub. She gently polished the little piece of stone with a clean corner of the cloth, then placed it on the brass. It seemed to smile a little more, as though in thanks. A hot soaking bath, shared with her little golden carp on the old ammo case-turned-netsuke stand, made Jade feel prepared for anything, even Palovoi and Furgato in full riot.

Jade actually returned home late, to find that Megan had been waiting outside her door for almost half an hour. Jade apologized, and opened the door, and stepped inside. When Megan caught sight of her she exclaimed, "Good lord, what happened to you?"

It was a fair question. Jade's hair was tossed, her clothes were ripped in a dozen places, and she was covered with cuts, bruises, and scrapes. She walked over to one wall and said, "First aid, Val," and a cabinet with various items opened for her.

There was a tickling around her ankles. Despite her own soreness, she reached down to pet the frizzlic nuzzling her legs. "Well, little pain in the ass, it looks like we came through. We're both tougher than we look, aren't we?"

"What happened to you?" Megan asked again.

"All in the line of duty," Jade said offhandedly as she began rubbing some healing ointment into her wounds. "There was a party at the ingesterie—a Bolinaki family were celebrating their daughter's defloration. The party started long before I got there, and was scheduled to go well into tomorrow. Near the end of my shift, one of the young lady's suitors who was . . . passed over for the honor came in and started making a scene. It just took a while for the whole thing to get calmed down. Ow . . . there's one scrape on my shoulder blade I just can't get to. Can you rub some of this stuff in for me?"

Jade stripped off her top as Megan took the jar of medication from her. She made sure she was facing the mirror so she could watch every move the other woman made.

"I've come to my decision about you," Megan said as she began to rub the ointment into Jade's skin—and then deliberately ignored the muscle tension this produced in her patient. "For the time being, at least, you're far too valuable a resource for me to simply throw away. As long as your past has no bearing on the work I may need you to do for me, your secrets can remain your own. I protect the people who work for me, as long as their indiscretions remain in the past. Of course, if your history ever interferes with your work, I may have to reevaluate—but I'll let you know I'm doing it."

Jade's neck and shoulder muscles relaxed slightly,

both from relief and from the skilled massage Megan was applying. "You keep mentioning future work. Are you staying here once the Palovoi business is done?"

"That's the good news," Megan said. "The Caf-Tech board—at my insistence—has decided there's enough potential business out here for us to open a permanent office. I'll be setting up shop for a while. I hope that won't bother you—I mean, you'll lose your monopoly as the only Terran around. But I do expect we'll be working together again."

"Only if you keep paying like you did."

"Maybe not quite that well all the time—but most people say I cut a fair deal."

Jade fell silent for a moment—not a surly, withdrawing silence, but a thoughtful one, broken only by the wood-rasp sound of a happy frizzlic gnawing on a bone. "What's the matter?" Megan asked. "Was it something I said?"

"Not at all. I just . . . when I came back to the house after being away, it seemed almost strange and alien. But then I got back to work, and everything feels right again. This is my world, I'm comfortable here. I haven't had a place like this for some time, but, for better or worse, Cablans is my home."

"Yup," Megan said as she daubed at the scrape with some of the ointment, adding cynically, "And we all know there's no place like home."

About the Authors

Stephen Goldin is the author of more than 20 science fiction novels. He has a bachelor's degree in Astronomy and has worked as a space scientist for the Navy. *Jade Darcy and the Affair of Honor* is his first collaboration with his wife, Mary Mason. They currently reside in Sacramento, California, where they live with their stepson, Kenneth.

Mary Mason makes her debut as the co-author of *Jade Darcy and the Affair of Honor*. She has worked as a counselor for emotionally disturbed children and as a teaching assistant. She has lived in California all her life.

In the vast intergalactic world of the future
the soldiers battle

NOT FOR GLORY

JOEL ROSENBERG

author of the bestselling
Guardian of the Flame series

Only once in the history of the Metzadan mercenary corps has a man been branded traitor. That
man is Bar-El, the most cunning military mind in
the universe. Now his nephew, Inspector-General
Hanavi, must turn to him for help. What begins as
one final mission is transformed into a series of
campaigns that takes the Metzadans from world to
world, into intrigues, dangers, and treacherous diplomatic games, where a strategist's highly irregular maneuvers and a master assassin's swift blade
may prove the salvation of the planet—or its ultimate ruin . . .